A
Cold
White
FEAR

A Meg Harris Mystery

The Meg Harris Mysteries

Death's Golden Whisper
Red Ice for a Shroud
The River Runs Orange
Arctic Blue Death
A Green Place for Dying
Silver Totem of Shame

A Cold White FEAR

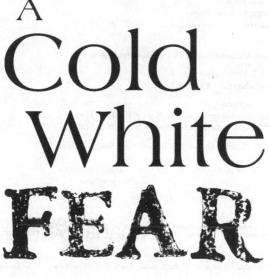

A Meg Harris Mystery

R. J. HARLICK

DUNDURN
TORONTO

Editor: Allister Thompson
Design: Laura Boyle
Cover design: Courtney Horner
Cover image: © wildcat78/ veer.com
Printer: Webcom

Library and Archives Canada Cataloguing in Publication

Harlick, R. J., 1946-, author
    A cold white fear / R.J. Harlick.

(A Meg Harris mystery)
Issued in print and electronic formats. ISBN 978-1-4597-3199-8 (pbk.).
--ISBN 978-1-4597-3200-1 (pdf).--ISBN 978-1-4597-3201-8 (epub)

    I. Title. II. Series: Harlick, R. J., 1946- . Meg Harris mystery

PS8615.A74C64 2015   C813'.6   C2015-901489-1
                                             C2015-901490-5

1 2 3 4 5   19   18   17   16   15

Conseil des Arts   Canada Council
du Canada   for the Arts

Canada

ONTARIO ARTS COUNCIL
CONSEIL DES ARTS DE L'ONTARIO
an Ontario government agency
un organisme du gouvernement de l'Ontario

We acknowledge the support of the **Canada Council for the Arts** and the **Ontario Arts Council** for our publishing program. We also acknowledge the financial support of the **Government of Canada** through the **Canada Book Fund** and **Livres Canada Books**, and the **Government of Ontario** through the **Ontario Book Publishing Tax Credit** and the **Ontario Media Development Corporation**.

Visit us at
Dundurn.com | @dundurnpress | Facebook.com/dundurnpress | Pinterest.com/dundurnpress

Dundurn
3 Church Street, Suite 500
Toronto, Ontario, Canada
M5E 1M2

To Jim

ONE

I was sitting in the kitchen, agonizing over my Christmas grocery list, when I heard the noise. It wasn't a knock or even a tap. More like a thud from the front of the house. But since a blizzard had been howling all day, I ignored it. I assumed it was a branch the wind had broken free, given the force with which it was lashing snow against the windows.

With only four more days until the big day, I was planning to drive into Somerset tomorrow to ensure I could get everything Eric wanted for our first family Christmas, like the three dozen fresh oysters he wanted to serve as the starter to the moose stew he was preparing for Christmas Eve. But the way the snow was filling up the driveway, I might have to wait another day before my road would be cleared enough for my aging pickup to crawl through.

Though I was looking forward to seeing my sister Jean and her family, and Eric's daughter Teht'aa, whom we hadn't seen since she'd moved north, I couldn't understand why my husband wanted to share our second Christmas as a married couple with so many people. We could have a perfectly wonderful time with just the two of us. Mind you, given the way he'd slammed the door on me when he left for Regina on Saturday, maybe we wouldn't be celebrating Christmas at all.

The thud sounded again. This time with more force. Since the likelihood of a branch falling on the same place twice was nil, I made my way down the hall to the front door, wondering what kind of an idiot would be out in such terrible weather.

It couldn't be Pierre delivering one of his fabulous farm-fresh turkeys. He wasn't supposed to drop it off until the twenty-third, the day Eric was scheduled to return. Besides, he would take it to the back door.

Nor could it be Jid. Though the boy was outside, he was replenishing the dwindling supply of firewood on the back porch with logs from the wood shed. There was no need for him to wade through deep drifts to the front door.

Through the sheers covering the narrow window next to the door, I could make out a shadow, but not much else. Living in such an isolated location with kilometres of empty forest between my closest neighbour and me, I tended to be wary about opening the door without knowing who it could be, especially when I was alone.

Before Eric and I were married, I'd become used to living by myself in the remote wilderness of Three Deer Point with Sergei, my wimpy standard poodle, as my only company. But he could hardly be called a guard dog, though he did have a ferocious bark on him. Sadly he'd passed on, and now my current guard dog was Shoni, another standard, who at ten weeks old wouldn't scare anyone away.

Since it was a winding kilometre-and-a-half drive up the Three Deer Point road to my rambling Victorian cottage, most people called to ensure someone was home before making the trip. Today, with the amount of snow that had fallen, it would be nearly impossible to get here without getting stuck. Unless this individual had come by snowmobile. But a Ski-Doo wasn't exactly quiet, and I'd heard nothing to suggest one was parked outside my home.

"Who's there?" I called out.

"Open the door," shouted a male voice, followed by another thump against the heavy oak door.

Forget it. No way was I going to open it with that tone, especially to a voice I didn't recognize.

I backed away, almost tripping over Shoni. Recently separated from her mother, she followed my every step. I lifted her up and gave her a kiss on the top of her soft, furry head by way of an apology. She gave me a big lick on the cheek, along with a nip from her sharp puppy teeth. She hadn't yet sorted out the distinction between licks and nips.

A shudder went through the house as another blast of wind pummelled it.

"Madame, please let us in. We need help."

That was better. At least he was now being polite.

I decided to get the portable phone from the living room, thinking it would be a good idea to have it handy, just in case. But the minute I reached for the receiver, I was plunged into the semi-twilight of the storm. The hall light had gone out, along with the lights in the living room.

The power was out.

Given the velocity of the wind, I'd been expecting it to happen all day. However, now was not exactly a convenient time. Hoping it was a momentary flicker, I waited for the lights to return. They didn't. It meant the phone also wouldn't work. With no cell coverage in the area, I couldn't use Eric's spare cell either.

"Open up, madame. My friend's badly hurt." Another round of loud pounding.

I didn't like the feel of this. It made no sense that these men would be at my place in such weather.

Still … perhaps there had been an accident.

I hated to open the door without some form of protection, but Eric's hunting rifles were locked up, and the key was likely on his key chain with him. Besides, I didn't have the foggiest idea on how to use one.

But if someone really was hurt …

I moved the sheers aside and found myself staring into a pair of startling amber eyes framed by a swirl of tattoos, which gyrated up over his forehead and onto his bullet-shaped head.

I let the curtain fall back into place.

He knocked on the window. "Please, madame, my friend might die."

No way I was going to let this guy in. "I can't help you. There's a health centre on the reserve. Go there."

"We can't go anywhere in this shit. Our car's stuck. You have to let us in. It's damn cold out here."

"Miss Aggie, that you?" came another, much weaker voice. "It's Willie's boy."

Miss Aggie. Did he mean my great-aunt Agatha?

I inched the curtain aside just a crack. The tattooed man had moved away, giving me a clear view of another man, half-standing, half-leaning against the porch railing. Snow swirled around him, momentarily hiding his face. When it cleared, his face was equally unfamiliar, though it bore the familiar bronze tinge of my husband's skin and many of my friends, but in his case it bore the unhealthy yellowish pallor of more time spent indoors than outside. His duffle coat was crusted with snow, as was the tuque pulled down over his forehead and ears. His eyes were closed as if in sleep, until they winced in pain. Then I noticed the snow turning red where his hand pressed against his side.

"How do you know my great-aunt?"

"My dad used to do odd jobs for her."

"But she's been dead almost fifteen years."

"Yeah, well, my dad died about that long ago."

"You from the rez?" The Migiskan Anishinabeg Reserve bordered my land.

"Yeah."

"I don't think I've seen you around."

"Yeah, well … I haven't lived there in a while."

"What did you say your name was?"

"Ah … Larry. Look I'm not feeling so hot. Can you let us in?"

I hated to turn away someone from the community where many of my friends lived, particularly someone who was in trouble. I knew Eric wouldn't want me to either.

"What's your last name?"

"Whiteduck."

"Are you related to Tommy?"

"You talkin' about Marie's kid? Him and me were in the same class at school."

He did look to be about the same age as Tommy, in his early thirties. And he did know that Tommy was Marie's son.

I felt a pang at the thought of Marie. She'd been a valued friend when I first moved into Three Deer Point and was having difficulties adjusting to the disparities in my life. Even though it was many years since her tragic death, I still missed her.

Wanting to believe him, I opened the door.

TWO

I scooped the puppy up into my arms to keep her from getting in the way. By now my poor departed Sergei would've been in full barking frenzy, but Shoni was too young for the guard dog instinct to kick in, so I would have to rely on my own. It was on high alert.

The force of the wind slammed the front door against the wall and brought with it a cloud of snow, which was beginning to melt on Aunt Aggie's treasured hardwood flooring. Though the light maple was no longer as highly polished or as unscathed as it was when I inherited Three Deer Point from her, I didn't want puddles of melt water ruining it further. I was about to ask the two men to go around to the back door when I noticed what a struggle it was for Larry just to walk over the threshold.

"There's a sofa in the den where you can lie down."

The tattooed man surprised me. He kicked off his wet shoes with a muttered "Sorry, madame," while struggling to keep his injured friend from falling. He didn't, however, attempt to remove Larry's shoes. I found it curious that both men were wearing low-rise running shoes, which looked to be soaked, instead of sturdy winter boots. On the other hand, men weren't necessarily known for their practicality.

I tried to ignore the snow dripping from their clothing and the odd drop of blood following their path down the hall to the den. But I managed to cover the leather sofa with the worn wool blanket kept for cold winter mornings before Larry dropped onto its cushions with a groan.

"What happened?" I asked.

I thought I could make out a rip in the coat where he was pressing his hand. The blood that had seeped into the heavy wool fabric looked to be more dry than wet. I hoped it meant that the bleeding was stopping.

"It was a car accident. We drove into a tree," the other man answered while keeping his eyes fixed on his injured friend.

"Easy enough to do in a whiteout. It must've happened close by."

Shoni, tired of being held, began to squirm. I struggled to keep her from falling.

"It occurred on the main road near the start of your road."

"That's a difficult walk in deep snow, especially with an injured man."

"It was rather a challenge, but we persevered, didn't we, little buddy?" He gave his friend a gentle pat. "Larry believed your place closer than it turned out to be."

Given his less than savoury appearance, his educated English surprised me. His use of the French "madame" suggested that he also spoke Canada's other official language, or else he was putting on airs.

"Are you hurt too?"

"No," he replied a little too abruptly, and then, as if having second thought, continued. "I might have a few bruises, but nothing more. It's rather dark in here. Can't you turn on some lights, or are you being eco-friendly?"

"I'm afraid the power's just gone out, but I've got plenty of oil lamps and candles. Unfortunately, it also means there is no phone service, so we won't be able to get the paramedics in here to look after your friend."

At the mention of the power outage, the two men exchanged glances. But instead of looking upset, they appeared to relax. The tattooed man even cracked his thin lips into a sort of a smile.

Shoni continued squirming, so I took her into the kitchen and placed her in her crate. She whimpered but quieted when I bribed her with a dog cookie.

I could hear Adjidamò, or Jid as we friends and family called him, on the back porch stacking the wood. Sometimes I called him Little Squirrel, the English meaning of his Algonquin name, though at twelve years of age he cringed whenever I used the English version. The "little" reminded him too much of his small stature.

He was staying with me for a few days to help with Christmas preparations. This morning we'd tramped out into the woods to chop down this year's "perfect" tree, a spruce just short enough to provide sufficient space under the ceiling for the *de rigeur* flashing plastic Santa that had lorded over my Christmas trees since childhood. At the moment, the tree was dripping the last of its snow onto the pantry floor.

I brushed past its prickly branches and stuck my head out the back door. "Jid, we have company. I would feel better if you stayed out here for the moment, okay?"

There was something about these two men that didn't sit right. Their turning up in a major snowstorm in the middle of nowhere, for nowhere was where I lived, wasn't normal. The only strangers that came to this isolated corner of West Quebec were hunters and fishermen, and this wasn't the time of year for either activity. If things became too tense, I would have Jid leave without their knowing he was here.

"I guess. Who's here?" He raised questioning brown eyes up to mine.

He and I had become good friends after my beloved Sergei saved him from freezing to death. At the time, he had been living with Kòkomis. I learned later that she was actually his great-grandmother, or *ànikekòkomis*, but everyone had called her Kòkomis, meaning simply "grandmother." When she passed on, I wanted to adopt him. His mother was dead and his father in jail. But an aunt came forward, insisting that he had to stay with his own kind. The rest of the Migiskan Algonquin agreed. So, against his wishes and mine, he went to live with his aunt on the reserve.

We'd remained close. For the past several months he'd been spending more time at my house than at his aunt's. She had two boys of her own, and Jid was often ignored. His aunt had recently taken a job in Ottawa, leaving him alone with her sons, who didn't hesitate to bully their much younger cousin. Though he was adept at deflecting their jibes, he preferred to retreat to where he could be assured of some peace and could play with Shoni. The boy loved dogs. Sergei and he had been the best of buddies. He still mourned the dog's loss as much as Eric and I did.

"A couple of men I've never seen before. There is something about them I don't trust, so I think it best you stay out of sight for the moment."

"I know how to shoot. Give me one of Eric's rifles, and I can handle them." He jutted out his jaw with stubborn determination in an attempt to look tough, which was difficult. The impish gleam in his eyes kept sneaking through.

"I know you do, but not this time. I want you to stay in the pantry or on the porch until I let you know everything's okay. But if you hear me yell or something strange happens, leave. Use my snowshoes."

Though his aunt's house was five to six kilometres by road from my place, it was half the distance through the woods along an old hunting trail Jid frequently hiked.

At my insistence he'd put on his puffy down-filled jacket to get the firewood but hadn't bothered with any other warm clothes. "Put these on." I passed him his Gore-Tex mitts and his wool hockey toque. "And do up your jacket and tie your boots."

He smiled sheepishly as he zipped up the jacket.

I'd no sooner closed the door on him than a voice came from out of the darkness. "Were you talking to someone?"

I jumped. The tattooed man was stepping across the kitchen threshold onto the linoleum floor.

"You know how it is when you live alone. You talk to yourself." The second I said the word "alone," I realized it was a mistake. "Actually, I don't live alone. My husband will be here shortly. I just like to talk to myself."

"When do you expect him?"

"In a few hours." I was hoping this would persuade them to leave.

"He'll need a Hummer with chains if he wants to get through this shit."

"A snowmobile will do."

"I'm looking forward to meeting him."

I wasn't quite sure how to take this. Did it mean they planned to stay longer than a couple of hours?

"Expecting anyone else?"

"It is close to Christmas, and I am expecting deliveries." Might as well pile on the lies. But why did he care?

He peered down at me from his six-foot height. "Like I said. Not in this shit. I came in to ask if you have any first aid supplies."

THREE

"I'll get the bandages as soon as I get us some light," I replied, returning to the pantry.

I squeezed past the tree, endeavouring, albeit unsuccessfully, to avoid its sharp needles. On tiptoes, I reached up to the top shelf to retrieve a couple of oil lamps and then fumbled around on another shelf for the bottle of lamp fuel that was supposed to be there. It was proving difficult to see in the growing darkness. In another hour it would be pitch black.

It would remain so until the hydro trucks eventually made it to this remote wilderness, which likely wouldn't happen until the storm had stopped and all the downed lines and poles leading here were repaired. One time it had taken eleven days, but that was during an ice storm, when inch-thick ice toppled the hydro poles like dominos. With blizzards, the outages tended to be shorter. However, two years ago it took crews three days to turn the lights and heat back on.

I cringed at the thought of being trapped inside my house with these guys for longer than a few hours. Surely they would leave once the injured man was patched up.

Setting the lamps on the kitchen counter, I poured oil into both, adjusted the wicks, and lit them. The tattoos on the face of my unwanted guest sprang menacingly into view. Snakes, big ones, little ones, with long, flicking tongues, slithered over his cheeks, down his neck, and up over his forehead onto his bald pate. Not being a big fan of snakes, I stepped back.

Although he was slim, he held himself in a way that suggested he was all muscle. I suspected he could bench press considerably more weight than Eric could — though that wasn't a fair comparison. With his busy business travel schedule, my husband seldom had time these days to work out on the equipment he'd set up in one of the upstairs bedrooms.

"Take this lamp into your friend," I said. "I'll get the first aid kit."

As the lamp's glow headed down the hall, a jolt ran through the house from another strong gust. Snow scraped against the kitchen windows. I threw a couple of logs into the cookstove. Although the house was warm at the moment, with no electricity to fire up the baseboard heaters it would be freezing by morning. I made a mental note to stoke up the fireplaces in the living room and den too.

I was about to check on the boy when a voice behind me said, "My throat is feeling somewhat parched. I imagine you have a well-stocked liquor cabinet somewhere in this palatial cottage of yours. Bring me a bottle."

There was no way I wanted this guy drunk in my house. Should I pretend I didn't have any? But that would only get him searching through my cupboards, and I didn't want him finding Eric's cherished bottles of single malt.

"There's some beer in the fridge."

"Hardly. You must have something more in keeping with my palate."

Thankfully, Eric kept a bottle of rye for a friend who only drank rye and ginger. I pulled it out of the cupboard.

His nose squinched up with disdain. "Nothing better?"

"No." He wasn't going near Eric's Lagavulin.

He uncapped the bottle and sniffed. "I guess it will have to do. At least it is Crown Royal." He greedily gulped down the burning liquid. "Aaaahhh, it's been too long." He took another long swig.

If he continued to drink this stuff straight, he'd be drunk in no time. I passed him a glass and a can of ginger ale.

"It takes me back to my university days." He poured a good measure of rye into the glass, followed by a lesser amount of ginger ale. "Ice?"

I gave him the ice tray in the hope that a good quantity would dilute the alcohol.

He dislodged a single cube and dropped it into his glass, but instead of heading back to his friend, he started leafing through yesterday's mail sitting on the counter.

He pulled out an envelope and read, "Mr. Eric Odjik. Your husband, I take it. Name sounds Native. Is he Algonquin, like Larry?"

"Yes." He didn't need to know more, like the fact that Eric had once been the Migiskan band chief and was currently running for Grand Chief of the Grand Council of First Nations.

"Ms. M. Harris. What's the *M* stand for? Mary? Marilyn?"

"No, Margaret." I wasn't about to give him "Meg," the name used by people who were part of my life. He definitely was not.

"I'll call you 'Red.' It seems more fitting."

I shrugged. Cursed with a head of shocking red hair, though it was a tad faded now, it wasn't the first time someone had called me by that name, nor would it be the last.

After another long draught, he sauntered back down the hall. Although he moved with a dancer's grace, I doubted he was a dancer. More like a viper poised to strike. The bottoms of his jeans were soaked, but I wasn't about to suggest he put on a dry pair of Eric's. He'd unzipped his black nylon windbreaker, which I thought rather lightweight to be wearing outdoors in such weather. But I imagined he hadn't planned on trudging up my long drive in a snowstorm.

I wondered where these guys were going when the accident occurred. The main road dead-ended at the reserve, but perhaps they were going to visit Larry's family for Christmas. On the other hand, neither had mentioned the need to contact anyone to let them know about the accident.

Once satisfied the tattooed man was in the den, I headed back to the pantry. I'd decided to send Jid on his way. Not only would he be safely away from here, but he could also alert Will Decontie. Though Will was the chief of the Migiskan tribal police force and therefore not responsible for the policing at Three Deer Point, I knew he would come. He could also send emergency personnel to take care of the injured man. But I'd no sooner stepped into the narrow room than I heard the tattooed man returning to the kitchen.

"Red, I need your assistance. My friend is out cold."

I glanced out the pantry windows, hoping to catch sight of the boy to signal him to leave, but it had become too dark outside to see properly. Nonetheless, I waved in the direction of the reserve, hoping he would see it and understand its meaning.

From her crate in an out-of-the-way corner of my large country kitchen, Shoni whimpered and squirmed.

"Look, my puppy has to go outside." I would use this chance to tell Jid to go straight to the police station.

"She can piss in the cage. My buddy needs you."

FOUR

The black cherry panelling and floor-to-ceiling bookcases had never made the den the brightest room in the cottage, but with daylight almost gone, it was like a cave, except for the bright swath where the man had placed the oil lamp. Unfortunately, it didn't reach the injured man, so I moved it to the end table nearest the sofa.

Larry was still, almost too still. But the gentle rise and fall of his chest told me he lived. His hand had fallen away from where it had been gripping his coat. The blood soaked up by the coarse wool looked to be almost dry. Earlier I thought I'd noticed a tear in the fabric, but now I wasn't so certain. I wondered what kind of car accident would cause such a wound, particularly since he didn't appear to be injured or bruised anywhere else.

I removed his wet wool tuque to reveal a head of thick black hair in desperate need of a trim and a wash.

"We need to get this wet coat off him. Could you hold him up while I remove it? By the way, do you have a name?"

"They call me Professor."

Professor? "Snake" would be more appropriate.

He wrenched the unconscious man up into a sitting position with more force than necessary, which caused Larry to groan. But it hadn't hurt enough to rouse him into consciousness.

I eased his arm out of the sleeve on the opposite side of the wound and carefully removed the coat from around his back, trying not to tug too hard when it became caught. When I started to remove the front part covering the wound, I realized the material had stuck, so I left it for the moment.

The coat's wetness had penetrated to his thin white T-shirt. I could feel the poor man shivering. When I finished treating him, I would replace it with one of Eric's and a heavy wool sweater.

"Okay, you can put him back down. But do it gently."

His friend eased him onto the sofa with considerable more care. "Sorry, little buddy, if I hurt you." He turned his yellow eyes in my direction. "Will he live?"

"I've no idea. I'm not a doctor. But I need to check the condition of the wound. For that I need better light."

I got up and turned to leave.

"Where are you going?"

"To the kitchen to get a headlamp."

I was hoping for another chance to tell Jid to run, but the man followed right on my heels. I could smell his perfumery aftershave lotion a little too intensely. "Look, stay with your friend to make sure he doesn't have a seizure."

"Hell, is that likely?"

"I've no idea, but it's best to watch him closely, just in case."

"Pour me another rye and ginger." He slapped his empty glass into my hand and strode back to his friend.

Jid was no longer on the back porch. Through the waves of blowing snow I could barely make out the indentations left by his snowshoes. They were heading in the direction of the old hunting trail, though when I saw the rate at which they were being filled in, I was worried I'd sent him into a maelstrom that was more than he could handle.

Yet he was a very determined and very resourceful young man. He might be only twelve, but he'd grown up in these woods, knew the dangers, and how to handle them. Generally it took him about forty minutes to walk to my place from the rez, thirty if he ran. In this weather it could take him close to two hours. Give the police chief a half hour to corral enough skidoos, another half hour to get here, and I could expect rescue in three hours.

Three hours to keep Professor sober. Three hours to keep myself safe. Three hours to keep Larry from dying, for I had no idea how Professor would react if his friend died.

My optimism rose when I saw that the boy had taken Eric's headlamp from the drawer. Though he knew every twist and turn of the trail, snow can change the landscape, especially in the dark. Light would help keep him from getting lost.

I let Shoni do her business on the porch where the snow wouldn't bury her, then gathered up some firewood for the den. When I walked into the room with the puppy pattering behind me, Professor was leaning over his friend, watching him intently.

"You must be good friends."

"What makes you say that?"

"The way you're worrying about him."

"He's such a little guy, he's an easy target. So I look out for him."

"Were you on your way to visit his family?"

"Pardon?"

"To spend Christmas with them. That's your reason for being in this area, isn't it?"

He took a gulp of his drink and stood up. "Stop asking your fucking questions and do something about him."

His windbreaker swung open to reveal the head of a cobra stamped in red on the front of his black sweatshirt. He padded over to one of the leather armchairs bookending the chesterfield and sank into the soft cushions. After another mouthful of rye, he slammed the glass onto the end table, sending a scared Shoni cowering into a corner. After a few seconds she summoned up the courage to gingerly approach him for a pat. Without thinking, he reached down and gently patted her.

What was with this guy? One minute he was as polite as by your leave and the next as rude as a mindless boor.

FIVE

The fire flared with the fresh logs, bringing renewed warmth into the den. I switched on the headlamp and surveyed the coat where the blood was drying. I worried that if I removed it, I might cause the bleeding to restart. But if I didn't, it might lead to infection.

I slipped my fingers under the coarse wool and inched them toward the wound. The T-shirt was stuck to the coat where the blood had collected. I gently pried the two fabrics loose. They parted slowly. At one point I thought I felt fresh bleeding, but when I pulled my fingers away there was no sign of new blood.

I was concerned about Larry's continuing unconsciousness. Since his clothes weren't drenched in blood, I didn't think it came from blood loss. Internal bleeding could be another cause. But I had no idea what symptoms to look for, though I knew enough to realize that if he was hemorrhaging, he could die without prompt medical attention. The coma could also be the result of a head injury, which was equally life-threatening.

"Did Larry's head hit something during the accident, like the dashboard?" I asked, though I didn't see any obvious marks on his face or bumps on his head.

"Not that I noticed, but I was too busy trying to keep us from being killed."

"He could be seriously hurt. He needs proper medical attention." I stood up. "Since we can't call, one of us should go for help."

"You're staying right here, as am I."

"But he could die."

"It's up to you to make sure he doesn't."

"If you're expecting me to save him, forget it. I don't know the first thing about first aid."

Not quite true. Twice before, I'd been involved in trying to save someone's life. The first was when I was eighteen and doing lifeguard duty at a local pool. It had been a busy day with lots of kids, making it difficult to keep track of them all. Suddenly someone shouted that a girl was at the bottom of the pool. Frantic, another lifeguard and I dove in and brought her to the surface. She wasn't breathing. Gloria and I worked on her until the paramedics arrived. She never revived. I blamed myself for her death. I hadn't been vigilant enough. A short while later I quit lifeguarding altogether. Although I learned months later that she'd died from an unsuspected heart condition and not from drowning, I continued to blame myself and still do to this day. Irrational, I know. But that was me. I didn't handle guilt well.

As for the second case? That person died too.

Not exactly a stellar track record, was it?

I continued to work my fingers between the two fabrics. Fortunately, the blood hadn't melded them into one.

Finally, the coat came free. I carefully lifted it from his body, removed his arm from the sleeve, and set the bloody coat on the bare wood behind me, away from the oriental carpet, one of Aunt Aggie's prized belongings, though somewhat frayed from years of use.

The puppy was being a little too quiet. I looked around to discover her nestled in the lap of Professor, his long fingers gently stroking her.

"It's been awhile since I had my own dog." He smiled, revealing a mouth of surprisingly white and well-cared-for teeth.

Maybe I'd misjudged these guys and had overreacted in sending Jid after the police. Regardless, Larry still needed medical attention. Sending the boy was the only way to get it, since this man wasn't about to do it. The mantel clock pointed to a quarter after five. Jid had been gone about thirty minutes. Another two and a half hours before help would arrive.

Night had closed in, leaving the world outside an ominous black hole. Judging by the reduction in sound, the wind's intensity had lessened. Flakes, however, continued to tap incessantly against the den windows.

Larry moaned but remained in a coma. I took this to be a sign that he might be coming out of it.

His T-shirt was caked in mostly dried blood in the area above the injury. A little pressure confirmed that it was stuck to the wound. I felt the best way to remove it was to cut the fabric around the area and gently pry it loose.

I stood up.

"Where are you going?" Professor asked, brushing Shoni aside with a shove, sending her tumbling to the floor. Confused, she ran to me. I picked her up.

"Relax. I'm only going to get a pair of scissors and my first aid kit."

"Get me another drink." He tossed me the empty glass.

Taken by surprise, I almost missed it but managed to hang on to it, and with the puppy under one arm, I headed to the kitchen, where the first thing I did was put her in her crate.

Although most of her fur was black, her muzzle was silvery grey. Eventually her coat would turn completely silver. I'd chosen this colour so she wouldn't remind me of my old companion, who'd been a rich, inky black except for a dusting of grey on his muzzle that had appeared in his later years. Eric had named her, appropriately, *Shóníyá*, the Algonquin word for *silver*, which was quickly shortened to Shoni.

I left her quietly munching another bribe while I went upstairs.

I'd no sooner switched on my headlamp and placed my moccasin on the first step than Professor called out again, "Where are you going?"

This was getting boring. "To get the first aid kit in the bathroom."

"I'm coming with you."

What was it with this guy?

He creaked up the wooden stairs behind me.

"Red, this is a remarkably fine cottage you live in. You aren't pinched for money, are you?"

I didn't like where this was going. "I don't have a bean. I inherited what little you see here."

"Hardly little. I've seen millionaires' cottages in the Charlevoix smaller than this."

Our footsteps echoed as we followed the funnel of light from my headlamp up the stairs. I could feel the cold air rushing down to greet us.

"Much cooler up here," he remarked. "With a house this old, you must have a fireplace in one or two of the bedrooms."

"I do."

"You need to get them going to keep your pipes from freezing."

He had a point, but I'd worry about it later. My only desire at the moment was to get what I came for and return downstairs as speedily as possible. It unnerved me being up here alone with him in the frigid darkness.

But he had other ideas.

"How many bedrooms do you have?" he asked, stopping to glance through the open door of the room we were passing. I shone my light onto the sparse furnishings to get the message across that I wasn't rich.

Aunt Aggie hadn't bothered to furnish the spare rooms properly, and I hadn't either, which invariably sparked complaints from Jean on the rare occasions when she visited. For the coming visit I was attempting to head off her complaints with new linen, goose-down pillows, and goose-down duvets for the four beds they would be using.

She and her husband didn't share a bed, she'd told me on their first visit not long after Eric and I were married. "We can't be bothered with that nonsense," she'd said with one of her judicial stares, doubtless of the variety she directed at the poor victims in her courtroom. I'd merely replied that there was nothing like a good romp, which got the outraged reaction I'd intended.

"Six bedrooms," I said as I continued walking to the next room, the bathroom.

"Good for lots of kids."

I could feel his eyes on my back, querying where mine were. There weren't any. Eric's daughter was the only offspring we had, and this was going to be her first visit, though not through our choice. Her busy broadcasting schedule and move to the Northwest Territories hadn't permitted a stay until now.

"That's how they built them a hundred years ago," I said.

"I figured this was built in the late 1800s."

"In 1891. My great-grandfather built it."

"My great-grandparents could have used a place this size. They had eighteen kids. But they were poor French Canadian farmers with only a four-bedroom farmhouse, not rich like you English."

I didn't reply, knowing any answer I gave would lead to places I didn't want to go.

SIX

My headlamp lit up the bathroom, bounced off the mirror above the sink, and onto the lion claw bathtub behind me. I rummaged through the cupboard until I found bandages, sterile pads, gauze, tape, and hydrogen peroxide. Living in the wilds, where all manner of accidents can happen, Eric insisted we keep a well-stocked first aid supply.

"You can take these downstairs." I tossed Professor some old towels and facecloths.

Placing the supplies in an antique porcelain washbasin, I headed to the front of the house to my bedroom for a clean T-shirt and sweater for Larry.

Behind me, the bathroom door clicked closed.

"Don't flush the toilet," I called out. "The electric pump won't be working."

I selected one of Eric's old T-shirts and a sweater an old girlfriend had knitted him. I figured it didn't matter if it got blood on it. Since the house was only going to get colder, I pulled out a sweater for myself, the heavy Aran fisherman cardigan with its distinctive O'Brien clan pattern that Mother had brought me back from Ireland when

I was a teenager. She'd wanted to remind me of my distant Irish roots from her side of the family.

Though Mother and I had grown apart after I forsook the Harris family home in Toronto for the wilds of Quebec, I was still mourning her loss from heart failure in September. It was the main reason for Eric's insistence on a family Christmas. Since we were so few and so spread out, Jean and family in Toronto and Teht'aa in Yellowknife, he felt it would be a good time to renew our family ties.

I flashed the light around the large room. looking for anything else that could be useful. It lit up the antique mahogany chest of drawers and the matching armoire, both inherited from my great-aunt. Her three-quarter brass bed had been just a little too cozy. We had replaced it with Eric's queen mattress from his bungalow on the reserve and blown a bundle on a mahogany sleigh bedframe to give our marriage bed that special touch.

As the light shone on the crowded bookcases filling the inside wall, I noticed Aunt Aggie's black rotary phone peeking out from behind some books. I'd forgotten all about it. Unlike the portable phone, its modest electricity requirements came through the telephone wire. This old phone usually worked in outages, as long as the phone lines hadn't been affected. Sure enough, when I plugged it in, I heard the welcoming sound of a dial tone.

I was dialling the police chief's number when the bathroom door creaked open. Stocking feet padded down the hall toward me. I hung up, shoved the phone farther behind the books, and headed out into the hall. As much as this man seemed to care about his friend, I sensed that he didn't want me bringing in authorities of any shape or variety. I'd make the call when he wasn't stalking me.

"Grab the blankets off that bed, will you?" I indicated the open door of the guest bedroom next to mine.

"These look like genuine Hudson's Bay Company blankets, complete with the short black lines," he said.

"They likely date from my great-grandfather's days. Weren't those lines used to indicate the number of pelts a trapper had to pay for the blanket?"

"Not so. The lines were invented by French weavers in the eighteenth century to indicate the finished size of the blanket."

"You seem to know your history."

"I dabble."

With my arms full, I headed back to the stairs. Surrounded by blinding darkness but for the ribbon of light from my headlamp, I felt like I'd been transported to another world. It was as if nothing else existed but the hallway, the storm, this strange man, and me. The air throbbed with the eerie moaning of the wind as it whipped around the house and through the pines.

The house had been built beside a stand of ancient white pine, one of the few to survive the logging ravishes of the late 1800s. Although no giant had fallen directly onto the house, massive branches had come down in storms such as this. For the most part, they had missed the house, but there had been a few direct hits over the years, including a memorable one a couple of winters ago that partially caved in the verandah roof. Last summer, Eric had hired a logger from the rez to remove some of the lower and dying limbs of nearby trees. But it was no guarantee that an unusually strong gust of wind wouldn't send a branch, even a tree, crashing onto the house.

Larry remained as still and silent as when I'd left him, though I thought his right arm might have shifted. His breathing was steady, and I couldn't detect a fever, all good signs. Like Professor, he had tattoos, but only two, an eagle feather caressing the side of his face and a single teardrop underneath his eye. His skin was pockmarked from acne. A single feather earring dangled from his right ear. I threw another log onto the fire to ensure he would have enough warmth while Professor covered his legs with the blanket.

"What happened to my glass?" Professor demanded.

"I left it in the kitchen. I'll go get it."

Not that I wanted to be his servant, but my plan was to pour less rye and more ginger ale into the glass.

"I'll do it. You won't put in enough rye."

"That's the only bottle. When it's gone, it's gone."

"Bullshit. I'm certain there is plenty more liquor in this house. What else does a person do on cold dark nights like this other than drink?"

Used to, I thought to myself, but no longer. Eric had cured me of that.

I gave him the glass and watched his back disappear into the blackness of the hall.

SEVEN

The dried blood had caused Larry's T-shirt to bunch up, making it difficult to determine the extent of the wound underneath. When the fabric refused to budge with a gentle tug, I decided it might be stuck to his skin. I then noticed a curious tear in the cloth near the centre of the stain, which suggested that the area of the injury was comparatively small.

"You said this was caused by a car accident," I said to Professor as he walked into the room, his full glass tinkling.

Sticking out of his jacket pocket was the metallic blue end of a flashlight. It unsettled me to realize he'd gone snooping through my kitchen drawers without asking. I wondered what else he had helped himself to.

"That's right."

"Was he thrown against something sharp?"

"In a car?"

"That's why I'm asking. His wound looks like something stabbed him, but it's too low on his body for it to be from a cracked windshield. Besides, his face would be covered in cuts. Do you have any idea what it could have been?"

"Does it matter? The key thing is to cleanse the wound and cover it with a bandage." He resumed his seat in the armchair and concentrated on his drink.

I felt Shoni's warm muzzle on my back. He'd let her out. I started to get up to return her to the crate, when he called out, "Here puppy, puppy, puppy," and held out a dog cookie. She gamboled over to him. Traitor.

"Please keep her with you. I don't want her bothering me while I am dealing with your friend."

"No problem, eh, *p'tit*?" He placed her on his lap and hid his face in her soft puppy fur. He seemed to care more for the dog than for the man on the couch.

I snipped away the free edges of the T-shirt and removed most of it, except for the front piece and the back when it wouldn't easily slide out from under him.

I returned to the kitchen, this time without my escort, and filled the washbasin with a blend of hot water from the kettle simmering on the woodstove and cold water from a container kept on hand for power outages. Back in the den, I moistened the bloodied patch of cotton with a wet facecloth until it started running red. I gently pulled at the fabric, lifting it gradually from the wound. When it remained stuck, I added more water, until finally it came away free. Larry grunted once or twice as if from pain, but otherwise remained unconscious.

Before I had a chance to inspect the wound, Shoni was jumping against my back. She nibbled my ear before turning her attention to the dirty water in the washbasin.

I pulled her away. "Professor, could you please look after her?"

My answer was the soft snoring of sleep. He was slumped down in the chair with his head flopped uncomfortably to one side. On the table beside him stood the half-empty glass.

Without another thought, I draped a blanket over Larry, scooped up the puppy, and hotfooted it to the kitchen as stealthily as I could. After placing her in her crate, I headed upstairs to the phone. Big mistake. Before I reached the second floor, Shoni was whining, loudly. I debated returning to quiet her down, but since I was so close to the phone, I keep going. I crept along the hall to my room, but as I reached the door, the tattooed man called out from downstairs, "Red, where are you?"

I ignored him and rushed to the phone, but as I did so, I heard him running up the stairs.

"You up here?"

My headlamp flashed momentarily on the phone hidden in the shadows of the shelf. So close and yet so far. Dare I? But I decided against it. I feared the risk was too high. When I made the call, I wanted to be assured that I could bring in the police without raising the man's suspicions. If he knew they were coming, I wasn't sure what he would do.

I stuck my head out the door. "I'm getting some dry socks for Larry. You could probably do with some too."

"Don't you dare disappear on me again," he growled, coming up to me.

EIGHT

Larry's eyes fluttered when I knelt down beside him.
"Are you awake?" I asked.

They fluttered again and opened.

"How are you feeling?"

He tried to sit up and then fell back onto the sofa, groaning with pain. "Holy fuck, where am I? It sure don't look like the —"

Professor brushed his hand over his friend's lips. "Ssssh…. It's okay. We're in that fancy old house you're always talking about."

Larry shifted his eyes questioningly around the den. "How'd we get here?"

"Drove, remember? We hit that damn tree and had to walk in through the goddamn snow."

"Yeah, but —"

"Ssshh. You're here. That's all that counts."

"Sure, Professor, whatever you say. Jeez, I hurt like hell. What happened?" He inched his hand down to where his wound gaped. A trickle of blood oozed from the hole.

"The car accident, remember? You got stabbed by something in the car."

But now that I could see the injury clearly, I noticed that it didn't have the ragged edges I would expect from an object sharp enough not only to penetrate the man's flesh, but also to go through two layers of fabric, including the thick wool of the coat. Nor did I see any bruising that would be expected from being hurled against a dash. Rather, the hole was perfectly round, about the diameter of my baby finger, with the edges puckered and blackened. A few scattered fibres were stuck to the edges of the wound. Redness radiated out from the hole.

"Are you sure he was injured in a car accident?" I asked.

"Yes." Professor's unwavering amber gaze stared back at me, as if daring me to challenge him.

So I bit my tongue and kept my opinion to myself. Although my experience was limited, I was convinced it was a bullet hole. This, of course, led to the obvious questions. Who had shot him, and why? And more importantly, why pretend it hadn't happened?

I shivered from more than just the cold. The room had grown darker, the shadows deeper. Through the window only sightless black. The wind had ratcheted up several notches and changed direction. The agony of the pines filled the room. The snow no longer scraped the den window, but from the kitchen its scratching came loud and clear.

I was worried about Jid. At least the tightly packed evergreens of the forest would protect him from the worst of the blizzard. If the snow became too deep, he knew enough to burrow under the protection of spruce boughs and wait until the worst was over. It would mean that he wouldn't be alerting the police. But that was okay. It was more important that he remained safe.

Ever since Sergei had found him passed out from a drug overdose in an abandoned shack on my land, I'd had a special place in my heart for this orphan boy with the elfin grin. Small for his age, he'd looked so forlorn and lost and in need of love. I soon learned, though, that he'd plenty of love from his *kòkomis*, who was doing the best she could to raise her great-grandson despite her blindness and her poverty. It was a very sad day for all of us when she died.

Jid and I had developed a special relationship. He would often come to Three Deer Point to play with his buddy Sergei and to talk to me. Keenly curious, he would ask me endless questions about the broader world beyond the reserve, while at the same time he would help expand my knowledge of Algonquin ways. His grandmother had been a highly respected elder within the community and did her best to follow the traditional ways. But sometimes they collided with the modern world. Rather than ridiculing them and tossing them aside, as any child his age would do, Jid, knowing how much they meant to his grandmother, would find a place for them in the modern life he wanted to lead.

I remembered the time he came down with strep throat. Kòkomis, who had little trust in modern medicine, threw away the antibiotics the nurse had given him and brought in a shaman to heal him properly. His face flushed, his eyelids heavy from fever, Jid had calmly lain back and accepted the ministrations of the medicine man and the healing powers of the tobacco tie. But as I left the room, he winked and surreptitiously showed me the bottle of antibiotics retrieved from the garbage.

It wouldn't matter if the boy were delayed in reaching Will. I still had Aunt Aggie's phone. I watched the tattooed man take another long drink of his rye and ginger and settle farther into the comfortable chair. The glass was almost empty. If he continued drinking at this rate, he would hopefully pass out, and I would be able to call without fear of being caught. I only had to keep him in an amenable state until then.

For the moment I had a bigger problem. I might not know much about gunshot wounds, but I did know that where there was a bullet hole, there would be a bullet. Unless the bullet had passed straight through Larry's body, it was still inside him, somewhere in his abdomen. I also knew that it couldn't stay. It had to come out, or infection and all sorts of other nasty side effects would ensue. But I didn't have the foggiest idea how to take out a bullet.

"Do you know anything about removing a bullet?" I asked, deciding to bite the bullet myself, so to speak.

The tattooed man stared at me without blinking. I stared back at him, equally noncommittal. If he wasn't going to admit his friend had been shot, I wasn't going to either.

"Maybe," he finally said.

"You're going to have to help me. If we don't remove it, your friend's going to die."

He ran his hand over the snake slithering over his head.

"There is another way, a much better way," I continued. "I can go for help."

I left the words hanging in the sudden stillness. The first time, he'd turned me down. What would he do this time, when the need for medical attention had become all that more imperative?

His answer was to brush me aside. "I'll do it." He knelt down on the floor beside his friend and shone the flashlight onto the wound.

My suspicions grew, along with my uneasiness.

NINE

"No way you gonna dig around inside me," Larry squeaked, placing his hand over the wound. He grimaced at the touch. In his other hand he gripped a tiny leather pouch hanging around his neck as if his life depended upon it. It looked to be similar to the amulet Eric wore.

"P'tit Chief, you're going to die if I don't," Professor said almost in a whisper.

"So … my life ain't worth shit."

"We've gotten through worse shit than this. You're going to make it. Here, drink this down." He passed his friend what remained of his drink and then turned to me. "Get the bottle. We have to get him drunk."

Larry turned his head away from the glass. "No way. You know I go crazy when I get smashed."

"It's going to hurt like hell. Get drunk and you won't feel a thing."

Larry grabbed the glass and downed it, but a little too quickly. He coughed and sputtered, which caused him to wince in pain. "Jeez, that hurts." He closed his eyes as he waited for the pain to subside. Then he took another sip, slower this time. "Sure feels good, eh? Been a long time." When he finished the drink, he passed Professor the glass and then gingerly ran his fingers over the wound. "Pretty small hole to hurt so much. How'd I get shot?"

I tensed, dying to know the answer myself. I'd been nervously tossing around a few scenarios, none of which fit the definition of law-abiding.

Instead of answering, the tattooed man cast an angry scowl in my direction. "Get the damn bottle."

"Okay, but are you sure it's a good idea?"

"Do you want my help?"

"He's your friend, not mine."

"Right, so go get that goddamn bottle." He slammed his fist down onto the coffee table, which sent me scurrying.

By the time I reached the kitchen door, I could hear feverish whispering. I turned around and tiptoed back to try to catch what they were saying, but the voices stopped abruptly when I stepped on a particularly noisy floorboard.

When I returned with the half-empty bottle of rye and a couple of cans of ginger ale, Professor was gently pushing down on Larry's abdomen.

"What are you doing?" I asked.

"Trying to see if I can feel the bullet."

"Is that a good idea? It might cause more bleeding."

"It's okay. I've seen them do this in the infirmary."

Infirmary? Sounded like the military to me, but he didn't strike me as being a soldier. "Where was that?"

"No place you'd be interested in."

Maybe he didn't want to tell me, but I was beginning to have my suspicions.

I noticed an old scar, possibly from the removal of his appendix, on the opposite side of the bullet wound, and another smaller, older scar farther up on Larry's chest. This one appeared too jagged to be from an operation.

"Looks like you were shot once before, Larry."

He fluttered his eyes open. "Yeah, almost died. Long time ago." He smiled a faint half smile. "Just a kid, doing something I shouldna been doing."

"Was this on the rez?"

"Yeah, I was sticking my nose where it don't belong. My uncle thought I was a bear, and wham. Got a bullet in me. But he saved me too. Loaded me onto his Ski-Doo and hightailed it to the nurse. They got me to the hospital in Ottawa pretty quick. Almost died in the ambulance, though."

"I have a feeling you're going to be okay this time too. Professor, I'm wondering, since the bleeding has stopped, if the injury is as bad as we think. Maybe you don't have to get the bullet out now but can wait until the roads are cleared and you can take him to a doctor."

Larry grew quiet as he waited for his friend to answer.

"You have a point. I've seen guys bleed a lot worse than this and survive. But rather than waiting, let's get this sucker out now, okay, little buddy?"

Larry nodded numbly, then yelled out "Jesus!" when Professor pushed a little too hard on his abdomen.

"Sorry, P'tit Chief. You better have more rye. It's going to get a lot worse."

"Ya sure you need to do it now, Professor?" Larry squeaked. "Like the lady said, maybe it can wait until later."

"I have to do it now. But the good news is since the wound is on one side of your abdomen and not in the middle, the damage to your internal organs could be minimal."

"If you say so." Larry squeezed his eyes closed and held on to his amulet as if seeking strength.

I didn't blame him. I wouldn't want to be awake while someone dug around inside of me either.

"Red, you don't happen to have some forceps or something similar with which to extract the bullet?" Professor asked.

"I'm not exactly an infirmary, but let me check in the kitchen to see if my husband has something that might work."

"Speaking of husband. You still expecting him to get through in this stuff?"

I froze. I'd forgotten I'd told him Eric was coming. "Yeah, he should be here soon. If he can't get through in his Jeep, he'll borrow a Ski-Doo."

Maybe this would entice the man to take his friend and leave. I had a feeling he wouldn't want to meet up with Eric any more than he wanted to meet up with paramedics.

"Like I said, I can't wait to meet him."

"I'm sure he will be interested in meeting you too," I answered, moving toward the door.

But my way came to an abrupt halt when I stumbled over Larry's coat lying where I'd tossed it onto the floor. I slung it over the back of the armchair Professor had been sitting in. The light from the oil lamp brought the bloodstain into sharp relief against the light grey wool. It covered most of the lower half of the coat and had penetrated deeply into the fabric. I figured the garment was ruined, but maybe it wouldn't matter to Larry. He could get a lot of mileage out of it with his beer-drinking buddies, maybe even free beer.

Then I realized I was looking at the back of the coat.

"Professor, check his back. I think the bullet might have gone through."

He slipped his hand underneath as Larry hollered, "Hey, watch it, that hurts."

"Yes, there's a hole back here." He pushed the wounded man onto his side a little too roughly, causing Larry to yell out again.

"Jeez, what are you trying to do, kill me?"

My headlamp lit up another bullet hole, this one larger and more ragged around the edges, with more tissue showing through the hole. Like the front entrance wound, this one was no longer bleeding.

"Your lucky day, P'tit Chief. I don't have to go digging around inside you." He slapped his friend on his backside before lowering the man back onto the sofa. Larry groaned with pain.

"Be careful," I warned. "Just because he doesn't have a bullet inside him doesn't mean that he hasn't been seriously injured. We don't know the extent of the damage it left behind."

"You're going to live, little buddy." Professor ruffled his friend's thick black hair before pouring himself another stiff drink. He sat back down on the chair without bothering to remove the coat underneath him.

"Hey, what about me?"

"You don't need any liquor now, P'tit. Besides, you said it makes you crazy, and we can't have you going crazy on us, can we?"

I was more worried about it making the tattooed man crazy. Though he'd already drunk almost a half a bottle, I couldn't detect any change in his behaviour, not even a hint of drowsiness. So maybe I would be lucky, and he would remain relatively normal until he finally passed out.

I noticed threads stuck to the side of the abdominal wound. "We need tweezers, which are upstairs. I'll go get them."

The man started to get up.

"I don't need any help. It's better if you stay here to make sure Larry doesn't go into a coma again."

He nodded and slumped back with the glass firmly clenched in his hand.

TEN

I slipped upstairs before the tattooed man could change his mind. I didn't want to lose this chance to call the Migiskan police. I stopped when I reached the door to my room and listened carefully. Apart from the sound of the trees arguing with the wind and the snow creeping across the bedroom windows, I couldn't detect any other sound, especially footsteps coming up the stairs.

I tiptoed into my room, crossed the carpet to the bookshelf, pulled out the phone, and checked to ensure there was still a dialtone. I hastily dialled the phone number for the detachment. Dialling 911 wasn't an option. It would direct my call to the police force that handled the policing for my area, the Sûreté du Quebec in Somerset, forty-five minutes away on a good day. In this storm, easily double that time.

"Get the hell away from the phone!"

I jumped and almost dropped the receiver but managed to hang on as I yelled, "Will, it's Meg!" while praying like hell that I'd completed dialling.

The tattooed man twisted the handset out of my hand, yanked the cord from the plug, and flung the phone against the wall with such force the dial came loose. "Who in the hell are you calling?" He shone the flashlight into my eyes, blinding me.

I turned away from the light and concentrated on rubbing my sore hand while trying to settle my spiking nerves before blurting out, "I was calling the Migiskan Health Centre." The minute I spoke the words, I knew it was a bad move, almost as bad as telling the truth.

"Do you not understand the word 'No'? I said no paramedics, no doctors, no nobody." He brought his snakes within inches of my face.

"Look, I'm sorry, but I'm worried about internal bleeding. I think we should know what signs to look for and if there is anything we can do to treat it."

"Is Will a doctor?"

"Head of the health centre."

"Did you get through?"

"No," I said.

For several long seconds his amber eyes seemed to bore through me, as if seeking the truth. I tried not to flinch.

"You said you had no working phone."

"I forgot about this one."

A sudden thud against the side of the house had us both whirling around.

"What the hell was that?"

"Probably a branch." I shone my headlamp through the window and onto a broken branch lying half buried in the white expanse covering the verandah roof. The snow had drifted against the bottom quarter of the window, which likely meant more than double the amount on the ground.

"Why did you stop me from calling? I thought you were worried about your friend."

"We can fix him up." A tic sprouted in his right eye.

"He can't be that good a friend if you're willing to gamble with his life."

The tic worsened. "Shut the fuck up!" A knife suddenly appeared in his hand. I could feel its icy point pricking the skin under my chin.

"Look, you don't need to do that. I'm not going to do anything."

"Get downstairs and work on Larry. He is my special friend, you hear, my ace man. Anything happens to him, and I will kill you."

ELEVEN

For the first time since these strangers had barged into my house, I felt my life could truly be in danger. Until the knife appeared — a hunting knife I recognized to be Eric's — I'd been assuming, somewhat naively I realized now, that they would leave when they could without causing me harm. I no longer thought that.

Maybe I shouldn't wait for the police. With Jid gone barely an hour, it was still another couple of hours before I could expect them. Anything could happen in two hours.

I decided to leave.

But I'd have to wait until Professor was asleep or occupied in another part of the house, which was unlikely, given the man's penchant for keeping me in his sights. I'd also have to make sure the puppy was away from him. I couldn't leave her behind. I didn't trust him.

I didn't think I had ever felt so alone. If only Eric were with me. He'd know how to handle a man like this. Ever the diplomat, he'd convince him to let the paramedics come and take Larry to the hospital. And he'd convince the man to give himself up from whatever the two of them were running from, for I suspected they were running from something and not on their way to visit anyone on the reserve. It was the only explanation for Larry's gunshot wound and their unexpected arrival at Three Deer Point. My house had become their hideout.

But Eric wasn't here. And given his anger when we'd parted, I wasn't sure if he was coming back.

The only way I knew to survive was to obey this man's demands and wait for the right moment to escape.

With the tweezers in hand and Professor on my heels, I returned to the den considerably more nervous than when I'd left. Larry lay on the couch, his eyes closed, with the blanket pulled up to his chin. He'd managed to prop himself up with the sofa cushions to keep from lying fully on the exit wound.

"Larry, I'm back," I whispered, not wanting to startle him.

His eyes snapped open. "Am I dead?"

"No, you're very much alive. I'm going to remove some threads that are stuck to your wound. It might hurt, so be prepared."

I knelt beside the sofa and lifted the blanket away. He was shivering, so I kept his legs covered. Since his forehead didn't feel abnormally warm, I doubted he had a fever.

"Professor, do you mind adding wood to the fire? It's cooling down in here. There's more on the back porch if you need it."

I waited until I heard his footsteps echoing along the hall to the kitchen before beginning to work on Larry. It bothered me having the man watching my every move.

I sterilized the tweezers first in the pot of boiling water I'd left near the heat of the fire and then in rubbing alcohol. Steeling myself, I brought my hand to the open wound. Larry sucked in a breath, making me even more nervous. Once again he gripped the tiny amulet hanging around his neck as if his life depended on it. I tried to steady my trembling as I plucked first one and then another fibre. Larry's stomach quivered.

"I'm almost finished."

The next threads were easy to remove, until the last one, which had become stuck in the blackened edges of the opening. I tugged as swiftly as I could.

"God!" Larry cried out when it finally broke free.

The wound started to bleed, but only a trickle.

"What in the hell are you doing?"

I could feel Professor's hot breath on my neck.

Larry smiled weakly. "It's okay, Professor. It's just me being a sissy."

"You hang in there, P'tit Chief. You're going to be okay."

He patted his friend on the shoulder and then dropped the logs he was carrying into the rack and threw one onto the fire. He resumed his seat in the armchair. As I knelt over Larry to examine the bullet hole, I caught the sound of ice tinkling. *Good, drink until you pass out.*

"Larry, it looks very clean now, but I'm going to put some hydrogen peroxide on it as a disinfectant. Brace yourself. It's going to hurt."

"Okay," he whispered, squeezing his eyes closed.

I dribbled some of the clear liquid onto a sterile pad and dabbed the area as gently as I could.

He whimpered, "Oh … oh … oh," and then slowly let out his breath.

I felt the puppy's muzzle against my thigh. When she started sniffing at the peroxide bottle, I picked her up. "You're not supposed to be here, little one."

"She was getting lonely," the tattooed man answered.

"She needs to be in her crate. Could you please return her?"

"She's staying with me. I'll keep her out of your way."

"Make sure she doesn't go to the bathroom."

"Already done on the porch."

Enough with this jousting. It was as if he sensed my intention. I'd have to wait for another opportunity to separate the puppy from him.

I leaned back on my heels. "I'm worried about the house cooling down too much. Do you mind checking the fire in the living room and adding more if it needs it?" I stood up. "Just so you know, I'm going to the kitchen to wash my hands after touching Shoni."

As he rose from the chair, he brushed his jacket aside to reveal Eric's sheathed knife tucked into his belt. His lips creased into a thin warning smile before he scooped up the puppy and headed out the door.

Though the kitchen was comfortably warm, I added more wood to the firebox of the cookstove to keep it that way. I heated up a basin of cold water with hot water from the kettle simmering on the burner and plunged my hands in. While I washed them with antiseptic soap, I ran my headlamp around the kitchen in search of ideas for transporting Shoni.

The glossy white paint on the wooden cupboards glimmered in the light's brilliance. Dating from Aunt Aggie's time, I'd never bothered to replace them, believing solid pine, even if it was painted, and not vinyl-covered plywood, belonged in a century-old kitchen. The polished chrome of the cookstove gleamed, although not with the same intensity as it used to in Aunt Aggie's time. Keeping everything spotless and shiny wasn't exactly my thing.

Several grocery bags hung on the knob of the door into the pantry. I imagined Shoni could fit inside one, but my arms would feel like lead after carrying her a short distance. She might be only ten weeks old, but she wasn't exactly a featherweight. A bucket wouldn't work either, for the same reason. Besides, she could jump out of it.

Finally, my light lit up Eric's backpack hanging on a hook next to the dripping Christmas tree. Perfect. My back could handle her weight without any difficulty, and my hands would be free.

I was finishing washing my hands when Professor arrived with Shoni trotting behind him. The puppy jumped up against my legs. "Sorry, Shoni. Pats will have to wait. Why don't you put her in the cage?" I might as well keep trying.

He ignored me.

"You have quite the antique collection in the living room," he said on our way back to Larry.

Pretending I hadn't heard, I continued walking.

"I should check out this room too." He stopped at the archway and shone his flashlight into the dining room.

As luck would have it, I'd recently polished the silver tea service, the candelabra, and the other silver pieces in anticipation of my sister's visit. They didn't hesitate to advertise their worth in the glare of his light. Many of the pieces dated from Aunt Aggie's marriage to a German baron a few months before the First World War. Given how the marriage had worked out, I was surprised she hadn't tossed them into a pot and melted them down.

Professor whistled, and then whistled again when he saw the painting of a forest at sunset over the buffet. "Amazing. That's a Lawren Harris. I've only had the pleasure of enjoying his paintings in a museum."

It would appear that he knew his Canadian art. Too bad. Doubtless he'd also recognized the value of the paintings hanging in the living room, several by other members of the Group of Seven and other well-known Canadian artists. Aunt Aggie had had a keen artistic eye. Unwilling to leave Three Deer Point, she'd tasked my father, when he was alive, to acquire them when they had come up for auction.

Though I enjoyed living with these family heirlooms, they were just things. Maybe if I wasn't able to escape or the police didn't come, I could use them to persuade Professor and Larry to leave.

TWELVE

Larry was trembling like a leaf and was about as thin as one.

"It won't be for much longer," I said. "Once I'm finished you can put on some of my husband's warm clothes and wrap yourself in the blanket."

He nodded grimly.

His forehead continued to feel cool, though a bit sweaty.

Instead of following me into the den, the tattooed man returned to the living room with Shoni nestled in his arms, where he no doubt was taking inventory. The largest and most beautiful room in the house, with its floor-to-ceiling stone fireplace, wall of windows overlooking the lake, and corner turret, was filled with antiques, as the man had already noted. My great-grandfather acquired many of them during several trips to Europe. My great-aunt had added the Quebec pine pieces, like the eighteenth-century folk art sculptures and metal-edged grain bin that had long been used as a woodbox.

I was rather proud of my handiwork. The wound was clean, with almost no discharge of blood. I prepared the bandage, applying some antiseptic ointment to the gauze. With Larry gritting his teeth, I spread it gently over the wound and affixed it with tape.

"Roll over on your side so I can dress the wound on your back."

Despite considerable groaning, he seemed to move easily, which suggested that the bullet had caused minimal internal damage. Although the exit wound was larger and more ragged, it appeared relatively clean, with no embedded threads.

Once I finished dressing it, I had him sit up so I could remove the remnants of his T-shirt. Although he favoured his injured side, he continued to move with ease. I was feeling more hopeful that his injury wasn't as bad as initially thought. Nonetheless, I found his shivering worrisome, considering that the room had warmed up to almost tropical levels with the recharged fire. I'd even been forced to remove my sweater.

"This'll make me better." He pointed to the traditional four-coloured medicine wheel on the front of Eric's T-shirt. "Been a long time since I seen one of these. My grandmother used to believe in all that shit. Even had her own medicine bundle."

After struggling into the T-shirt and the former girlfriend's sweater, he lowered himself gently back down onto the sofa and pulled the blanket up to his chin.

"Did your grandmother live on the rez?"

"Yeah, all her life. But she's probably dead now."

"You don't know?"

"Like I said, been a long time since I lived on the rez."

"I might know her. What was her name?"

"Flora. She was my mother's mother."

"I know a few Floras. What is her last name?"

"Commanda."

"It sounds vaguely familiar, but I can't place her. She might've passed on before I moved here."

"How long you been here?"

"About eight years."

"Yah, coulda happen. Been about thirteen years since I seen her."

"Well, the rez is just around the corner. You can go look for her when you leave here."

"Yah, be nice to see her again. She was real good to me when I was growing up." He wiped his runny nose with the back of his hand.

"Do you have other family who might still be living on the rez?"

"Don't know. Like I said, I haven't kept in touch." He turned his eyes away and began picking at a loose thread in the blanket.

So much for my visiting-relatives-for-Christmas theory. "Do you want anything to drink?"

"Some of that rye and ginger would be good."

"How about just ginger ale? I don't think the rye will do you any good."

"I guess."

I poured some into Professor's empty glass.

Larry greedily drank up the ginger ale, finishing with a resounding burp. "I never been inside this house before."

"But you've seen it?"

"Yeah, a ways back, when I was little. My dad did odd jobs for Auntie. He sometimes brought me. She used to give me an apple and a glass of lemonade. Not much of that stuff on the rez back then. If I was extra good, she'd give me a chocolate chip cookie. The first I ever had, eh? I sure loved 'em. Still do."

"I'm rather partial to chocolate chip cookies myself. Aunt Aggie's were particularly tasty. She always added extra chocolate chips. I have some of my own in the kitchen, but I can't vouch for them being as good. Do you want some? Perhaps with a cup of tea?"

I felt the puppy's muzzle sniffing my hand and picked her up. "Where's your babysitter?" I expected him to arrive at any second.

But he seemed content to remain in the living room. As long as he wasn't leaning over my shoulder, that was fine by me.

Larry reached over to ruffle the puppy's ears. "Sure cute. Had me a dog when I was a boy. Called him *Nàbek*. Means 'bear' in my language. Been a long time since I spoke any Algonquin. Used to speak it with Kòkomis." He raised his dark brown eyes up to me. "Kòkomis is what all us Algonquin kids call our grandmothers."

"I know."

"Anyways, Nàbek was a mix, not high class like this one. He was sure a great dog, till he got run over by my dad's truck, eh? Never had another one. Mom hated dogs."

Larry seemed more relaxed and more trustful of me. With Professor occupied in the living room, I thought I would see what more I could learn.

"Larry, I'm curious to know why you've come to my place? It isn't exactly a top tourist attraction."

He took his hand away from Shoni's head and tucked it under the blanket. His smile vanished, as did the warmth in his eyes. "Professor didn't tell you?"

"No."

"You better ask him."

"I doubt he'll tell me. To tell you the truth, the two of you turning up at my place in this awful storm and your gunshot wound make me nervous."

His eyes shifted everywhere but on me. He breathed in slowly and then let the air out just as slowly. "You been nice to me. I make sure he don't hurt you, okay?"

"So where are you from? Who shot you?"

He sighed. "Better you don't know. Look, I'm feeling kinda hungry. Think you could get me one of those cookies and some tea?"

I tucked Shoni under my arm and tiptoed as silently as I could down the hall to the kitchen. Larry's words, or more correctly the lack of them, made me even more jittery. They had to be escaping after committing some crime.

If the police didn't come, what would Professor do with me when he finally decided to leave?

THIRTEEN

I didn't for one second think of getting Larry a cookie or making him tea. Instead, with Shoni under my arm, I aimed straight for the pantry, where I snatched up my down-filled jacket, wool hat, down-filled mitts, Sorel boots, and Eric's backpack, and threw them out onto the porch.

I listened one last time to make certain that Professor wasn't coming after me, and then I closed the back door softly, very softly, behind me. I threw on my clothes and then stuffed my feet into the boots and the puppy into Eric's pack. She squirmed and scratched, but with the appropriate bribe, she settled down long enough for me to zip up the pack, leaving a small opening for air. She had just enough room to move around and curl up into a warm ball. I slung the heavy pack onto my back and grabbed the snowshoes and the ski poles hanging on the outside wall.

I stumbled through the snow clogging the stairs, almost losing my balance when my foot missed the last step and I landed knee-deep in the white stuff. It was deeper than anticipated. Crunching through it was going to be a challenge.

I fought with the snow as I jammed my boots into the snowshoes and cinched them up tightly. After a last glance at the windows, half expecting to see the tattooed man's writhing snakes, I set out with my headlamp off. I would turn it back on once I was out of sight of the house.

I felt the icy prick of the flakes against my face. My world was an all-pervasive swirling white, while around me the trees roared with the anger of the wind. I lumbered toward the slightly darker shape of the woodshed, thinking it would be best to put its sturdy log walls between the house and me. But it was hard going. The snowshoes sank in the light powder, forcing me to lift up each leg like a high-stepping horse and kick the snowshoe forward through the snow.

Shoni squirmed and whimpered. I reached back and touched her nose poking through the gap. "Go to sleep, little one." I found another treat in my pocket, but I would soon be out of them. I mentally kicked myself for not bringing a good supply.

Not being familiar with every twist and turn of Jid's bush trail, I decided to take the Three Deer Point Road to the main road. If the gods were with me, I would meet up with a passing motorist on Migiskan Road. If not, I would keep walking until I reached the reserve.

The snow was so blinding that I almost bumped into the woodshed. Only a sense of a looming presence prevented a collision. I hazarded a backward glance at the house for signs of Professor, but the whirling white obliterated it too — which was fine by me. The man wouldn't be able to see me either.

I was very glad to be wearing Eric's lightweight aluminum snowshoes. With Aunt Aggie's old-fashioned willow bearpaws, I'd still be back at the house trying to move.

Once I reached the woodshed, I decided to keep going past the rest of the outbuildings and away from the house, instead of taking the most direct route to the driveway. This was parallel to the house, in full view of the den windows. Knowing my luck, Professor would be gazing out one of them.

After what seemed an eternity, I stepped beyond the shelter of the old stable, the last of the outbuildings, and into the full onslaught of the storm. It almost blew me over as the snow lashed against my face. I tucked my head deeper into my hood and cinched the wolf ruff tightly around my face. It reduced the pinpricks marginally.

I switched on my headlamp, hoping to see the start of the forest, which I knew was less than a tree length away. But it merely lit up whirls of flying flakes and little else. I trudged forward, terrified I might trip on my snowshoes and fall. Unable to get solid purchase in such deep powder, I would find it practically impossible to get up.

Once again, I felt as if I were in my own separate surreal world, only this time nothing else existed but the snow, the wind, and the tunnel of light. The only sounds were the moaning of the forest canopy and the rhythmic scrapping of my snowshoes. For some strange reason it seemed to envelop me in a protective cocoon. I began to feel more relaxed, more confident that I would make it … until I caught the sound of gunfire.

At first I wasn't sure I'd heard correctly until the second shot was fired.

The tattooed man had discovered my escape.

I picked up my pace.

Where had the gun come from? Had he managed to break into Eric's gun cabinet?

Another shot boomed.

With one of Eric's deer rifles, he could hit me at two hundred metres, and he wouldn't need to step off the porch.

I turned off my light.

Another few metres, and I was entering the protection of the trees. I stopped behind a particularly wide tree trunk and listened for the crack of another rifle shot.

I waited a minute or two but heard no more gunshots. He could be caught up in following my tracks, but without proper gear, I doubted he would leave the dryness of the porch. Nonetheless, I wasn't going to wait around to find out.

I treaded deeper into the muffled silence of the forest. Under its protective canopy, the blizzard's intensity was lessened. It was almost like walking in a gentle snowfall. It also meant the snow was not as deep. Since I could make out the black shapes of the tree trunks, I kept my headlamp off and turned in the direction of my road.

I was hoping the two of them would leave for wherever they were headed before their detour to my place. Professor would know that I would send the police after them as soon as I reached civilization.

I no longer felt Shoni squirming in the backpack. Hopefully she'd fallen asleep with the rhythm of my walking. I was now fully in stride and was maintaining a good pace. I decided to stick to the woods and follow alongside the road when I reached it. Staying off it would also prevent Professor from knowing my route, should he decide to leave.

As I wended my way through the trees, my thoughts strayed to Eric. I wondered if he had tried to call. But with the power outage, he would only get a busy signal. After several failed attempts, he would know it wasn't me occupying the line. I hated talking on the phone, so I kept my calls short. Besides, Eric was the only person I talked to on the phone. My friends were few. Eric was the only friend I needed.

He probably knew by now that Three Deer Point was being pummelled by a blizzard. Would he call Will to have someone come check on me? Before our decidedly frigid parting, I would have said likely. Now I wasn't sure.

God, I was stupid. He was the best husband a woman could have. Yet I couldn't shove aside my insecurities. I couldn't understand how he could love me. I was not what anyone would call a beauty. Even though I had lost weight, I would never be called slim. My hair might be red, but it needed a lot of help from Clairol to hide the emerging grey. And I wasn't exactly a witty conversationalist.

Eric could have any woman he chose. I watched the way women, young and old, gathered around him at events, hanging on to his every word, trying to catch his attention, batting their eyelashes, blowing kisses. Well, not quite. But that's how it seemed to me. So when I heard the same voice for the fourth time in two days asking to speak to my husband in a breathless Marilyn Monroe whisper, I got mad and hung up. Eric was furious.

This had happened as he was packing to fly to Regina to meet with a number of First Nations chiefs. In his bid to become the next GCFN Grand Chief, he was criss-crossing the country to meet with the chiefs of as many of the six hundred or more First Nation communities, as best he could. He believed that to be an effective Grand Chief he needed to have a solid understanding of the issues and needs facing them.

He gave me only a perfunctory kiss on the cheek as he hefted his bag over his shoulder and headed out the door to make the two-and-half-hour drive to the Ottawa airport. He didn't call from the airport, something he always did before hopping onto the plane. I was too chicken to call him. That was three days ago. We hadn't talked since, so he probably hadn't bothered to call to see if I was okay.

The second the door slammed behind him, my heart sank. I knew I'd done it again. The last time he'd slammed a door on me, we barely survived. It took a near tragedy to cut through the months of silence and bring us back together again.

This time jealousy was added to the mix. He hadn't told me who the woman was. And I was too afraid to ask.

FOURTEEN

I breathed deeply and tried not to think of Eric. I needed to put all my focus on getting to the main road and to safety. Though I was fairly certain the tattooed man wouldn't try to follow me, I didn't know whether the two of them would eventually be coming up behind me along the Three Deer Point road.

I increased my pace. By the time I saw the top of the snowbank bordering my road, I was sweating. It wasn't frigid enough to keep me cool, especially since I was encased in feathers. I unzipped the jacket, removed the hood, and stuffed the mitts into my pockets. The icy pricks on my face felt good.

I stopped to listen for Professor. Though it would be nearly impossible for the two of them to have come this far, I wanted to be absolutely certain that there was no danger. As an extra assurance, I decided not to walk on the single-lane road but to follow alongside it within the protection of the forest. Despite the number of inclines, dips, and turns, it should be a fairly straightforward kilometre-and-a-half hike to Migiskan Road.

The track the two men had left on their way to my place was little more than a meandering dip in the road's flat expanse. In another hour their passage would be as if it had never happened. If only it were true.

I wondered if I would stumble across their car. I found it difficult to believe that they would choose to come to such an isolated wilderness, especially in such a blizzard. More likely in their haste to get away from whomever they were fleeing, they had got lost.

On the other hand, with hundreds of square miles of empty forest, anyone who didn't want to be found could hide out in these woods for years by living off the land. But not these guys. They struck me as the kind of men who relied on getting their meat from fast-food joints and not by a rifle. And they certainly weren't dressed for surviving outside one day in this weather, let alone months.

The high winds were having a greater impact on the trees along the edge of the road. I was forced to detour around several downed trees and was almost skewered by a falling branch. The gentle snowfall of the forest had changed to sheets of snow, making the visibility worse. I tried the headlamp, hoping it would help, and ended up walking straight into a low-hanging branch. I turned it off and inched my way forward, hands out in front to prevent another collision.

I was beginning to tire. My legs were starting to feel like lead, and my shoulders were aching from the weight of Shoni. For once I wished I'd follow Eric's advice about working out regularly on his fitness equipment, instead of my usual on-again/off-again exercise regime.

I thought I was more than halfway to Migiskan Road, after which it would be another five kilometres before I reached the police detachment. If no one picked me up, I was going to be a walking zombie by the time I arrived. But it didn't matter. The puppy and I were safe and well beyond the reach of the tattooed man and his threatening gun and knife.

I stopped to rest, took some deep, calming breaths, and continued. I soon established a good walking rhythm, albeit at a somewhat slower and more cautious pace. I was paying so much attention to the potential obstacles in front of me that I failed to notice a faint clinking sound until it was almost upon me.

It sounded like metal knocking against metal. I wasn't certain if it was coming toward me or I was moving toward it. Likely it was something metallic caught in a tree that was being blown about by the wind.

Or so I thought until I heard voices. They were too far away to make out the actual words, but from the tone I sensed anger. For a horrid second I thought it was Professor, until sanity prevailed. These people were coming toward me along the road, and not from behind me.

Was it Will? But it was too soon. My watch said Jid would be just arriving at the police station, unless he'd lucked out and met someone on a Ski-Doo. But the police chief would be travelling by snowmobile, and he wouldn't be alone. These people were walking, and it sounded like only two of them.

Since I'd been surprised once already by one set of unsavoury strangers, I didn't want to meet up with more. I moved further into the safety of the trees.

When they were nearer, I heard a male voice growl, "Shut your mouth, boy."

"You're hurting me."

It was Jid. What was going on?

While I could make out the swishing of movement through snow, the trees obscured my view of the road. I shuffled closer and saw a single light beam streaked with white coming towards me. About several car lengths away, it seemed to be following the track left by Professor and Larry. But I couldn't see who was holding the light, only a dark, amorphous shape.

I needed to get closer. I scrambled as silently as I could over the snowbank onto the road. I stayed hidden behind an overhanging bough and watched the relentless forward march of the beam. It seemed higher off the ground than it would be if Jid were wearing it.

Who was he with?

The black shape separated into two figures, one short and slim, the other considerably taller and wider. They seemed linked, with the taller person in front of the smaller one. As they came closer, I realized the man was pulling the boy behind him through the deep snow. He was also wearing Jid's headlamp and snowshoes, which were the source of the tinkling sound.

This was too much of a coincidence. This man had to be connected to the two in my house. No one else would be crazy enough to be walking along my road in this weather.

I didn't know whether to retreat back into the woods and continue my trek to the police station or try to rescue Jid myself.

The resounding thud of a slap and a cry from the boy made up my mind.

I waited until they were past me. The man, oblivious to everything but the way ahead, kept the headlamp fully fixed on the snow in front of him.

Unfortunately, Shoni was starting to stir. Maybe she'd recognized Jid's voice. So far she was being quiet, but at any moment she could start to whimper. I would have to act before she announced my presence.

It looked as if the man had a firm hold on the boy with one hand, while in the other he carried an object impossible to identify in the darkness. I supposed I could try to pull the boy away from the man and run like hell. But running in snowshoes was a nonstarter.

The only other option I could think of was to create a distraction and hope the man would leave my buddy alone while he went to investigate. But what kind of a distraction? As if reading my mind, a branch suddenly snapped in the forest across the road from me. It knocked against a tree before landing with a thunk on the ground. The man barely stopped in midstride. So much for distracting him with deadfall.

It would have to be something unnatural, not a forest sound. A noise, like the metallic clinking that had caught my attention? Or a human voice? Mine. Or what about a whimpering dog?

After they passed, I scrambled back over the snowbank and into the forest. I followed them, careful to stay concealed by the trees. The man's pace was so slow that I caught up and passed unnoticed, though Jid's head seemed to turn in my direction.

I searched for likely places to hang Eric's backpack and found the broken stub of a branch on a hardwood close enough to the road to entice him to check it out. On another tree, a piece of deadfall caught in a lower branch appeared strong enough to knock the guy out. Amateur hour, I know. But I was desperate. If I didn't rescue my buddy now, there was no way I would be able to once this man joined up with his comrades.

I slipped the loop of the pack over the broken end of the short stubby branch, poked, and prodded poor Shoni until she whimpered. It soon grew to a yelp. I hid behind the trunk and waited, branch in hand. I was beginning to lose hope when I heard the man's panting as he broke through the snow. I raised the branch, ready to strike.

When I heard, "What the fuck?" I came from behind the tree and slammed the branch as hard as I could onto his head.

Except I missed.

"Fuck!" was followed by a gunshot and then another.

FIFTEEN

"Who the fuck you?" the man yelled.

Blinded by his headlamp, I lay with my heart pounding where I'd fallen the second his gun fired. I didn't think I'd been hit.

"Get that thing out of my eyes. I can't see!" I shouted back.

"Auntie, is that you?" Jid cried out.

He crawled through the drifts toward me.

"Get fuck away, kid."

"Leave him alone." I struggled to get up but found myself floundering, unable to get purchase in the deep powder. "Jid, can you help me?"

Shoni was in full yelping mode and scratching desperately at the pack's zippers. I hoped they held. Poor thing. She was as scared as I was.

Jid's worried face appeared in the light. "You okay, Auntie?"

"I'm fine. I just need a little help getting up. Can you find my ski poles? They're buried somewhere close by."

He scuffed through the snow around me until he found them.

"Get up, woman," the man shouted.

"I'm trying to."

Trying to get purchase was like punching a cloud. Whenever I placed any weight on my hands to hoist myself onto my feet, they sank deeper. The snowshoes didn't help, so I removed them. Finally, putting my full weight on the poles, I managed to get myself upright, but no sooner was I on my feet than I heard the pack's zipper give, and out tumbled Shoni.

She sank like a stone into the white stuff. Both Jid and I scrambled to find her, banging our heads together in the process. Her yelps rose several decibels as she thrashed around. Jid was finally able to grab her and up she came into his arms, squirming in panic.

"What fuck doing?" the man shouted.

"Getting my dog."

"I no give fuck about dog."

While Jid struggled to calm the puppy down, I flicked on my headlamp and shone it straight into his eyes.

"Who are you?" I asked with more bravado than I felt.

"Turn off fuckin' light."

"I'll do it when you do." Even with my eyes closed, his light was penetrating.

For a second neither of us moved, then I shifted my beam away. After waiting several long seconds, I was about to shine it back on him when he finally turned his away.

"You lady who live here?" He spoke with a thick accent, possibly Slavic.

"Yup. What are you doing on my land?" Unable to see the man behind the headlamp, I had little sense of him other than from his voice. The harsh, demanding tone was telling me he was the kind of man who shot first and asked questions later.

"Auntie, he's got a gun," Jid warned.

"So I heard. So we won't do anything to make him want to use it, will we?"

"Nope, he made me come with him. I didn't get to Will."

Worried he would say more, I asked, "How's Shoni doing?"

"Will, who he?" came the demand.

"A friend. What are you doing with the boy?" I inserted my feet back into the snowshoes.

"He yours?"

I wanted to say yes, but was afraid the guy would use it to his advantage. "The son of a friend. Let him go. His mother will be getting worried."

"I not stupid. He tell his mother about me."

"I won't, honest," Jid replied.

"I no trust you, not after you bite me and try to run away. It fuckin' cold. We go to house."

As an added incentive he shone the light on his gun, a menacing black revolver of the kind I was used to seeing on TV and not pointed at me.

"I need to get the puppy back in the pack." I pulled it down from the branch.

"I no care. Move."

"I can hold Shoni, Auntie. She's gone to sleep," Jid said.

"Let me know when she gets too heavy, and I'll take over." I slung the pack onto my back.

"You go first, woman, and then boy. No tricks or I shoot." To emphasize the point, he waved his gun at both of us.

I wasn't particularly keen on returning to my house. I had no idea of the kind of reception I would receive from the tattooed man, but I doubted it would be friendly. However, with a handgun aimed at our backs, we had no choice but to walk back.

As we moved away from the trees and into the openness of the road, I noticed that the intensity of the snow and wind had lessened, making it easier to see with the headlamp. Framed by the high banks of ploughed snow, the lane was a smooth plane except for the faint trench left by my other unwanted visitors. I followed it, hoping it would provide firmer traction for Jid.

Half expecting to run into Professor and Larry, I kept my eye out for a dot of light coming toward us. I wasn't certain which would be worse, meeting up with them on the road or back at my place.

"How far away the house?" the man rasped between gasps.

Good. Pushing snowshoes through the snow was taking its toll. Maybe he'd collapse from a heart attack.

"About half a kilometre."

"The Injun say you an old lady."

"She was my great-aunt."

"You seen my buddies? They at the house?"

"Why my house? There are better places to hide out."

"Injun's idea. Say old lady live alone. No family. No friends." He paused. "I think you were at house. So what you doing here? You run away?"

Big mistake letting on I knew about his friends. "Larry's the man's name. Call him that. He's hurt badly and will die without medical attention. I was going to get a doctor."

"I don't believe you. You can phone."

"The phone's not working. Let us go, so we can get the help Larry needs to survive."

He spat. "I don't care if he die. He not important. No, you go after police. Now move."

"Are you guys bank robbers?" I figured I might as well find out who they were.

He guffawed. "No, convicts. We escape from Joyceville."

"Joyceville?" I would've thought a maximum security prison like Millhaven would've been more appropriate.

"They move me there for good behaviour." He laughed even louder. "Now go, or I shoot boy."

SIXTEEN

I went numb. Escaped prisoners had crossed my mind, but I'd rejected the idea, believing it too preposterous. Three Deer Point was too far away from the penitentiaries in Quebec and Ontario. Joyceville was located near Kingston, easily a five-hour drive away. So why in the world did they end up here?

With the reassuring sound of Jid tramping behind me, I plodded up my drive to the house in silence, all exhaustion gone. I was too worried to talk. I was afraid of what this could mean for Jid and me. Other than saying a few words when he passed Shoni to me, he was quiet too.

All hope of rescue had vanished. I knew deep down that my plea to Will had failed to get through. That left Eric. If everything were normal between us, I knew he wouldn't hesitate to get Will to drive over to check up on me. But things weren't normal.

Why was I so damn stupid? Why couldn't I have just pretended that it was fine by me having another woman call him? Instead I had to make a big deal of it, which had only made matters worse. Was my outburst enough to drive him into the arms of this other woman? I shuddered at the thought.

Not wanting to consider for even a nanosecond life without Eric, I continued trudging forward. Apart from the incessant droning of the storm, the only sound was our captor's laboured breathing. It would appear that exercise wasn't part of his routine in prison. I hadn't yet given up hope for a heart attack.

But he was still moving, albeit slowly, when the timber structure of my home finally loomed into view. At one point, when we were closing in on the house, he ordered us to stop while he rested, though he pretended it was to fix one of the snowshoes. When we resumed, he demanded that we slow our pace to his and threatened to shoot if we didn't.

I had mixed feelings when I saw the faint glow filtering through the windows of my house. It would be a relief to get out of the storm and into its warmth. But Professor was going to be one very angry man.

As if reading my mind, he flung open the door at the sound of us clambering up the back stairs. His bullet head backlit by the kitchen light made him appear even more menacing. Without a single word, he slugged me across the jaw. I fell into Jid and tumbled the two of us down the stairs and back into the snow.

"Why fuck you do that, Viper?" shouted the man behind us.

"Slobo, is that you? It's about time you showed up," Professor said. "Did you get rid of the car?"

"Fuckin' snow make plenty problems. Fuck, I hate this country. But the snow bury it good. No one find car until snow gone in summer." He guffawed.

I tested my jaw. I didn't think it was broken, but it sure hurt. I helped Jid out of the snow, and then myself.

"You okay, Auntie?" he whispered. "Where's Shoni?"

I'd forgotten about her. The two of us dug around in the snow, frantic to find her.

"What you doing?" our captor shouted.

"Looking for the puppy."

"She's where she belongs." Professor smiled smugly, holding Shoni in his arms while she licked his face. "A cute little thing. I might take her with me. It would serve you right for trying to escape."

Pretending to ignore his threat, I bent over to release the straps on my snowshoes. My aching jaw was telling me I would have little say in my puppy's future.

"You gonna let us in? I fucking cold," Slobo said, attempting to kick the snowshoes off his feet.

"It would help if you undid them," I said.

"Stupid shoes. Only crazy people wear them." He glared at me before bending down to release the straps.

"They got you through the snow, didn't they?"

He ignored me as he continued to struggle with them.

Professor stared down at us from the top of the stairs. I sensed a standoff developing. But after a few minutes, he turned around and walked back inside the house with the puppy perfectly happy in his arms.

With Slobo prodding us from behind, Jid and I stumbled up the steps. Snarling "Move!" he pushed us through the door, past the Christmas tree, and into the kitchen.

Waves of heat from the woodstove washed over me. Though this wasn't where I had expected to be, the warmth still felt wonderful. I hadn't realized how cold I had become. At least Professor had kept the fire going.

There were no signs of impending departure. He must've thought I would get lost and end up freezing to death. Otherwise, if he thought there had been a chance that I would make it to the police, the two of them would have left. But perhaps Larry was the deciding factor. I doubted the injured man would have made it very far.

"Who's the kid?" the tattooed man asked.

"Don't know. Find him on road."

Road? He should've been miles away on the reserve.

"Fuck, he got sharp teeth." Slobo held up his hand to reveal red teeth marks on the back of it.

In the glow of the oil lamp, Jid's smile covered almost as much of his face as the splotch of redness spreading across his cheek.

"You okay?" I mouthed.

He nodded and beamed more broadly.

The man yelled, "Boy, no smile or I hit you again."

The smile vanished, but not the glint in his eyes.

"Don't you dare!" The words shot out before I could stop them.

"Or you'll what?" Slobo patted the gun tucked into the waistband of his jeans.

I shoved Jid behind me.

"Calm down, everybody," Professor interjected. "Slobo, why did you bring the kid here? We don't need more people knowing our whereabouts."

"You know I no like name Slobo. Call me Slobodan or Tiger."

The new arrival wasn't as tall as the tattooed man and was considerably broader, with a hint of a beer belly pulling at his wet ski jacket. Given the way he smoothed back his thick mane of dirty blond hair after removing his hood, I'd say he prided himself on his chiselled looks. Doubtless a lot of women would find his notched chin and commanding jawline attractive. Not this one.

"Ah yes. A Serbian mother's diminutive for her little boy," Professor replied.

If I'd expected an angry retort, it didn't come, other than a firming of his lips. Instead the new arrival said, "The boy saw me hiding car. I worry he tell his mother. He make good hostage, *ne?*"

"That makes two," Professor said, pointing to me. "If it comes to that. Any sign of the police?"

I supposed about the only good thing you could say about being a bargaining chip was they would want to keep us alive.

"*Ne.* Nobody on road in this shit. But good for us, *ne?*"

He ran his pale blue eyes over the kitchen, letting them linger on the line of copper pots hanging over the cookstove. They might not be as gleaming as they were in Aunt Aggie's day, but they couldn't hide their value in the soft glow of the oil lamp. "Nice house."

"Remember what we agreed," Professor said. "We leave it the way we found it. So don't even think of taking anything."

Slobodan shrugged by way of an answer, not bothering to hide his smirk. "Where the Injun? He okay?"

"You are being disrespectful. If we are to work together, we need to respect each other. Larry is doing as well as expected." Professor nodded in my direction. "She fixed him up."

The Serbian grunted, removed his wet jacket, and tossed it over the back of one of the fuchsia kitchen chairs before dropping down onto it. He pulled out a cellphone and flipped it open. "Fuck, no service." He shook the phone, as if that would help. "Nothing. You, woman, why not working?"

"We're in a blackout zone. No cell coverage. My landline isn't working either."

"Fuck. I got to talk to Jo."

"I thought you set it up for there to be no communication with her in case the cops are monitoring the phones," Professor said.

"She has burn phone like this. Pigs know nothing about them."

"I thought everything was all set up with Jo. We do nothing but wait here until she arrives. What did you want to talk to her about?"

"Tell her we are at house."

"She'll find out when she gets here tomorrow morning."

Did this mean come morning they would be gone?

"Jo did good job, *ne?*" Slobo grinned. "The crash work perfect." He breathed in deeply and flung out his arms, narrowly missing a shelf on the wall behind him. "Feel good to be free."

"I couldn't agree more. And let's keep it this way by not doing anything stupid, okay?"

"*Da*, sure." Slobo turned his eyes on me.

I found myself staring at a single teardrop tattoo under the corner of his right eye, similar to the one Larry had.

Slobo touched the teardrop. "Prison tat. Mean we kill somebody."

He'd just confirmed my worst fears.

"But I not like Viper. I have only two tattoos. Jo no like them."

I noticed that the letters *D.F.F.D.* were tattooed across the knuckles of his left hand, one letter per finger. "What does that mean?"

He held up his hand as if admiring it. "Devil forever. Forever devil."

I guessed once you were committed to the dark side, there was no point in pretending otherwise.

"Red, it means he's a full patch Black Devil." A smile stretched Professor's snakes into a coiled mass.

I gulped. "You don't have a teardrop, so what were you in for?"

"Tax evasion." Another broad grin was accompanied by more raucous laugher from the Serbian. "But enough questions. I'm starving. Start making dinner. You had better have some decent food in this establishment."

SEVENTEEN

The nightmare had gone from bad to worse. Three escaped convicts, two of them murderers and one a member of the notorious Black Devils, or Les Diables Noirs, as they were known in Quebec. I'd already had one bad run-in with members of this powerful biker gang. I dreaded another. But for the moment I couldn't do anything other than ensure neither Jid nor I did anything to provoke their anger. I would worry about the morning when we got there.

But if these cons were expecting a gourmet dinner, they weren't going to get it. My culinary skills were limited to boiling water and opening cans. I couldn't even make proper coffee. My tea, though, wasn't bad, since it basically involved boiling water.

When Eric moved in, he realized he had to take over the cooking or starve. I agreed to do the wash-up. Since he was an excellent chef, I felt I received the better end of the deal. Often, when he took off on a trip, he would leave me a few tasty dishes that only required microwaving to fill the kitchen with their enticing smells. But this time he had left me nothing, not even a pot of soup.

In an attempt to placate him, I had ironed his shirts, something I hated doing. But he merely grunted as he threw the shirts I'd carefully folded into his bag and zipped it up without so much as a smile, let alone a thank-you.

More signs of the extent of his unhappiness.

Despite changing into a dry pair of jeans, Jid continued to shiver. So I sat him in Aunt Aggie's rocker, next to the hot woodstove, where I could also keep him within sight while I made dinner. The tattooed man glowered at me from his perch at the kitchen table, the sheath of Eric's knife in plain view. After vacuuming up her kibble, the puppy, no worse for her excursion in the storm, pattered between the man and the boy in an attempt to get as many pats as possible. The biker had gone to the den to check on the injured man, and I suspected the rest of the house.

I figured I couldn't do too much damage to Kraft Dinner, since it basically involved boiling up noodles and adding the package of ready-made cheese sauce. Moreover, I hadn't met a person yet who didn't like KD.

But when I pulled a couple of packages out of the cupboard, Professor groaned, "Not that shit. Make something else."

I showed him a can of beef stew.

"No, I'm a vegetarian."

That stopped me for a moment. He probably practiced yoga too. "How about baked beans?"

"Does it have pork in it?"

I thought of lying, but wasn't sure what he'd do if he encountered one of the few chunks of pork they put into these cans.

"I've got a jar of tomato basil sauce. What about that with spaghetti?"

"Sounds good. Do you have any vegetables?"

"A couple of cans of peas."

"We're served that junk all the time. I want some fresh stuff."

"If you know how to cook it, go right ahead. There's some green beans in the fridge."

He sat bolt upright with his hand resting on the hilt of Eric's knife. "I told you to make dinner, so do it."

"She'll burn them," Jid piped up.

Thanks, Jid.

"Red, if you burn them, I think you know what you can expect from me."

Maybe he was only joking, but I didn't want to test it. I pulled the remaining beans out of the fridge. Though they dated from my last dinner with Eric, I didn't think they looked too old.

"I know how to cook them," Jid volunteered, dumping the bag onto a cutting board. "Shome showed me."

He used the short form for *mishomis*, meaning grandfather. It was an endearment he used for Eric. I'd kidded my husband the first time I heard it. He was hardly the grandfather type. But Eric had replied that he felt very honoured to be given the name.

"Good for you, kid, just don't burn them."

Other than reaching down to pat Shoni or lifting her onto his lap, the man didn't budge from his station on the chair the entire time we struggled to make dinner. It was a challenge working in the meagre light from the one oil lamp and the narrow beam of our headlamps. Without a working electric stove, we were forced to cook on the six-burner wood cookstove, which dated from the time of Great-Grandpa Joe. According to Aunt Aggie, he'd gone to great lengths to transport the latest in stoves from Detroit via lake transport and canal barge to Ottawa before having it hauled many dusty miles via horse-drawn wagon to his newly built cottage.

I, however, was neither my great-aunt nor my husband. Although Aunt Aggie had eventually installed a rudimentary two-burner electric stove, she continued to cook most of her meals on the cookstove. Eric thought it perfect for simmering stews and soups. I, on the other hand, used it as a source of heat. I also kept a kettle of simmering water on one of the burners to add humidity to the dry winter air. The only time I attempted to cook on it was during power outages like this one.

By the time I finished stoking the firebox with enough wood to provide sufficient heat to boil the pasta water, the three of us were removing our sweaters and jackets. This prompted Professor to push up the sleeves of his sweatshirt, revealing more snakes writhing up his arms.

No doubt psychologists would have countless theories for his snake obsession. I figured with this guy it was a simple matter of wanting people to be afraid of him. Jid, though, seemed more intrigued than put off. After exclaiming "awesome," his latest favourite word, he asked what kind of snakes they were. And so ensued a conversation about snakes in greater detail than I wanted to hear.

"Jid, watch out, your beans might burn." The pot's lid was clattering from the force of the rising steam.

Because I'd generated too much heat, I had to wait until the fire cooled enough to put the pot with the tomato sauce onto the burner. Jid had his beans perfectly cooked and ready long before my sauce was hot enough to be poured over the spaghetti, which had cooled too much despite attempts to keep the pot warm with a towel. All of this took time, more time than my unwanted guests were prepared to wait.

"Where the fuck food?" Slobo poked his head through the kitchen door, causing Professor to wake up with a start.

So intent was I on ensuring dinner wasn't burned that I'd failed to notice the man had fallen asleep. Damn. We'd missed a chance to escape. Regardless, it told me that he was very tired, particularly with all that alcohol in his system. After watching the Serbian struggle up my road, I was certain he was close to dropping from exhaustion too. I had no idea how long it had been since their escape, but I doubted they had stopped to rest. Before the night was too far gone, these dangerous men were going to finally fall into a sound sleep, and when they did, Jid, Shoni, and I would be ready to slip out the back door and be gone.

Slobo held up the bottle of rye from the den. It was empty. "Need more."

I was about to tell him it was the last when I realized more would make them go to sleep sooner. "Yes, I'll get it for you."

Reluctant to leave the boy alone with these men, I brought him along with me. But if I was looking for some privacy, it was not to be. As Professor had done earlier, the Serbian followed our every step into the dark, frigid dining room.

He whistled when the headlamp lit up the silver tea service.

"Like I've already told you, Slobo, we leave everything as we found it," Professor said, sauntering into the room.

"Milos give top dollar for stuff like this."

"Please, don't take the tea service." Even to me it sounded weak, but it was worth a try. "It belonged to my great-grandmother, a wedding gift from her grandparents. See the crest. It's the Harlech family crest. Family history has it that King George III gave it to an ancestor for his loyalty during a difficult time for the king."

This tea service had been a source of contention with my mother. She'd wanted it. She thought it was the kind of family heirloom that should be passed down through the male line, namely to my father. Instead, Great-Grandpa Joe had given it to his daughter, Agatha, instead of his son John, my grandfather. And in turn, Agatha, with no children of her own, had bequeathed it to me along with the rest of her estate, including the 1,500 acres of Three Deer Point.

"It's not something that could be easily sold without proper provenance," I continued.

"It is a worthy treasure to have in one's possession," the tattooed man replied. "Don't worry, Red, I'll make certain Slobo doesn't take it, or anything else in your house. It's not the reason for our visit."

"So why you are here?" I asked.

Ignoring me, he said, "I envy you your rich heritage. I once had a friend with a similar family background. But we are off topic. I believe you came here for more liquor. Get it for us."

I reached into the cabinet and pulled out the only remaining liquor in the house, a bottle of Eric's precious Lagavulin.

Professor's amber eyes lit up. "Finally something worthy of my palate."

EIGHTEEN

Though dinner didn't come close to meeting Eric's lofty standards (the pasta was overcooked, while the once perfectly cooked beans were limp from sitting too long), at least nothing was burned. I suspected this was the first real food the men had eaten since escaping. They devoured every last bean, strand of spaghetti, and molecule of sauce, even Larry's portion, and insisted that I make more. Thankfully, I'd stocked up on pasta and sauce a week ago.

The two men also consumed a good portion of Eric's Scotch. I waited for them to pass out. But other than an occasional drooping of an eyelid, they both remained stubbornly awake.

I'd had no opportunity to forewarn Jid about my intention to escape. The chance came when I offered to take soup and a slice of bread to Larry, who hadn't felt well enough to join us at the kitchen table. Professor and Slobo were laughing boisterously over some raunchy jail joke and didn't notice the boy and me leave. Instead of heading straight to the den, I detoured into the dining room.

Outside, the storm continued to rage. Though the verandah protected this side of the house, the odd stray gust still managed to rattle the French doors. This monster of a storm had been thrashing us since early yesterday and didn't look to be letting up any time soon. It might even beat Eric's once-in-a-lifetime blizzard. Whenever we were being pounded by winter's wrath, he would bring up the record-breaking storm more than thirty years ago that buried the reserve in roof-high drifts and kept the community cut off for days.

I shuddered at the thought. There was no way I wanted to be stranded inside my house for days with these guys.

I checked one last time to ensure neither man had followed us before saying, "I'm so sorry you're caught up in this mess."

"Did they really escape from jail?"

"You heard the guy."

"Awesome."

"It's not awesome. They're dangerous. Look what the guy did to your face."

Jid gingerly touched the puffiness. "Yeah, but I kicked him good in the you-know-what." He grinned.

"Don't do it..." I stopped at the sound of a creaking floorboard coming from the hall. When it didn't sound again, I stuck my head around the doorframe to make certain Professor wasn't there. Their laughter was still going strong in the kitchen.

"I'm hoping that they'll soon pass out from too much alcohol, and when they do we'll leave. But in case they don't, I want you to take off without me if you get the chance and go straight to the police."

"No. I don't want to leave you alone with these bad guys."

"I'll be okay. It's going to be easier for you to slip out unnoticed than for the two of us to try to do it together.

When these guys leave the kitchen, I want you to sneak back in, get your gear, and run. I'll do what I can to distract them."

I tried not to think about the backlash on me. But it was more important for him to be safely away from these thugs than to spare me more bruises. Besides, I felt it would be easier to protect just myself than both of us. I could see these men threatening to harm him to force me to do something.

He remained silent, his mouth firmed in stubborn resistance.

"Make sure everything you need is at the back door."

"I need a headlamp. That guy took mine."

"There's a spare one in the kitchen drawer."

"I don't want to go without you."

"Someone has to let the police know about these escaped convicts. That's your job."

Chewing the inside of his lip, he fiddled with the deerskin amulet he wore around his neck as if seeking strength from its powers. He'd first started wearing it to please his grand-mother, but after her death he tossed it aside until the day Eric sat down with him and chatted about the importance of upholding Algonquin traditions. Now he wore it proudly.

Finally he nodded sombrely. "Okay."

I ruffled his wavy brown hair, which had grown enough to tickle the collar of his red Senators sweatshirt, his favourite hockey team. Wanting to emulate the thick mane of his hero, Eric, he'd decided last summer to grow out his brush cut.

"Good. Shome will be proud of you," I said. "Tell me, how did you get caught? I thought you were miles away on the trail to the rez."

"I started out along it. Snow wasn't so deep in the woods, so I could go fast. But I came across some fresh wolf tracks going after a deer. Shome says best not to get near a wolf and his prey, so I took the trail that goes out to the main road."

"Where did you meet up with the biker?"

"When I was walking along the road, I saw this guy acting real strange. The snow was coming down real hard, so I couldn't see what he was doing very well. So I went closer."

"Where were you?"

"You know the old gravel pit near the Hawk Lake turnoff? He was trying to push a car into it."

"Did he succeed?"

"Not totally. It got hung up on a big rock, so he left it. But you can't see it very well from the road. Looked like a really awesome car, one of those fancy Range Rovers, like you see on TV."

By now it was likely hidden under a thick layer of snow, so there was little chance of anyone seeing it in the dark. Come daylight, though, maybe someone would notice.

"I guess he saw you."

"Yeah, he started yelling at me, so I ran. But I tripped on my snowshoe and fell. He fired his gun at me. That part was scary. He made me take off my snowshoes. That's when I bit him and kicked him in the nuts."

"Jid, your language."

"Sorry, forgot. Boy, I sure made him mad." Another grin erupted. "That's when he slugged me and made me go with him."

"How passable was the main road? Did you see any cars?"

"Lots of snow. Think the snow's falling faster than they can plough. We passed a truck stuck in a snowbank. Looked like Billy's Ram, but it was empty. The guy made me check to see if anyone was inside. He kept pointing his gun at the window. Looked like he was going to shoot. Just like the bad guys in the movies."

"Lucky Billy wasn't in the truck."

"Yeah, I was really scared. I've never seen anyone get shot. Only animals."

"And no sign of the police?"

"Nah. Snow's too deep. You need one of those Hummers to get through."

I jumped at a sudden loud clatter. My initial thought was the men in the kitchen had broken something, before I realized the sound was closer and came from outside. Figuring it was another branch falling onto the verandah roof, I shone my headlamp through the dining room window. It lit up a porch filled with snow, and thankfully the underside of a roof that appeared sound.

The laughter in the kitchen had changed to shouting.

I thought I caught the words, "Why you? It my job," before something metallic was slammed against a hard surface.

"Jid, let's take this soup in to Larry."

At that point, Shoni padded through the archway and promptly squatted down for a pee.

Deciding the condition of my hardwood floor was the least of my worries, I motioned for the boy to pick her up, and off to the den we went.

NINETEEN

Larry lay huddled under the blanket, his eyes closed. Apart from sinking more comfortably into the sofa cushions, he hadn't moved since I'd dressed his wounds. The blanket trembled with his shivering. Little wonder. With only a handful of coals remaining in the fireplace, the room had taken on refrigerator temperatures.

"Could you get the fire going again?" I asked Jid.

At the sound of my voice, Larry's eyes sprang open. He looked around anxiously. I turned off my headlamp to keep from blinding him and placed the tray with his food on the table next to the sofa. The oil lamp still had enough fuel, but it was getting low. I would have to add more.

A curious Shoni was sniffing along the edge of his blanket. His hand slipped out and patted her gently on the head. She licked it in return.

"How are you feeling?"

"Is that you? I thought you'd gone."

"I'm afraid I'm back."

"Jeez, you sure had Professor mad. He wanted to kill you." He raised a shaking hand to brush a hunk of greasy hair out of his eyes. "I was glad you'd got away. It's not safe for you here. Why did you come back?"

"I ran into the third member of your team, Slobodan. Unfortunately, he was holding a friend of mine prisoner."

Larry twisted his head around to look at the boy, who was standing off to one side in the shadows. "You talking about the kid?"

"Yeah. Jid, meet Larry, and vice versa. I couldn't leave him alone with that man, so here I am."

"You're a nice lady. Take the kid and run as far away from here as you can."

Though he was acting sympathetic, I wasn't about to tell him our plans. "Look, I brought you some hot soup. You need to eat something."

"Nah, I'm not hungry." His top lip was moist from a runny nose.

"How're you feeling? Any pain?"

"It don't hurt so much, not like before. You done a good job fixin' me up. Thanks."

His brow glistened with sweat.

"Let me take your temperature. I'm worried you might have a fever."

The basket of medical supplies still rested on the floor where I'd left it. I removed the thermometer and was about to place it in the man's mouth when he pushed my hand away.

"It's not a fever."

"Let me make sure. A fever could be a sign of infection."

"So what. Nothing you can do."

He was right. If the gunshot wound was infected,

antibiotics would be the only way to deal with it. Without medical help, that wasn't going to happen.

After stoking the fire back up to a glowing roar, Jid sank into one of the leather armchairs and lifted the puppy onto his lap.

"What's wrong with him?" he asked, his eyes glued to the prone man.

"He was shot."

"While he was trying to escape?"

"I imagine. Do you know who shot you, Larry?"

"I don't remember." He wiped his runny nose with the back of his hand. "So ya know we escaped from jail, eh?"

"Yeah, from Joyceville."

"Do ya know anything else?"

"I think the three of you were in a vehicle. The Serb said something about a staged crash. He mentioned a woman being responsible for it. Do you know her?"

"Nope. Just know her name's Jo. She's his woman. Supposed to be one tough broad. I remember the van, one of them prison vans. They were taking us to another facility. I remember a big bang, nothing after that."

"Was there anyone else in the van with you?"

"If you mean prisoners, nope. Just Professor, Tiger, and me. But there were a couple of hacks."

"Hacks?"

"Yah, guards. One of them was Nick. Nice guy for a hack."

"Do you know what happened to them?" I wasn't sure if I wanted to know.

When he turned his eyes away, I had a pretty good idea.

"Like I said, I don't remember much," he said.

"Do you think you can sit up? I need to get some soup into you."

"I'm not hungry." His eyes shifted away from me again and then back. Once again he wiped his wet lip with the back of his hand. "I need something else. You got any pills around here? You know, stuff like Oxycontin, something that's got a kick in it? Maybe even horse?" His eyes reflected the desperation I heard in his voice.

The minute he said the word "horse," I knew what I was dealing with.

"Ya see, Tiger didn't bring any. He usually gives me the stuff."

Just what I needed, a heroin addict going into withdrawal.

"You need to eat. A little chicken noodle soup will make you feel better." A tried and true grandmother recipe for all that ails one, at least that's what they say — whoever "they" is. But the soup wasn't homemade, just straight out of a can with all the goodness processed out of it.

I brought a spoonful of tepid soup to his lips and kept it there until he reluctantly opened his mouth. He'd no sooner swallowed it than I gave him another spoonful. This time he readily took it. A couple of more, and he was trying to push himself more upright. I helped him to sit up as far as was comfortable. He finished the rest of the soup on his own.

"Thanks," he said.

"Do you want more? I can reheat it."

"Later. But I'll have that piece of bread."

He munched on the bread while Jid and I watched him in silence. With flames licking at the fireplace's metal screen, the room had warmed up to almost cozy levels. Behind us, flakes scraped a staccato beat against the window, reminding us that danger lurked as much outside as it did inside. The two men continued to argue in the kitchen. I figured it was probably the Scotch taking over.

"You got some nice decorations." Larry jerked his head in the direction of the mantel, where I'd draped a garland of emerald tinsel and set up a streetscape with the last of Aunt Aggie's china Christmas houses, some more chipped than others.

"My *kòkomis* used to decorate her house for Christmas. It was kind of nice. I liked going there. Mom never did much of anything." He sighed than turned to the boy. "You from the rez?"

"Yeah."

"How old are ya?"

"Twelve."

"Not very big for your age, are ya? I figured you were younger."

That wasn't something the boy wanted to hear. His small size was a source of embarrassment. Often bullied by the bigger boys, he'd learned to get back at them with his quick tongue. Eric had taught him a couple of effective moves he'd employed as a professional hockey player. The one time Jid had been forced to use them, they'd worked, leaving one bully lying with a broken wrist on the ground and the other running as fast as his legs could carry him away from their victim. He'd had no further run-ins.

"Who's your dad?"

"I don't have one."

"How about your mom?"

"She's dead."

At that point the shouting in the kitchen stopped, followed by the thump of footsteps echoing along the hall toward us.

TWENTY

The three of us stopped talking. It sounded like only one man was stumbling down the hall toward us. I tensed as I waited to see whose face would appear. I supposed if I had my choice, I would choose the tax evader over the murderer. He hadn't killed anyone, at least not that I knew of.

I heard the thump of a body against a wall before I saw Professor's snakes etched in the glow of the lamp. His face twisted into a smile.

"How's it going, P'tit Chief?" he rasped.

He clung to the doorframe before lurching into the room. He made straight for the chair where Jid was sitting and fell into it, barely giving the boy enough time to escape. It would appear that consuming a bottle of rye and good quantity of Eric's Scotch had finally caught up to the man. The big question was whether he was a benign drunk who would slide into a drunken stupor or an angry one who would become belligerent and violent.

"Hey, Red, I should kill you for taking off on me." He pulled out Eric's knife and ran his finger along the sharp edge.

I froze. I had my answer.

Jid scrambled out of the way, his eyes huge with fear.

Not exactly the kind of behaviour I associated with a tax evader. I tried to act as nonchalant as I could and remained seated in the leather armchair by the fireplace as if having a knife pointed at me happened everyday.

"Professor, she's good people," Larry said. "She ain't gonna do it again." His eyes pleaded.

"You're right, she won't. I'm going to tie her up. Kid, get me some rope."

My heart sank. There went my chance to escape. It was now up to the boy.

He turned frightened eyes toward me as if seeking direction. In the ensuing silence I heard the third escaped convict clamber up the stairs.

"You know where we keep the rope, eh?" I said.

Nodding imperceptibly, he silently acknowledged that he knew it was in the woodshed. With no one in the kitchen, he could make a run for it and take the puppy with him.

"Okay?"

He nodded and mumbled, "Okay."

Stepping back, I said out loud, "Take Shoni. She needs to go to the bathroom."

"The dog stays with me." Professor pulled the whimpering puppy from the boy's arms.

Jid tried desperately to hang on to her, but when Shoni cried out in pain, he let go.

"The dog has to go outside. I don't want her making a mess on the carpet," I persisted.

"You telling me what to do? The dog stays with me." He clumsily grabbed her leg as she struggled to leave his grasp. She yelped.

"Let go, you're hurting her."

"The only one I'm going to hurt is you." Locking his eyes on mine, he ran his long fingers with a surprisingly gentle touch along the puppy's back and behind her ears. She quieted down.

Jid remained standing, unsure of what to do, until the man shouted, "Go!" and off he ran, his face twisted in apprehension. I prayed he understood that he had to leave right away.

As I listened to his footsteps fade into the kitchen, I knew I had to distract the tattooed man to take his mind away from the boy. But my thoughts were in a whirl. All I could think to say was, "So you like dogs."

He buried his face in her silky coat, and then, sitting back up, he said, "Nothing like a puppy." He tickled her under the chin. "Yes, you could say I'm a big fan of the canine species. Once I settle into my own place, I plan to get one. Maybe I'll take Shoni. She does rather like me, don't you think?"

Over my dead body, I thought, and then shuddered when I realized it might come to that.

"I had a dog in prison. A rescue dog. A Rottweiler/German Shepherd mix, not a refined specimen like Shoni." He ran his fingers through the soft fur.

At least the distraction seemed to be working. "I didn't think they allowed dogs in jail."

"He wasn't allowed in my cell. They didn't trust us. Though I did manage to sneak him in once. He had his own personal cell, a crate. Poor bugger had to be incarcerated like the rest of us.

"It was one of those do-gooder programs that are supposed to make us nice people." He sniggered. "They teach us dog training techniques, and we in turn transform these badass dogs into pussycats to make them more adoptable. Yeah, right. They hadn't bargained on us liking the aggression in our dogs. We had some terrific dog fights, and mine usually came out on top." He growled at Shoni.

"You'd better not give her any ideas."

"Nah, she's a sweetie, just the way I like my women, docile and submissive. That's right, eh, Larry?"

He stared so pointedly at the injured man, who beamed back at him, that I began to wonder about his definition of "women." "Since you like dogs so much, I'm surprised you'd want to leave him behind."

"The dog's dead. He got sick one day and was gone the next. I figured he'd been poisoned."

"I'm sorry."

"As they say, easy come, easy go. I figured my cellie did it. He hated Mom."

"Yeah, Hammer probably done it," Larry added. "I liked Mom. I used to play fetch with him, remember?"

"Mom would've made some kid a terrific dog. I had him expertly trained."

"Mom?" I asked.

"After Mom O'Reilly, the biggest boss biker of all time."

Not another one. "Are you a member of the Black Devils too?"

"Nope, I'm an independent. I prefer to work on my own. But you have to admire a man who transformed the biker gangs in Quebec and made them into a major player. Too bad he's doing time."

"Mom's in SHU at Saint Anne's," Larry added. "That's where that stupid judge sent me before they transferred me to medium."

"I assume you mean medium security."

"Ya, I didn't belong with all those hardcore killers, ain't that right, Professor?"

"You just had the bad luck to get that particular tough-on-crime judge. Your legal aid lawyer didn't help either," the tattooed man answered.

"What is SHU?" I asked.

"It's super-maximum. No way you can escape from there," Larry replied.

"Mom's got one hell of an organization behind him," Professor cut in. "I'm willing to wager he won't complete his sentence. They'll find a way to get him out." He winked. "Look at how easy it was for us to escape, eh, P'tit."

Larry giggled until he gripped his stomach in pain.

"Mom was ratted out by one of his own. If anyone does that to me, they're history." His eyes pierced Larry with their glowing amber threat.

"Professor, we're buddies. You know I'd never do that to you." Larry shrank farther into the couch.

The tattooed man continued to hammer his fist into his other hand with such intensity that I wondered if he'd ended up in jail because someone had squealed on him.

An exceptionally strong blast of wind slammed against the house. I could feel it shake from front to back and top to bottom. This storm wasn't going to let us forget that there was as much havoc happening outside as inside. By now the boy would be well under the protection of the forest canopy and on his way to Will.

My diversion seemed to be working. Professor was more interested in dogs and being ratted out than about wondering why the boy hadn't yet returned with the rope.

I relaxed too soon.

The sound of two sets of approaching footsteps filled the hall, one lighter than the other.

Jid appeared first, his shoulders slumped, his face a mask of dejection. Melting snow dripped from his down-filled jacket while his boots left a trail of water.

Behind him glowered Slobodan, dangling the rope from his fist.

TWENTY-ONE

Slobodan pushed the boy into the room. "The kid try to run away. I tell him, he go, I shoot you."

I was numb. Gone was all chance of being rescued.

Jid barely glanced in my direction. For a second I thought he would burst into tears, but he took a deep breath, firmed his jaw in resolution, and shook himself free of the biker's grip. The red splotch on the side of his face had grown.

I motioned for him to come to me and put my arm around his trembling body. "It's okay," I whispered. "You tried your best."

Turning to the man, I said, "He wasn't leaving. He was going to the woodshed to get that rope you're holding." I summoned up my courage. "Don't you dare hit Jid again."

"You do what, lady. Hit me back?" He snorted. "Kid go after cops. I stop him. He do it again, I shoot. Why he need rope?"

I'd let Professor answer that one.

But Slobodan didn't wait. "What this boy to you? You say friend, but he call you auntie. You no look like him." Slobodan let the rope fall to the floor. "You very white with your red hair. He Injun, for sure."

I cringed. The word was as insulting for me as it was for Jid. "Don't call him that."

"I call him what I like," he sneered. "So you his aunt?"

Worried he would use our close relationship against us, I exaggerated the distance and hoped Jid would understand. "He's just a kid from the reserve who does odd jobs for me. 'Auntie' is the term used by children for older women within their community."

"Hey, other Injun. Wake up. You know boy?" He thumped the sofa with his foot.

Larry, who looked to be battling his own demons, flung his eyes open. He glanced around as if not sure of where he was. "Whaddya say?"

"The boy. He Injun like you. Ya know him?"

He stared intently at a shuffling Jid. "Nah, too young. He wasn't born yet when I was sent away. Besides, I was gone from the rez long before that."

"Maybe you know his parents," Slobodan said.

"What was your mother's name?" the injured man asked. "Jid's your name, right? Short for Adjidamò, eh? Little Squirrel. See, I haven't forgot all my Algonquin. Had me a friend called Jid when I was gro —" Larry sputtered, started coughing, and gripped his side painfully. I passed him some water, which he gulped gratefully. "Jeez, that hurt." He continued breathing heavily for a few minutes before continuing. "Gimme your mother's name again. We mighta growed up together."

"No way. My mother was good. She wouldn't be friends with a bad person like you."

The biker chortled. "I like boy with spirit." The man stepped forward to ruffle his hair. But Jid ducked his head and backed out of reach. The grin vanished from the man's face. "But not too much."

I hastily intervened before anger took over. Walking over to the sofa with Jid firmly by my side, I said, "I want to check your bandage, Larry."

The biker grunted and clenched his fist but didn't move from where he was standing.

I saw no indication that blood had seeped through the gauze. "Good. Now roll over so I can check the back dressing." Although I could detect some seepage, I felt it wasn't enough to cause concern. "How bad does it hurt you, Larry?"

"It feels okay now. Guess I'd better not cough, eh?" He smiled wanly. Reaching down with shaking hands, he drew the blanket up over his chest as far as his chin, careful to tuck his sides and arms fully under. He looked up at the Serb. "Sure you don't got any stuff? I could sure use a fix."

"You be okay. Jo bring it."

"But when's she coming?" Larry made no attempt to hide the desperation in his voice.

The man glanced out the window at the howling darkness. "In morning."

"That may be difficult with this amount of snow," I said.

"When will your road get ploughed?" Professor asked, suddenly taking an interest in the conversation.

"It doesn't get done until the main one is cleared, and since Migiskan Road is a dead end, it's one of the last roads in the municipality to be ploughed."

"Fuck," Professor said, while the Serbian cursed in his own language. Both voiced my sentiments exactly.

"We have to be able to leave in the morning," the tattooed man said.

"Then pray for the snow to stop." Something I was going to start doing nonstop. I wanted them to be gone as much as they did, if not more so.

Larry groaned.

"How bad is this withdrawal going to get? Is there anything we can do to help?" I asked.

"Don't worry about him. He's been through this before," the tattooed man answered. "We've got bigger problems. Slobo, you may have to walk out in the morning to wait for Jo."

"No, I no do," the biker snarled. "You go. You the man they want. I stay here in nice warm house."

I didn't like the sound of this.

My nose suddenly twitched at a stench I knew all too well. Shoni had left a small brown sausage in the middle of Aunt Aggie's oriental carpet.

"Stop!" Slobodan shouted as I scurried toward the kitchen to get something to remove it.

"I'm not going anywhere," I yelled back. "You've got Jid, remember?"

Nonetheless, he followed me into the kitchen with the boy struggling to get free from his vice-like grip. He smacked him across the face.

"Leave him alone," I cried out, pulling Jid toward me. "He's not going anywhere. He's already proved that to you. Do you honestly think we're dumb enough to try to escape in the storm that's raging out there? We're miles from safety. We'd freeze to death before we even got halfway there. So quit hovering over us."

He stopped in midstride as if taken aback by my sudden boldness. "You got balls, woman. But you already escape. I no trust you. I give you same warning I give boy. You leave, I kill him." He formed his hand into a mock gun, pointed it at Jid, and fired. "Kerpow. Between the eyes, *ne?*"

My stomach clenched tighter. It hadn't relaxed since these men had pushed their way into my home. "Look, I get the message. I'm not going to do anything, so leave the boy alone. Now let me clean up that mess, otherwise the den is going to stink."

He shrugged. "You never smell a prison cell, *ne?*" He laughed uproariously and then pointed at the empty Scotch bottle lying on its side next to a couple of empty glasses. "You got more? Is very smooth. I like." He smacked his lips with appreciation.

I almost considered saying no, but he didn't appear to be anywhere near close to passing out. Hopefully another bottle would do the trick. "Jid, could you get the last bottle from the dining room?"

The man started to follow the boy.

"Leave him alone," I said. "We have our bargain, okay?"

"*Da*, sure." He sauntered over to the table, slumped down into one of the chairs, and gripped a glass in antici-pation. I grabbed a plastic bag, rug-cleaner spray, a sponge, and another cloth to clean the mess in the dining room and then headed back to the den.

I met Jid coming out of the dining room with another full bottle of Eric's Lagavulin. I didn't want him alone with that biker, so I called out, "Slobodan, bring your glass. The Scotch will be waiting for you in the den."

TWENTY-TWO

I hastily wiped up the puppy's puddle in the dining room before returning to the den to clean up her mess on the carpet. Larry's eyes were closed, as were Professor's. His head was slumped awkwardly against the back of the chair. I even detected some sputtered snoring coming from his open mouth. Good. One down. One to go.

I felt a frisson of hope when I saw the rope lying forgotten on the floor. As the biker was coming into the room, I hastily shoved it under the sofa with my foot. If they didn't tie me up, we still might be able to leave. With Professor passed out, I was hoping the Serbian would soon join him. Then the three of us could escape without fear of being shot at.

"Hey, Viper, wake up." Slobodan kicked the man's feet.

When he got no response, he kicked him again several more times. No response. Not even a lifting of an eyelid. Good. He was going to be comatose for a good long while.

"Stop," I said. "He's not going to wake up."

"*Da*. But it feel good." He grinned and kicked the man's foot again. "Only time I can do this. When he out cold." He snickered.

"I guess you don't think much of him."

"He think he is big shot. He push everyone around in prison. Make people do things for him. And he talk like he better than us."

"He does speak well-educated English. Is that why you call him Professor?"

"He say he go to university. He say he have many what you call 'degrees.' Larry tell me he work at university, was Dr. Professor."

"Are you sure?" I found this too incredible. With his snakes, he would've had the sweet young things trembling in their lululemons. "Do you know where?"

"Larry know." He kicked the sofa hard. "Wake up."

"Watch out," I cried out. "You could make his injury worse."

"Injun can take it. He is little, but he tough."

Larry's eyes sprang open. "Jeez, I feel awful." He glanced around as if trying to make out who was in the room. Finally, his eyes landed on his fellow escapee. "That you, Tiger? Ya sure you don't got any stuff? I sure could use some." He wiped his nose with the sleeve of Eric's sweater, making me wince. But it would be a good excuse to finally get rid of this former girlfriend's gift.

"Like I tell you, Jo bring it." The man sank his bulk into the armchair on the other side of the sofa and ran his hands over the leather armrests. "Very nice. Been long time since I sit in chair so nice. Woman, you lucky you got so many nice things."

Figuring he was just trying to goad me, I pretended I hadn't heard.

"Larry, tell woman name of university where Professor work."

"You mean McGill?"

"*Da*, big one in Montreal."

"Ah … Tiger, I gotta go, eh?" The injured man flicked his eyes in my direction. "Ah … you know what I mean.…" Another glance at me. "Do you think you can help me?" Larry winced as he pushed himself further upright.

"I don't know if this is a good idea," I said. "You're going to have to climb the stairs. I have a chamber pot. Why don't you use that?"

"A bottle more better." Slobodan guffawed.

"I'll get both."

"Make sure bottle have big opening," he called out as I headed out the door. His laughter followed me down the hall.

The minute I saw Jid in the kitchen, I made a snap decision. "Get your jacket and let's get out of here."

I pushed him through the door into the pantry. I was reaching for my jacket when I heard a click behind me. I turned to see the biker leaning against the kitchen doorjamb. He was pointing his gun straight at me.

"You go somewhere?" He smirked.

I lowered my arm. With my heart pounding, I said, "Just getting the chamber pot. Jid, can you squeeze by the tree to get it from the shelf?"

The boy dropped his jacket onto the floor with a muttered "fuck," voicing my thoughts exactly. And he swore again as he pushed his body against the wall to avoid the sharp needles. If looks could kill, I was sure his would as he glared back at the biker.

"Why tree in house?" the man asked.

"For Christmas."

"Christmas? When?" He seemed surprised. I guessed when you were locked away in prison, you preferred to ignore these kinds of family events that would only remind you of what you were missing.

"In four days."

"Good. I like Christmas. I have proper Serbian Christmas with Jo." The smile spreading across his face seemed to change him into the kind of man with whom a woman like this Jo could fall in love — as if anyone could fall in love with a thug like him.

The boy appeared from behind the tree hefting the white porcelain bowl with its dainty blue flowers triumphantly above his head.

"Take bowl to room and get Injun to pee in it. Is big enough. He not miss." He snorted.

"Don't you call him Injun," Jid shot back. "It's not nice."

"Shut your mouth, Injun," Slobo sneered. "I say Injun if I want. Now go." He motioned for me to move too.

While we waited in the hall outside the door to the den, he fondled the gun as if making up for lost time. I could hear a fair amount of groaning and cursing coming from the room. Finally, it stopped. Jid appeared in the doorway holding the chamber pot as far away as his arms would allow while he squinched up his nose in disgust.

"Empty it in the toilet," I said.

"Kid, you play trick on me and bam, I shoot your aunt," the Serb called out as Jid started up the stairs.

He shoved me into the den, almost causing me to trip over the carpet. "Go there." He pointed to the dining-room chair I used to reach the books on the top shelf. In front of it were piled the boxes of Christmas tree ornaments I'd retrieved from storage a couple of days ago.

Larry smiled weakly from the couch as I walked past. Professor, on the other hand, still snored. If only the biker would fall into as deep a sleep. But from the way he was jiggling his leg, I'd say he was a long way from passing out.

Pushing the boxes aside, I stopped when I reached the chair and waited.

"Sit. I tell you sit."

He bend down and retrieved the rope from under the sofa. "I not stupid, *ne?*" He smirked. "Sit on chair."

He began slapping it against his leg while I carefully moved the box containing the most delicate glass balls from the cracked leather seat to an empty shelf and sat down.

He continued to glare at me while the rope rasped against his knee. Finally he said, "I no trust you. I tie you up."

He started striding toward me. But before he reached me, a tremendous jolt screamed through the house, followed by a resounding thump.

"Shit! What's that?" I cried out, rising from the chair. "Jid, Jid, are you okay?"

TWENTY-THREE

As I ran into the hall, Slobodan fired his gun. My instinctive reaction was to duck, as if one could dodge a bullet. But I wasn't thinking too clearly.

"Get fuck back here," he shouted.

"What did you do that for?" I yelled, trying to calm my spiking nerves.

"Fuckin' cops are here."

As much as I wished and prayed they had finally arrived, I had my doubts. "Impossible. The only way they could get here is by Ski-Doo, and we would've heard them. I need to check my house."

"You stay here."

"What was that awful noise?" Jid asked, running into the room. He careened to a stop when he saw the gun.

"Do you really think it's the cops?" Larry rasped, bunching the blanket up against his chest as if for protection.

"It's not the cops," I said. "Something's fallen on the house. I need to check it out."

"Shut the fuck up."

Despite the noise, Professor slept on.

For what seemed interminable minutes, the three of us remained frozen where we stood. I clutched Jid's hand in an attempt to reassure him that everything was going to be okay, even if I didn't believe it myself. He held it for a few seconds and then pulled it free as if to say *I'm a big boy. I can hold my own.* I strained to hear anything other than the sounds of the storm. But apart from Shoni's whimpers coming from the kitchen, I heard nothing that suggested a line of policemen were on the verge of storming into my house.

"Move," Slobodan ordered and pushed the two of us out into the hall in front of him. "Walk very slow. You run, I shoot." To emphasize the point, he shoved the barrel of his handgun into my back.

"Where are we going?" I asked.

"Front of house, where noise is."

I held Jid close to me as the three of us walked as one down the hall toward the front door. He stopped us when we reached the archway leading into the living room with its wall of windows. Only opaque blackness stared back at us.

He shone his headlamp into the room. My heart leapt at a sudden flash from outside.

"Cops!" he hissed, shoving us into the room. He brought the pistol up beside my head, in full view of anyone who might be watching.

The flash appeared again.

Maintaining his position behind us, he stopped us when we reached the window.

"I shoot hostages," he shouted.

Nothing. No response.

The beam of his headlamp lit up the inside of the screened porch and the snow on the floor. It came to rest on the wind chime, a present from Eric that he'd hung from a rafter to catch the breeze. The wind catcher was dancing. With each flutter it exploded with another burst of silvery light.

"No cops," I said, feeling the chill of disappointment.

"Good," Slobo grunted. He thrust us back into the hall. "We go to door."

The gun barrel pressed farther into my ribs.

He halted us just short of the door. "Boy, look outside."

Jid started to open the door.

"No! Use window." He added a few choice Serbian swear words.

Jid jumped back. But in the beam of my headlamp, I saw more stubborn defiance in his eyes than fear.

"Look through the window next to the door," I said. "And tell us what you see."

By now I was convinced he wouldn't see any police here either. It was too black out there. If they had somehow managed to track down these escaped convicts to my house, they would have it lit up in an orgy of light. And they would be shouting through a megaphone, demanding these guys come out with their hands up.

I had a fairly good idea of what Jid would see.

He moved the curtain aside and tried to shine the beam through the window. But its brilliance bounced off the glass, obscuring any view.

"Take off your headlamp and use it like a flashlight," I said.

Jid pressed his face against the glass and directed the beam outside. "I can't see anything. Looks like something's in the way."

More concerned about my house than the gun, I wrenched open the door.

Instead of wind and snow blowing through the opening, there was just an eerie, creaking stillness. At first I couldn't see anything other than what looked to be a jumble of wood, and then I realized the porch roof had caved in. Sandwiched in with the broken planks were disembodied pine branches.

"Like I tried to tell you, a tree has fallen against the house."

It would be the lone pine on the other side of the driveway, the one I'd stopped Eric from cutting down. A good two hundred years old or more, I was hoping it would live another two hundred years. But Eric had suspected the high number of dead branches meant it was dying and was in danger of falling. I should've listened.

The caved-in roof made it impossible to tell if there was damage to the outside wall. But I suspected if there were any, it would be minimal. It would take more than a tree to dent the foot-thick timbers. On the other hand, the windows weren't quite so impenetrable. I headed back into the living room.

"Hey you, come back," Slobodan shouted.

I ignored him. "Come on, Jid. Let's check out the windows."

Fortunately, the windows overlooking this section of the porch were intact, although I could see that the sharp end of a broken branch had barely missed the pane of one of the windows. Because the tree had fallen perpendicular to the house, I started to worry about the upstairs windows, even the main roof.

Propelling Jid in front of me, I hastened upstairs. I could hear Slobodan stomping up behind me.

I felt the cold draft long before my light lit up the shattered window. Shards of glass, pine needles, and broken twigs littered the hall floor. Wind and snow rushed in through the gap.

"Fuck," the Serb said, coming up behind me.

"We've got to cover this up, otherwise the house will become a freezer in no time." The snow that was piling up on the floor beneath the broken window was no longer melting.

"Jid, run downstairs and get some large nails and a hammer. I'll grab a couple of blankets from one of the bedrooms."

"How about some plywood? My aunt uses it for her broken windows," he suggested. "I saw some in the woodshed."

"Great idea. Slobodan, could you help Jid?"

The man started to refuse, but, concluding I wasn't going anywhere, he followed the boy's retreating back.

TWENTY-FOUR

I listened to their footsteps patter down the stairs. I was scared, really scared. Jid and I had to find a way to deal with these men. But short of getting the hell out of here, I had no idea what else we could do to save ourselves.

Eric wouldn't hesitate to use his hunting rifles. But even if he kept a duplicate key to the gun cabinet somewhere in the house, I would only rouse suspicions searching for it. So far neither man had discovered the cabinet tucked away in a dark corner of his ground floor office. I thought it best to keep it that way. The last thing I wanted was for them to add his three rifles to their arsenal.

But there must be something I could do. I thought of the threat to tie me up. Maybe I should hide a knife in a pocket that I might be able use to cut myself loose. Unfortunately, my penknife was in the kitchen, but there might be something in the bathroom.

Keeping an ear open for sounds of their return, I rummaged through the vanity drawers and the linen cupboard. I tucked a pair of nail scissors into my front jeans pocket and a couple of paper-wrapped razor blades into the back pocket. Even if neither were strong enough to cut through rope, they could be used to stab or cut something, like skin....

I remembered that another of Eric's hunting knives was lying on his night table at the same time I heard the boy and the biker starting back up the stairs. There was no time to retrieve it at the moment, but maybe I would get the chance after we finished boarding up the window. I was at the end of the hall, removing the sharp shards and splinters of glass from the floor, by the time the two of them reached the top of the stairs. Each carried a good-sized piece of plywood.

"Auntie, we brought two in case one isn't big enough," Jid said, holding up his board, which was taller than he was when he held it up to its full extent.

Slobodan let his go with a clatter onto the floor. He stepped to one side to prevent it from landing on his feet. I heard the crunch of glass.

"Sranje!" he cried out. "Fuck!"

He bounced around on one foot, hurling more Serbian curses until he lost his balance and ended up on his back on the floor. "Bitch! You do this!"

With his face grimaced in pain, he clutched the injured foot. Something on the underside glistened in my headlamp.

"I didn't do anything. You stepped on some glass." I kneeled beside him. "Stay still and let me check it."

More Serbian swearing, but he kept his foot steady while I examined the piece of glass. An inch-long shard protruded from the dirty white sock. The only thing to do was to pull it out. So I did, careful not to cut myself in the process.

This resulted in another round of Serbian curses as the blood spread across the underside of his sock.

I'd no sooner removed the glass than I realized I'd blown it. I should've left it in. With it buried deep in his foot, there was no way he could chase after us. How could I have been so stupid not to think of using this chance to escape?

Still, his foot had to be causing considerable pain, making it impossible for him to put his full weight on it. Maybe there was still a chance.

I raised myself from the floor. "Jid, let's get the first aid kit from downstairs and some water and towels."

"Not so fast." Slobodan pulled out the gun from his waistband.

"The cut is deep. I need to stop the bleeding."

The blood was starting to drip onto the floor.

"The kid go. You stay."

"Look, I've already told you we're not going anywhere. We'd freeze to death in this storm."

As if to emphasize the point, a particularly strong gust pushed a stream of snow through the gap in the window, covering us in a veil of white.

"The boy can't carry everything on his own. He needs my help," I persisted.

I could see Jid was about to protest, so, turning off my headlamp, I shoved him in front of me and ran down the hall. I held my breath and tried to make myself as small a target as possible.

"Stop!" he yelled. He fired a shot.

He missed.

We kept going. Another metre and we'd be at the stairs and rapidly descending out of his line of sight.

But I hadn't bargained on the determination of the man.

I heard the groans and thumps but didn't fully understand what they meant until I was suddenly wrenched backward with a gun jabbed into my neck.

"Bitch, I tell you, stop."

"Don't you dare hurt my auntie!" Jid shouted.

I heard what sounded like a scuffle, but with the convict's light shining directly into my eyes, I couldn't tell what was happening.

"You leave the boy alone. I'll do what you want."

He walloped me across the face with his hand, much harder than Professor had. "Bitch, you do what I say." He slugged me again.

I reeled backward from the blows. My ears were ringing. Lights danced in front of my eyes. The entire right side of my face was filled with a burning pain, and I was plunged back to the days of my first marriage, a marriage I'd tried so hard to forget. I felt like I had a lead weight dragging me down. All the bravado was knocked out of me. It wasn't so much the physical pain but the terrifying awareness that a man could still so easily turn me into a quivering blob of jelly, and there was nothing I could do. I'd thought I'd left this behind.

"Are you okay, Auntie?" Jid's voice hovered over me as I realized I was lying on the floor.

"I'm fine ... just do what he says."

With my eyes still trying to focus, I sensed his nod more than I saw it. My only desire was to curl up in a ball and pretend none of this was happening. But Jid's hand on my arm wouldn't let me.

"I'll help you get up," he said.

The cold blowing through the window was penetrating my clothes. With the boy pulling on my arm, I struggled to stand but couldn't find the energy until Slobodan jerked me to my feet.

"You gonna be good, bitch?"

I nodded numbly.

"Good. It freezing. We fix fuckin' window, and then you fix foot."

TWENTY-FIVE

The man wasn't human. While he padded back along the hall, leaving a bloody trail, he didn't emit a single groan or screw his face up in pain. He didn't even favour the sliced foot.

When we reached the window, he pointed to the pile of glass where he'd cut his foot and snarled, "Get rid of fuckin' glass. I cut my foot again, I hit more than face."

With my cheek a stinging testament to the veracity of his threat, I obediently brushed the shards and splinters along the floor, using one of the broken pine branches as a broom. Jid joined me with another branch. We swept them into a nearby bedroom.

Though the thought of snatching up one of the larger splinters crossed my mind, I knew I didn't have it in me to stab anyone, not even this monster. But I noticed a familiar glint in Jid's eye when he slipped his hand into his pocket. It was the same reckless glint that would appear when he was weaving in and out of the other hockey players, intent on scoring a goal. But a twelve-year-old boy was no match for a man like Slobodan. Still, I didn't tell him to remove the shard from his pocket. Instead, I decided to go with the flow, so to speak, and let the gods determine the role it would play.

I whispered, "Watch out that it doesn't break."

Denial started to spread across his face until he realized he'd been caught. His answer was the cocky smile he flashed when he scored.

"What you say, bitch?" Slobodan's light blinded us.

"Just telling Jid not to hurt himself on the broken glass."

He shone his headlamp up and down the hall, exposing the dark holes of opened doors. "You got lots of bedrooms. How many?"

"Six."

"Many places to fuck. This the room where you get rammed?" The man shone his light across the hall and into the large master bedroom Eric and I shared.

Trying to ignore the icy pit in my stomach, I pretended I hadn't heard. I returned to the smashed window and brushed off the snow covering it. "Jid, do you have the hammer and nails handy?"

"He's got them." He pointed to my bedroom doorway. I could hear sounds of movement coming from inside.

The last place I wanted to be was in a bedroom with that man. "Do you mind giving us the nails and hammer?" I cried out with some trepidation. "We want to cover the window."

"Come get them."

Jid noticed my hesitation. "I'll get them."

I shook my head. He wasn't going in there either. "Slobodan, we'd like you to nail the board into the window frame. We aren't tall enough to reach the top of the window."

"Great big bed. Come, we try it out." He punctuated it with the raucous laughter that had become the embodiment of the man for me. Loud, sneering, and rude. I heard the bedsprings creak in the one spot where they were weak, a spot Eric and I carefully avoided.

Cold, gnawing fear crept over me. I couldn't go in there. In fact, I couldn't move, even if I wanted to. I felt Jid's hand briefly in mine. When he let go, something remained. I could faintly feel its sharp edge through the Kleenex wrapping.

"Thanks," I whispered, inserting the glass splinter carefully into the pocket of my fleece vest. It felt a good three or four inches long. Better than the scissors for stabbing.

With the wind from the broken window buffeting our backs, Jid and I waited for the next move.

"Slobo, get your ass out of there!" came a sudden shout from the other end of the hall, along with a beam of light. Professor walked toward us with an unwavering stride — no hint of the earlier stumbling gait. Amazingly, he was sober, stone cold sober.

The bed creaked again, followed by a thud on the floor and loud swearing. The biker limped out of my bedroom, almost colliding with Professor. "I cut fuckin' foot."

"I don't care. We've got to get the damn window boarded up before we become blocks of ice." He held out his hand. "Hand over the nails and hammer."

Crossing his arms, the Serb jutted his jaw out in defiance.

Neither Jid nor I dared move.

The hand with the snakes slithering around the fingers remained open.

Not a single word was spoken between the two men.

Finally, Slobodan pulled the hammer out from his belt and swung it down toward the outstretched palm.

But before it connected with flesh, Professor grasped the handle and pulled, forcing the other man to put his full weight on the injured foot.

He howled.

"Shut up and hold the plywood against the window for the lady," Professor said with barely an inflection in his voice.

Jid and I quickly moved out of the way as Slobodan slammed its flatness against the window frame. At this point I didn't care if he damaged the wood or gouged the plaster, as long as it stopped the wind, snow, and cold from storming in. Within minutes, Professor had the two pieces of plywood firmly nailed to the frame. I felt only a whisper of icy air along the edges. But it wouldn't be long before the cold would start penetrating the thin wood.

"Look at the blood you've put on this nice antique pine floor," Professor said. "You'll have to clean it up."

Bloody footprints, some wetter than others, criss-crossed the worn planks.

Slobodan's pale eyes narrowed in hatred.

"I'll do it," I broke in. The last thing I wanted was a fight between these two men. Mind you, if they killed each other, so much the better. But we could also die in the process.

"I want you to apologize for treating this lady so dis-respectfully." Professor brought his hand down onto the hilt of the knife at his waistband. "If you dare touch her, I'll kill you."

The Serb narrowed his eyes further and planted his feet as if preparing for action. He rested his hand on the grip of his gun. I felt as if we'd been plunged into a

B-movie Western. Normally a bullet fired from a gun should be faster than a flying knife, but in the hands of Professor I suspected it would be the opposite.

I backed up against the boarded window, pulling Jid with me.

Just when I thought it was going to end disastrously, the biker grunted and then slowly lifted both hands away from his body. "No problem." But the smile on his lips didn't reach his eyes.

I then noticed a brown leather sheath attached to his belt. Sticking out of it was the bone hilt of the hunting knife from the night table. I waited to see if Professor would do anything about it, but he merely pointed at the man's bloody sock and said, "Get that cleaned up."

TWENTY-SIX

I couldn't make sense of the relationship between these two men. They could hardly be called friends — more like enemies, and yet they had escaped together. They seemed to have little in common other than being convicts. One was a full patch member of a notorious biker gang. The other had supposedly taught at university. I doubted their paths would've crossed before their incarceration.

But if they weren't friends, why did they escape together? Or did Professor and Larry just happen to be in the van when the Serbian's friends arrived to free him? If so, it was more likely the three of them would've gone their separate ways. Instead they came here, together.

That was the other unanswerable question. Why Three Deer Point?

Professor obviously had some sort of hold over the Serbian; otherwise the biker wouldn't have given in. It made more sense for the relationship to be the other way around. After all, the Serbian was the biker, the tough guy, the bully who was used to getting his own way.

Whatever the source of his power, I was very thankful Professor could keep him in check. Maybe I should become the stalker and go wherever he went just to avoid being alone with the biker.

Slobodan sat on the edge of my bed, smirking while I removed his bloody sock. Afraid of revealing how effective his intimidation tactics were, I steadied my shaking hands as best I could as I worked on his wound. I was terrified that if he knew how much he frightened me, he would come after me again when Professor wasn't around. Fortunately, for the moment the tattooed man was standing directly behind me.

Though deep, the cut appeared clean, with no remaining silvers of glass and little sign of bleeding. After disinfecting it with the ointment Jid retrieved from downstairs, I covered it with a large Band-Aid and several layers of gauze in case it bled again when he put his weight on it.

"You'll need a clean sock," I said. "Jid, could you get one of Eric's from the drawer?"

"Viper, it very nice when woman caress your foot, especially when you sit on her bed?" He snickered. "But maybe you like more better man do it, *no*?" He let out another burst of laughter.

Disgusted by his behaviour, I snatched the sock from Jid's hand and threw it at the man. "Put this on yourself."

He roared. "I love woman with balls."

"Come on, Jid, let's go downstairs." The faster I got away from the man, the better.

I expected to be stopped, or at the very least followed, the way I'd been stalked before. But Professor remained in the room. I heard voices, along with shouting, as we headed down the stairs. Maybe they would kill each other this time.

"What are we going to do?" Jid asked.

"I don't know." I should've been more optimistic, but I no longer had the energy to pretend.

"Guess I'm going to miss my game, eh?" He sighed.

Game? What game? "You mean tomorrow night's hockey game."

"Yeah, Coach said I did so well in the last couple of games, he was gonna put me on the first line with Randy and Steve. I'd sure hate to miss it."

Nothing like a child to put priorities where they should be. I squeezed his arm. "We'll see what we can do to make it happen."

"We gonna go now?"

Dumb me. I should've been thinking about making a dash for it, but I hadn't. And now that my mind was finally focusing on escaping, it was too late. Footsteps thudded down the stairs.

"You got soap to clean floor?" Slobodan growled as he limped up to me. I relaxed at the sight of Professor's bullet head looming behind him.

"I'll do it." I didn't want him ruining the floor with too much water, as if it really mattered. The snow and broken glass had already done more than enough damage.

"Good. You my kind of woman," the Serb replied. "Get me more fancy Scotch," he yelled as I headed to the kitchen. "Viper want more too."

"Don't get any more, Red," Professor called out.

"What the fuck?" Slobodan rasped. "I need drink."

"You've had enough, as have I. We need to keep our heads clear."

So much for drinking until they passed out.

Shoni lay asleep, curled up in her blanket at the front of her crate. In the back corner were a couple of tiny brown sausages and a small puddle. Poor baby.

She yawned and stretched and wagged her tail and then gave Jid several sloppy licks when he opened the door. Picking her up, he nuzzled his face in her soft fur. "How ya doing, little one?" he whispered. "You've been a bad pup." He kissed her on the end of her nose. Turning to me, he said, "I think I'd better put her out."

"Good idea," Professor said, startling me. I hadn't heard him slip into the kitchen. "I'll do it." He pulled the puppy from Jid's arms. "Come to papa."

I ached for Jid as he helplessly watched the man take the ball of fluff into the pantry and out the back door.

"I guess I'd better clean the cage," he said.

"Don't worry." I hugged him. "He likes dogs too much to hurt her. You'll have plenty of time to play with her after they leave."

"When's that gonna be?"

"In time for your hockey game." I planted the broadest smile I could muster on my face. I was back to pretending.

TWENTY-SEVEN

While the cursing biker hobbled back upstairs with the mop and pail, I retreated to the den, leaving Jid alone with the tattooed man in the kitchen. Dead tired and emotionally exhausted, I wanted a few minutes of solitude in which I didn't have to try to pretend I wasn't scared for Jid's sake.

After the way Professor had intervened with the Serbian on my behalf, I was less worried about leaving the boy alone with him. I could even hear the boy's laughter. Still, if he didn't join me within ten or so minutes, I would retrieve him, particularly after the biker returned to the main floor.

I was amazed to see from the mantel clock that it was barely nine. The four and a half hours since these guys had invaded my home felt more like four and a half days. With close to twelve hours before daylight, it was going to be one very long and nerve-wracking night.

Come morning, I was praying they'd be gone. But judging by the amount of snow that had spilled through the broken window, it wasn't likely. The storm wasn't close to letting up. Tomorrow there could easily be half again as much as the amount already on the ground, which must have half-buried my pickup by now. There was no way this Jo would be able to drive in to get them, unless she knew enough to bring a snowmobile.

But let's get realistic. Why was I so anxious for them to leave? When they finally did go, Jid and I would likely be dead. They weren't about to leave witnesses behind.

But why not? It wasn't as if we could tell the cops anything that they didn't already know. I doubt these thugs would broadcast their next destination, and I wasn't about to ask.

Escaping was our best option. But with Professor putting the lid on drinking, it was pretty well ruled out. And if they carried out their threat to tie me up, that was the end of it entirely. Still, if by some miracle an opportunity presented itself, we'd be gone in a flash. But miracles were scarce at the moment.

That left some other way to deal with Slobo and Professor. I didn't view Larry as a threat. Stabbing them with scissors or the glass shard wasn't going to do it. I supposed I could take one of the carving knives from the kitchen, but I wasn't certain if I had it in me to actually stab someone, no matter how threatening. The same went for trying to slit one of their throats with the razor blade. I had to face it — I was the one most likely to be killed.

On the other hand, I wouldn't hesitate to have them ingest something that would incapacitate or kill them. I had some noxious gardening pesticides, but they were out of reach in the garden shed. The only item of that nature in the house was mouse poison, and I wasn't certain it had the strength to kill a man. Besides, how would I get them to eat it?

All of which didn't leave me much choice other than to do what they asked of us in the hope that when they finally departed, they would feel agreeable enough to leave us unharmed.

Very disheartened, I threw a couple of logs onto the fire and increased the flame of the oil lamp before sinking into an armchair. I noticed that more fuel had been added, likely by Professor. It wasn't something the Serbian would do.

The tinsel sparkled in the renewed light, reminding me that it was the Christmas season. Christmas. Peace and joy on earth. It seemed as if it belonged to another world.

Larry appeared to be asleep, although his body twitched under the blanket. I wondered how much worse his withdrawal would get. From the little I'd read about heroin withdrawal, I gathered an addict could become quite agitated. I hoped Professor would be able to control him and keep him from making the bullet wound worse.

I must've been sighing, for Larry suddenly spoke up. "You okay, lady? Tiger didn't hurt you, did he?"

"No, Professor came to my aid."

"Yeah, Professor's a good guy. He'll protect you the same way he protects me." He raised himself carefully into an upright position. The sweat on his face gleamed in the light.

"It must be hard living in a prison," I said.

"Yah, when you're a little guy, the big guys won't leave you alone, eh? But once you have a protector, no one comes near you."

"Other than your protector."

He raised his eyes to mine in alarm.

"Don't worry, I don't care if you're gay."

"Yeah, but I wasn't always this way. Before I got sent up, I had a girlfriend, eh? Just inside, you gotta do it, eh? Guys get killed when they don't. Besides, Professor treats me real good."

"What did you do to end up in there?" Though Slobodan had told me, I wanted to hear it from Larry.

"Fuckin' cops said I killed a man, but I didn't. Just 'cause my fingerprints were on the gun, they said I did it. I kept telling 'em I found it, but they called me a liar. Didn't like the colour of my skin, eh? And that Judge Meilleur screwed me royally, all because I was an Indian. So Professor says. He's gonna get me a good lawyer. He says it was harsement or some word like that."

"Harassment."

"Yup, that's it. Says it's against the law for the cops and a judge to do that. Says a good lawyer will get them to open up the case and get me off."

I supposed he could be innocent, but he was hardly the first convict to insist he was, nor would he be the last. "How long have you been in prison?"

"Thirteen years. Twelve more to go before I get parole, eh? You see, I got the max. First degree murder, all on account I was an Indian."

"You know, if you get caught now, you'll go back to jail for even longer."

"Professor'll make sure I don't get caught. We're going some place nice, where the cops can't catch us. You see, this is Professor's last job. He promised." A shiver ran through him, more like a convulsion. "I feel like shit. You sure you don't got any pills?"

"Only Tylenol." And the ibuprofen Eric used when he had too many aches and pains from trying to pretend he was twenty years younger. But neither would solve Larry's problem. However, they could solve mine. I wondered if a liberal dose of either would put the two men to sleep.

Jid came running into the room with the puppy scampering after him. "You should see the cool trick Professor taught Shoni."

He careened to a stop when he saw Larry sitting up.

"It's okay, kid. I'm not gonna hurt you or your auntie."

"You feeling okay?" Jid asked. "What's it feel like to have a bullet go through you?"

"Now, Jid, it's not polite to ask such questions," I said.

"It's okay. He's just a boy with a boy's curiosity. All I can say is it hurts like shit."

"Do you have the bullet? You know, like you see on TV."

Larry glanced over at me for the answer.

"It went right through him. So it's likely lying where he was shot."

"Do you know who shot you?" the boy asked.

Again Larry looked at me.

But before I could say I didn't know, Slobodan limped into the room. "A hack shot him."

"You mean one of the guards in the van?" the injured man asked.

"Yeah, before Jo shoot him dead. They kill other hack and driver too."

Shit. Triple shit.

I supposed if there were a positive side to this horrific act, it would be that the hunt for these escaped convicts would have gone up many notches with the killing of the guards. The police wouldn't stop until they'd captured all three of them. But would they know to look in the middle of nowhere?

"Jo good woman. Like I tell you, I love woman with balls." The leer that crept across the man's face made me shudder.

I'd been hoping that the arrival of this girlfriend would neutralize the killing instinct in these men. Instead, she was as cold-blooded a killer as her boyfriend.

TWENTY-EIGHT

I'd barely absorbed the implication of the guards' murders when the biker hauled me from the armchair and dragged me across the carpet to the dining room chair, kicking the boxes of ornaments aside. I was too stunned to resist.

"Sit," he ordered.

I sat.

I gritted my teeth to keep from crying out as my arms were wrenched almost out of their sockets when he pulled them around the back of the chair. Gripping my wrists together, he ordered Jid to tie them.

"Rope no good," he muttered. "You got zip ties?"

I held my breath, worried the boy would mention the ones lying in a pantry drawer. We'd used them yesterday to attach the Christmas lights to the verandah railing. But thankfully the boy remained mute while he finished tying my hands. He left the rope slightly loose so I might be able to work my hands free, something I couldn't have done with zip ties. *Thank you, Jid.*

But my hopes were short-lived when the Serb started wrapping the rope around my upper body, melding me to the back of the chair. Every time he ran the rope over my chest, he made a point of running his hand over my breasts. I tried my hardest not to flinch. I didn't want to give him the satisfaction of knowing he was unnerving me.

I strained to hear Professor's footsteps coming down the hall. I'd expected to see the man coming through the door behind the Serbian. But so far there was no sign of him.

"Jid, could you go find Professor?" I asked.

"Stay here, kid," Slobodan ordered. "Hold her feet."

I had a moment's panic when he whipped out Eric's knife and pointed it straight at me. But he was only interested in cutting the rope behind my back. He started wrapping the remaining length around my ankles, cinching it very tightly, so tightly I could feel it biting through my scratchy wool socks.

"Ouch, that hurts. Could you loosen it, please?"

"Shut up." He tugged it tighter.

"Professor!" Larry's voice rang out with more strength than I thought he had in him. "Could you come here a minute?"

"What's up, little buddy?" came the answer from the direction of the living room.

"I need you." Larry flashed a smug smile at the Serbian, who merely grunted.

The biker was just finishing cutting the rope around my feet when the tattooed man stepped into the room.

"Professor, she's good people," Larry said. "She doesn't need to be tied up." He turned imploring eyes in my direction. "Promise them you won't run away."

But before I could answer, Professor said, "Nope. She can't be trusted. Slobo, tie the kid up too."

It was the Serbian's turn to gloat.

Within minutes, Jid was trussed up as securely as I was on another chair brought in from the dining room.

They'd placed us side by side about a foot apart and within the circle of the fire's warmth, which I thought was considerate of them. Except they forgot to add more logs before the two of them left us alone once again with Larry.

I tried wriggling my hands, but I couldn't get much movement with the ropes tied around my arms. I thought if I managed to loosen them even a smidgen, my fingers might be able to make their way through the opening at the back of the chair to reach the razor blades in my back jean pocket, so I kept working them.

"You okay, Jid?"

"Yup."

"The ropes aren't too tight?"

"Kinda. I can't feel my hands."

"That's not good." But when I looked over to check on his hands, I saw faint arm movement going on behind his back. He waved his head in the direction of Larry to tell me this was his way of putting the man off.

"Good luck," I mouthed, then turned to see Larry watching both of us.

"They shouldna oughta done that," he said. "It ain't no way to treat a lady."

"Why don't you untie us?" I whispered.

"Can't." He turned his face away and closed his eyes.

"When's Shome coming?" Jid asked, lowering his voice so only I could hear him.

"Not for another two days," I whispered back. *If he comes at all*, I thought to myself, not wanting to let Jid know that all was not well between his hero and me. "When's your aunt coming home for Christmas?"

"I think it's Thursday, too. I guess Juicy won't come looking for me if I miss tomorrow night's game, eh?"

I didn't think his cousin would come either. He'd be happy to have another night free from babysitting.

"We're going to get you to that game, you hear," I persisted. "They have someone coming to get them tomorrow."

"Yah, I know." He paused and focused his brown eyes wide with trust at me. "They're gonna kill us, aren't they?"

For a second it took me aback that he, a child, should come to the same conclusion. Children shouldn't have to worry about death. But he could read their intent as well as I. "I don't know. If there is a way we can get out of here alive, we're going to find it, okay?"

"Okay," he answered but with little optimism.

"Don't worry," Larry piped up. "I'll make sure Professor don't hurt you. And he'll make sure Tiger don't either."

"Thanks, Larry. But are you sure you can do that? They won't want any witnesses."

"But you don't know where we're going after. So you can't rat on us. Besides, Professor owes me."

"Oh?"

"Yeah, I saved his bacon once."

"What did you do?"

"It happened shortly after Professor got sent up."

"How long ago was that?"

"Two years. He's up for parole next year."

"It doesn't make sense risking a longer sentence by escaping. So why did he do it?"

"They want him — no, I better say nothing. Better you don't know." He clamped his mouth shut and turned his face away from me.

I waited for him to continue and when he didn't, I asked, "Why do you say Professor owes you?"

"He got into a fight with a guy. And, well, the guy died."

"You mean another prisoner."

"Yah, a booty bandit. He was trying to make the moves on me, and well, Professor protected me. So I lied to the hacks and said it was self-defence. I told them it was the dead guy who attacked Professor with the shank, but Professor was lucky and got it away from him."

"Shank?"

"That's a knife, Auntie. Everyone knows that," Jid answered.

"How do you know?"

"TV."

"Right, all those cop shows you watch."

"Did he make it from a fork?"

"No, used his usual, a razor blade stuck into the end of a toothbrush," Larry replied.

"Cool."

"Professor's a knife man. That's his trade."

"He makes knives?" I asked, which earned me a groan from Jid.

"Okay, wrong question." Deciding I didn't want to know more, I continued, "So as a result nothing bad happened to Professor?"

"They coulda extended his sentence or sent him to maximum, but they didn't. Though they put him in the hole for a week."

"Hole?"

"Solitary. After that, me and Professor were buddies."

TWENTY-NINE

The murmur of voices drifted down the hall from the living room. I wondered what Professor and the Serb were up to. Despite Professor's protestations, they were likely doing an inventory of all the items they planned to steal. I doubted they'd left jail with any money, so they'd need something to pay their way. The Serb might not recognize the value of the small cigar box painting hanging next to the fireplace, but Professor would know it was a Tom Thomson worth enough to get them well beyond the reach of the cops. But as long as Jid and I got out of this alive, I didn't care what they took. Maybe I could use these treasures, even my great-grandmother's silver tea service, to guarantee our safety.

"Ending up in prison for tax evasion is a long way from teaching at McGill," I said to Larry. "His taxes would have been deducted from his paycheque, so where does the tax evasion come in?" I watched embers fly up the chimney from a sudden gust. "He must've had another source of income. Do you know?"

"You'd better ask him. He don't like people talking about him, eh?" The injured man didn't seem to be trembling as much as earlier, but his nose continued to flow. Occasionally he'd brush it away with his fingers or Eric's sweater, but mostly he ignored it.

"What about the snake tattoos? Hardly the kind I'd imagine a university would want for one of its professors."

"He weren't working there anymore. But I think he got the tattoos before he left. He's got this thing for snakes, eh?"

"All over his body?"

"Good a place as any, I guess. Some guys call him the Viper. He likes that. But me, I like Professor. It's more like who he is. I've learned a lot from him, eh?"

"Like what?" I asked.

"I don't got much of an education. Never went to high school, but Professor, he been teaching me. Says I'll soon know enough to get my diploma, eh?" He eased himself into a sitting position. "Jid, you better be going to school. Indian kids like you need an education, else you end up like me."

"Yeah, I go to school."

"Smart kid like you, I bet you're in grade six."

"Nope, grade eight. I skipped."

"Wow, that's terrific. I never made it past grade six."

"Why not?"

"My dad made me go trapping with him. Didn't want me moving to Somerset."

"Why would you have to go to Somerset?"

"You're from Migiskan, eh? Ain't that where you have to go to school after grade six?"

"Nope, I go to school on the rez."

"You gonna do high school there too?"

"Yup, all the way to grade eleven."

"So they built a school on the rez. Ain't you the lucky one."

"I guess."

"Take it from me, you are. They didn't treat us Indians too good in that white school in Somerset. Most of my buddies left after only a couple of years."

"This new one is a very good school," I said. "My husband was instrumental in getting it built. About ten years ago I think."

"Who's your husband?"

"Eric Odjik. He was Migiskan band chief for almost twelve years."

"Yeah, I remember the guy. He didn't think much of me. Chased me off the rez."

Just what we needed. Would Larry protect us now?

He chuckled. I looked up to see him grinning. "Yeah. I deserved it. I was a real scumbag. My girlfriend kicked me out too."

"What did you do?"

"I hung around with some pretty bad apples. They were into all sorts of shit. 'Cause of my size, they'd get me to go into houses through windows and stuff like that. I'd open the door so they could get inside and take stuff, mostly booze, but they also took TVs, microwaves, shit like that. One of the guys knew a fence in Ottawa."

"I guess you got caught."

From the corner of my eye I could see Jid working away on loosening his ropes.

"Sort of. I got stuck in a really small window. The other guys took off and left me there. The house belonged to your guy, Eric. When he got home he found me. Gave me a big lecture about going straight, then sent me home with a warning to get new friends. I was only sixteen. I guess Eric figured there was something worth saving."

"It sounds like something he would do."

"Yeah, he said I needed a chance to smarten up. Said I'd had a tough childhood. See, my dad used to beat me up when he got drunk. Said if I didn't act like a man he was gonna beat it into me. Anyways, your guy Eric got me playing hockey at the rec centre. Said it was good for building character."

Jid perked up. "What position did you play? Offense?"

"Yeah, the only position for a little guy like me. But you know what? I was pretty good at it. I was a fast skater. The big guys couldn't catch me. And I was good at scoring goals."

Jid smiled. "Me too."

"You keep playing hockey, you hear. Don't give it up like I did. My dad made me quit. He and Eric got into a big shouting match. Eric wanted me to go to school. He was going to pay for my lodgings in town. See, he'd made all this money playing hockey." He glanced over at Jid. "But I guess you know that, eh?"

"He was one of the best players and one of the first Indians to make it big in the NHL. They used to call him Lightning Odjik, because he was so fast." Jid beamed.

"Never heard that name before, but it fits. Anyways, my old man refused. He pulled me out of hockey and made me go trapping with him. I was gone all winter. When I got back to the rez, hockey was finished for the season. My buddies wanted me to do another job. So I did."

"What did you do to make Eric kick you off the rez?" I asked.

"He kept trying to get me to do stuff at the rec centre, but I wasn't interested. My buddies said only sissies hung around the place. I made sure I never got caught stealing again. But a couple of my buddies got caught and got sent up. Eric caught me giving some weed to a bunch of kids. He was real mad at me. Threatened to turn me in to the cops if I didn't tell him who the dealers were. So I did. He told me to leave the rez and never come back. I guess he'd given up on me by then." He sighed. "Wished I'd listened to him instead of my buddies. Never woulda ended up in the pen. I figured the dealer set me up."

"What do you mean?"

"When the guy discovered I'd squealed on him, he got his buddies to frame me. No way I killed that guy. But I'll never know. You see, I'd been drinking. Had too much and passed out. Professor thinks maybe they gave me something."

He lapsed into silence, staring at the fire. The wind continued to remind us that the blizzard was far from slowing down. The air wafting in from the hall seemed to have dropped a few degrees. I could feel coldness nibbling at my hands and ankles. Soon it would start to penetrate my clothes.

Larry shook himself away from his thoughts and turned back to us. "You guys getting cold? The fire's getting kinda low."

"Why don't you get Professor to put some logs on?" I replied.

"Nah, I can do it."

"Be careful. You don't want to make your injury worse."

"No problem. Don't hurt so much now."

He winced as he raised himself very slowly from the couch. Pressing his hands into his side, he shuffled over to the brass firewood rack leaning against the fireplace. He gingerly lifted one of the shorter logs and placed it on top of the coals. This he repeated a couple more times before shambling back to the sofa and collapsing with a painful groan.

"Man, that don't feel so hot. Guess I won't be practising judo any time soon, eh?"

"Wow, you know judo?" Jid asked.

"Yeah, something I picked up inside. Professor said I needed to defend myself. Said judo would be good, especially for someone my size." He glanced over at Jid. "I bet the bullies on the rez pick on you 'cause you're small, eh?"

"They used to, until Shome showed me a few tricks he learned playing hockey."

"I guess you mean Eric. He your grandpa?"

"Nope. I just call him Shome."

"Good. A kid needs someone to look up to and to keep you on the straight and narrow. I weren't so lucky. My *mishomis* was a drunk and died when I was little."

"I don't have any real grandpas either. One died before I was born and the other ran away and never came back. I guess he's dead now. Do you have your black belt?"

"Not yet. I got my green belt. Only two more *kyu* to go before I get the black." He picked away at some loose threads in the blanket, unravelling them more. "I've probably killed any chance of that happening now. The warden don't take kindly to escapees."

"You're never going to have to deal with the warden again, little buddy," Professor said, leaning against the doorframe. "You're not going to get caught. Neither of us are. We're free, you hear?"

"If you say so, Professor."

THIRTY

The tattooed man stepped behind me and tugged at the ropes.

"Ouch," I cried out. "That hurts."

"Your hands haven't turned blue yet, so they can't be too tight."

"Can't you loosen them a bit? My wrists are sore."

"Stop moving your hands."

I held my breath as Professor moved toward Jid's chair. Hopefully the boy hadn't managed to loosen his ropes enough to be noticed. But my worry was needless, for the man walked past without so much as a glance at Jid. He shone a flashlight through the window and growled, "When is this damn snow going to stop?"

As if in answer, the house voiced its displeasure as another gust rammed against it.

After poking at the fire, he sat down beside his lover and put his arm around him. "How are you doing, P'tit Chief? You've had a rough ride."

"The gunshot don't hurt so much anymore, but jeez, I need a fix. You sure you don't got something?" Larry pleaded.

"Just hang in there. Maybe this is a good time to quit."

"You know I can't do that. I don't got it in me."

"Sure you do. Remember, you didn't think you had it in you to finish high school, and yet you're almost there. No reason why you can't cure your heroin addiction. If you get through the next couple of days without the damn stuff you'll be well on the road to being drug-free."

"If you say so, Professor," Larry answered, barely above a whisper.

"Do they really call you Viper?" Jid asked.

"*Da*, Viper because he silent and deadly," Slobodan answered, limping into the room. He punctuated it with a mock throw of a knife before flinging himself into the leather chair next to me. Placing his hand on my knee, he said, "I gotta get chair like this. Where you buy?"

"Please remove your hand," I whispered between clenched teeth. Every nerve ending in my body flinched.

"Or you do what?" He let out a belly laugh while continuing to caress my knee.

Helpless to do anything about it, I looked to Professor for support, but he seemed more interested in communing with his buddy than being my protector.

"You leave her alone," Jid said.

"Or you do what, boy?"

"Untie me and I'll show you."

This caused an even louder crescendo of laughter. "You got balls, kid, like your aunt."

At that moment, a loud yelp from Shoni in the kitchen had Professor standing up. "Leave the woman and the boy alone," he said. "I suggest you move to that chair over there." He pointed to Eric's liberally duct-taped La-Z-Boy chair, which he'd finally had to retire after the back springs gave up. Not wanting to part with it entirely, he'd shoved it into a corner until he was prepared to give it a fitting farewell.

Slobodan firmed his jaw in resistance and then shrugged and stood up. "Sure, Viper, whatever you say." And he walked over and dropped his bulk into the chair with a loud clunk as more springs gave way.

"You had better be sitting in that chair when I return."

I watched with dread as the tattooed man left the room. I'd never felt so exposed in my life. If only I could convince him to untie me.

"You tell me, why woman like you fucking an Injun?" Slobodan rasped.

I wanted to spit on him and shout, "Shut up, you fucking racist." But I knew that was exactly the kind of response he wanted from me. So I ignored him and kept my eyes down, while I kept my ears peeled for Professor's speedy return.

Beside me I felt Jid tense up at the terrible insult to his hero, his friend. I willed him to remain passive too. He must've sensed it, for he did nothing other than start jiggling his leg.

"You probably like black meat too."

"Tiger, shut up," Larry said. "Or I'll tell Professor."

"*Da*, he like fucking red meat too."

I thought Larry was going to burst a vein.

Professor rushed into the room and slugged the Serbian's head sideways, cracking it against the wooden frame of the chair. *Good.* I hoped that hurt.

I tried to slink farther into my own chair while I waited for the biker to draw his gun and shoot his attacker.

But Slobodan merely firmed his fists and glared back. However, if looks could kill, this one would. Neither man said a word.

The tattooed man continued to tower over the biker until the man unclenched his hands and shrugged. "Only a little fun. I do no harm."

Yeah, right. He'd only offended everyone in this room. I couldn't understand why the man continued to goad Professor. He knew what the response would be. So far he'd deferred to his fellow con. But for how much longer?

"Give me your gun," Professor demanded.

Slobodan crossed his arms over his chest in refusal and jutted out his chin to emphasize the point.

"If you don't, I'll report you to the boss."

The Serb continued to resist. Finally, he shrugged and reached behind his back, but before he could pull the gun out, Professor grabbed his elbow.

"Remove your hand. I'll get it."

Just as well Professor couldn't see the hatred etched into the other man's face as he leaned behind him and eased out the gun.

He handed it to Larry. "I give you leave to shoot him if he insults you again."

"But you know I don't like guns. They get me into trouble."

"You've been very brave with this gunshot wound. I need you to remain strong for me, okay?"

Larry swallowed. "I guess." He shoved the handgun under the blanket while I slowly let out my breath.

Like me, Jid had been afraid to move in case it diverted their rage to us. Now he visibly relaxed.

You okay? I mouthed.

He stretched his lips into a weak smile and nodded.

"Everything gonna be okay, kid," Larry said. "Professor will protect us."

I dared a glance at Slobodan. He continued to slouch in the chair, jiggling his leg. He shot me a look of pure venom when he realized my eyes were trained on him. I looked away.

I had no idea how much longer Professor would be able to control this man. I only knew that I wanted to be far away from the two of them when it finally erupted. Even though it hurt my arms, I started straining on the ropes, hoping to loosen them. I noticed Jid doing the same thing.

The biker thrust himself out of the chair and limped out of the room, muttering. "We no need you, big shot. I can do it too."

Only then did I realize Shoni was nudging my leg, wanting to be lifted onto my lap.

"Sorry," I whispered. "You're just going to have to wait until my hands are free."

I couldn't even bend down to kiss her on her head.

It was at that point that I felt the tears begin to well up. I'd been trying so hard to put on a brave face, but I'd reached the point where I could no longer pretend. My world had gone to hell, and there was absolutely nothing I could do about it. Down my cheeks they trickled.

THIRTY-ONE

"What's the closest town to here?" Professor asked, lifting the puppy onto his lap.

"Pardon?" I said, trying to gain some control over my emotions. I was so helpless, I couldn't even wipe the tears from my face. "Did you say something?"

"Yeah, the nearest town. What's its name?"

I took a deep breath and felt a modicum of control returning. "Somerset. You must've driven through it."

There were only two main roads to this isolated part of Quebec, one from the west through Somerset, a once-thriving logging town, and the other from the south through the village-dotted skiing country of the Laurentian Mountains.

"We took mostly back roads. But I think I remember seeing a sign for Somerset. How far away is it?"

"About fifty kilometres."

While I loved the remoteness of Three Deer Point, this was one time I wished the town were next door.

"In this weather, I'm guessing a good hour away," he said.

Likely longer, I thought bleakly.

"I assume Somerset has a police detachment."

"Yes."

"Hey, you're crying." He rose from the sofa and walked over. Pulling a tissue from his pocket, he wiped the tears from my face. Surprisingly, his touch was very gentle. This only brought on more tears. He wiped those too. "Look, it's okay. I know we're not your ideal houseguests, but we'll be out of your hair in the morning, and you can get back to your normal life. Just hang in until then, okay?"

I wished with all my might that I could believe him.

He patted me on the arm and resumed his seat next to his lover. "How big a police force in Somerset?"

I tried not to glance at Jid, who must have been wondering what was going on. "I've no idea, but it's part of the Sûreté du Quebec."

I didn't feel it necessary to mention that as the second largest provincial police force in Canada, the SQ would bring limitless resources into play to capture three escaped convicts who'd killed three guards. But they would only do this if they knew these killers had crossed the Ottawa River from Ontario into Quebec.

"Where did you cross the river? At Ottawa?" Maybe someone saw them driving through the city.

"Hardly. Like I told you, we took the back roads, staying well clear of towns."

That meant either they took the Cumberland ferry, which was unlikely given that they would have to come face to face with someone in order to pay, or they took the only other bridge crossing the Ottawa River before it flowed into the St. Lawrence at Montreal, the Hawkesbury bridge, which would require them to drive through the rural town to get to it. But no one would've noticed them. People would be more worried about navigating safely through the blinding snow than in noticing three escaped cons driving past them.

"It's like I told you, Professor," Larry piped up. "There's nothing close by. No way the police are ever gonna know we're here."

"Just checking," Professor replied.

I was surprised Larry hadn't mentioned the Migiskan reserve's tribal police, but perhaps he thought the force too small and inexperienced to be a threat. Maybe they were, but if Chief Decontie had even an inkling these killers were in the area, he would bring in every SQ SWAT team in Quebec to ensure their capture.

But Will had no idea these men were less than seven kilometres from his detachment, unless he'd heard my plea. And if he had, the SWAT teams would be converging on us even as we talked.

"So why Three Deer Point?" I asked. "There are lots of other places that are more remote."

"We need to be close —"

Professor butted in. "He knew of the house and thought it would be a good place to hide out for a few days. That's right, isn't it, P'tit Chief?"

"Yeah, that's right." Larry glanced nervously at me before returning his gaze to his protector. He shrugged, almost as if he were apologizing.

His actions only made me more suspicious. Close to what? Other than the Migiskan community and the odd cottage and farm sprinkled amongst the surrounding hills and lakes, there was nothing close by. Besides, few farms were occupied full-time anymore, and the cottages would be boarded up for the winter. So I had no idea what Larry could be alluding to.

Jid shifted in the chair beside me. "Can you untie me? I gotta pee."

"You should've thought of that before, kid," came the man's clipped response.

"I really gotta go."

"Please, untie him," I chimed in. "He's not going to cause you any trouble."

"The bitch lie," Slobodan said, stepping across the threshold. A glass of what looked to be Coke sloshed around in his hand, though judging by his smirk, I wasn't sure if something stronger hadn't been added. "The kid make plenty trouble." He held up his hand to remind us of the bite Jid had given him.

Maybe if I were lucky, that, combined with the cut on his foot, would give him blood poisoning and he would die.

"I trust you are drinking only Coke," Professor retorted.

The Serb shoved the glass under the other man's nose and sneered. "Smell! Only Coke."

I was glad to see Slobodan wince when he put too much weight on his injured foot. Good, it was hurting him. I tensed as he hobbled past, expecting him to brush against me. But he ignored me and headed to the broken chair. However, instead of sitting on it, he spat on it, and then, with a challenging stare at Professor, he dropped his weight into the leather chair farthest from me.

I waited to see how Professor would respond, but he chose instead to ignore the challenge as he patted Shoni, curled up in his lap.

Jid squirmed. "Pleeease, I really gotta go."

I tried to move my chair closer in a futile attempt to loosen the ropes around his wrists. But before I'd managed to rock it an inch, Professor was untying the boy.

"Try and escape and you know what I'll do to your auntie."

"Yeah, I know," Jid yelled as he fled the den. I didn't know anyone could run so fast up those stairs.

"It's been a long day. We're all tired," Professor said. "Larry, get some shut-eye. I want one of us awake at all times. Slobo, you get some sleep too."

"I'm hardly a threat tied up like this," I quipped.

"I wasn't thinking of you." His head jerked in the Serb's direction.

Was he trying to tell me that either he or Larry would be awake to ensure that monster didn't come near me?

THIRTY-TWO

By the time Jid returned, Larry's breathing had deepened into that of sleep. Although Slobodan hadn't yet succumbed, he'd finished his Coke and sat motionless with his eyes fixed on the flickering orange of the fire. In a matter of minutes, his eyelids should close.

Professor seemed lost in his own thoughts as he idly ran his hand back and forth over Shoni's soft fur. But when Jid stepped over the loose rope and sat in the hard chair, he roused himself enough to motion for the boy to take the other leather chair. He passed him the groggy puppy. The snake-fringed mouth even managed a twist of a smile.

I hoped this meant he wouldn't hurt Jid when it finally came time for them to leave.

My arms were aching and my feet and hands were growing numb. The circulation returned after moving and stamping my feet, but with the ropes so tight, there was little I could do to bring relief elsewhere. I debated asking Professor to remove the ropes completely, or at least the one wrapped around my upper body, but decided against it. A sense of calm had finally descended on these men. I didn't want to destroy it.

While the fire continued to send out waves of warmth into the dark room, the air drifting from the hall continued to grow colder. Likely the fires in the kitchen and living room were dying down, but I wasn't about to suggest Professor leave me alone with Slobo in order to stoke them.

My poor house. I anticipated by the time the power came back on, the water pipes would be frozen. I hated to imagine the flooded mess that would greet Eric when he returned on Thursday. Jean and her family were supposed to arrive a day later, on Christmas Eve. The plan had been to put the house in the kind of pristine shape she demanded. Jid and I had only cleaned the three bedrooms they would be using before these men barged into my home. That left the four rooms on the main floor yet to do, plus the kitchen. The way things were going, that wasn't going to happen. In fact, it was likely Christmas wasn't going to happen at all.

Thursday. Only two days away, and yet it seemed like an eternity. Was that going to be the day I would learn my marriage was over? I shuddered at the thought. But maybe I would no longer be around to find out.

The outside seemed to mirror the stillness that had descended inside. I no longer heard the snow scraping against the window. Though the trees continued to moan, it was more a backdrop than a hovering threat. The house seemed to have settled down too, no longer buffeted by gale-force gusts. It was almost as if the house knew the worst was over. I wished I could say the same for the tempest brewing inside. Maybe by the time dawn crept through the window, it would be all over, one way or the other.

I sighed, shut my eyes, and tried to pretend I was lying curled up in my bed.

Something startled me. I looked around. The Serbian's head was awkwardly flopped to one side, partially resting on the back of the chair. His breathing came in intermittent snorts and whistles. The boy too had fallen asleep. He and the puppy were curled up together in the large chair. A blanket covered both of them. I felt the cocoon warmth of wool encircling me. I glanced up at Professor standing next to the fireplace. He winked. The hands on the mantel clock pointed to a quarter after two. Amazingly, I'd been asleep for several hours. With my nerves tighter than a guitar string and my body trussed like a chicken, I hadn't thought it possible. It was then I noticed that the rope was no longer tied around my chest, and the back of a leather chair had been shoved against me to keep me from toppling over.

I mouthed a thank-you.

He smiled.

What a confusing mixture of compassion and menace.

Flames licked at the fireplace grate.

"Did you stoke up the fires in the living room and kitchen?" I whispered.

He nodded. "The storm is about over. By morning it should be completely stopped."

"And then what will you do?" I tried not to make eye contact.

"We'll get out of your life."

For whatever reason, this time I believed him.

THIRTY-THREE

"Have you had any sleep?" I asked. "You must be dead tired."

"I'm good, but thanks for asking." Professor sank down into the cushions at one end of the chesterfield and gently lifted Larry's legs onto his lap. He stretched the bottom of the injured man's blanket so that it not only covered his own legs but also his chest and shoulders. "I've taught myself to get by on very little sleep."

His hand moved slowly back and forth under the wool blanket, as if caressing his friend's feet. With his other he pointed to the plastic Santa in the faded red suit that was for the moment standing forlornly on an empty bookshelf. "Your Santa reminds me of my childhood."

"That old guy is from my own childhood. It's not Christmas without him. His usual place of honour is on top of the tree."

"It's a good thing to celebrate Christmas. I haven't done so in years. Maybe this year, eh, P'tit Chief?" He squeezed his lover's foot.

"You must really love Larry."

The disquieting snakes on his face seemed to soften as he regarded the other man's sleeping face.

"Let's just say he's the one bright spot in my otherwise paltry life. But don't tell him that. It might go to his head."

He bent over and kissed the feet. Larry smiled.

Jid made a slight noise, stretched, and then resettled himself in the chair. His eyes remained closed. Shoni crawled out from under the blanket and nestled in the crook of his neck. The boy's hand came out from under the cover, brushed the fur away that was tickling his nose, gave her another pat, and returned to sleep.

The fire spilled out its soothing warmth.

The scene seemed so peaceful that it was hard to believe danger was only a heartbeat away.

"What did you teach at McGill?" I asked.

"Who told you I taught there?"

Drat, was that supposed to be a secret? But before I could think of a way not to implicate Larry, Professor continued. "I imagine Larry told you. The silly fool's rather proud of it."

"I would be too. Not many can teach at the university level."

He shrugged. "I specialized in seventeenth- and eighteenth-century French philosophy."

"Sounds sufficiently esoteric. Where did you do your doctorate? At McGill?"

"The Sorbonne."

"Makes sense to study French philosophy in Paris. I hope you had a good long stretch there to fully enjoy it?"

"I lived there about eight years. I was working on another doctorate when I left."

"In a different area of philosophy?"

"Actually, it was in history, eighteenth-century French armaments."

"Rather a change from philosophy to history, isn't it?"

"Not really. I found it helped me better understand the philosophers and their thinking if I was familiar with French society during the time they lived."

"But French armaments?"

He laughed. "I like weapons, what can I say?"

I'm sure you do, I thought. And doubtless he liked to use them too.

"But I take it you didn't complete your doctorate in history."

"I had to leave rather abruptly. I've often regretted that I couldn't return to defend my dissertation. It would've knocked the Sorbonne's history faculty onto their collective ass."

"What prompted you to leave?"

"A small matter concerning a misplaced stiletto."

The thin line of his smile convinced me not to pursue this further.

"You mentioned that you grew up on a farm in Quebec."

"Seems a lifetime ago. But yes, I was born in the same bed my father was born in and his father before him, and so on and so forth. Although my family has farmed this land since the late seventeenth century, it has never been able to provide more than a subsistence existence. And of course, my parents were too afraid to go against the parish *priest*." He spat out the word. "They kept having kid after kid. I was lucky thirteen, the youngest and the brightest."

"A farm that old has to be near Quebec City."

"You know your New France history. It's located in the Charlevoix downriver from Quebec City. Separatist country, I might add." Another grin spread across his face, but more of a challenge than an expression of amusement.

Now was hardly the time to get into an argument over separatism, so I ignored it. "Beautiful country. I spent a few days at an inn near Cap-à-l'Aigle."

"The farm is inland from there. I grew up surrounded by jaw-dropping, spectacular beauty. But I don't think it rubbed off, do you?"

Any answer I gave would probably be wrong, so I said instead, "It seems a very big leap from a farm in the Charlevoix to the halls of the Sorbonne and ultimately McGill."

"You can say I was lucky. My mother worked at a nearby golf course that was patronized by Montreal Anglophones and Americans. She'd often take me with her so I could make extra money chasing after lost balls. One of the patrons, a Montrealer who spent his summers at the family cottage at Pointe-au-Pic, befriended me." He ran his eyes over the rich panelling surrounding us and up and down the floor-to-ceiling stone fireplace. "It wasn't very different from this place and about the same age. You've kept it in good shape."

"More my great-aunt's doing than mine. She lived here for almost sixty years."

"That's the woman Larry remembered, right?"

"Yes, his father worked for her. But we've become side-tracked."

He sighed. "Back to my life story, or the part of it I'm willing to share. Can't say I've ever told anyone this before. Must be something about this place. Reminds me too much of Mike's. Anyway, he decided to take me on as one of his good works. I was a mouthy brat back then. He somehow managed to see a spark of intelligence through the glibness and decided to develop it. He paid for my schooling with the Jesuits until I graduated from high school, at the top of my class no less." His shoulders lifted in a Gallic shrug.

"Very generous of him. But I imagine this schooling would've been in French, and your English is perfect. So you must've picked it up somewhere."

"From the very beginning of our relationship, he only spoke English to me, despite his French being very good for an Anglo. Maman didn't like it. She worried I would become too English, but she realized that this was one of the conditions of my getting properly educated."

"What were the other conditions?"

He shrugged. "I'm sure you can guess. You see, Mike wasn't married."

"How old were you when you met him?"

"Nine."

I didn't know how to respond to this. Surely his mother would've sensed something wasn't right about the relationship. But perhaps she saw only what she wanted to see, believing it was more important for her youngest to get the education she couldn't provide.

"He died when I was twenty but left me enough money to complete my studies. It was that money that enabled me to finish my BA at McGill and spend eight years in Paris. It's gone now. I spent every cent of it."

"What do you think he would say if he could see you now?" I knew I shouldn't be asking the question, but it flowed out before I could stop it.

"He say you dumb, stupid prick. You got caught, Dr. Big Shot Professor." Slobodan stretched out his arms and stood up. "How many time you fuck the guy?"

I shrank back into the chair, waiting for the knife to fly.

And when it didn't, I opened my eyes to see Professor continuing to sit on the sofa, with the blanket still covering him. The only change was he no longer caressed Larry's feet. Instead, his hands were very still, as was his body — too still. And while the snakes framing his face remained equally motionless, his amber eyes seemed to bore through the skull of the Serbian. In a low, even voice, he said, "When this is over ..."

Slobodan merely grunted and lurched out of the room. He stumbled up the stairs and slammed the bathroom door with such force, the banister rattled.

THIRTY-FOUR

"What's going on?" Larry struggled to sit up.

"Merely Slobo having a temper tantrum. Go back to sleep, P'tit Chief." Professor rubbed his lover's legs.

The puppy whined and jumped down onto the carpet. Before she had a chance to do any damage, a yawning Jid lifted her up. "Shoni's got to go outside." Doing his best to hang onto the struggling puppy, he headed out into the hall.

"Might as well stretch my legs too." Professor moved Larry's feet aside and stood up. He stretched his dancer's frame upward, raising his arms high over his head, then down to touch his toes. "My body's missing its daily yoga practice." He continued to touch his toes, really the floor, for another minute or so before walking to the open doorway, where he blocked it as if on guard.

I struggled to get comfortable. "Can't you untie me? My arms are killing me."

He continued to stare out into the dark hallway.

"Please, I promise I won't try to leave."

At that point, Slobodan padded down the stairs. The light from the den lit up another of Aunt Aggie's Hudson's

Bay blankets, slung over his shoulders as he limped past the tattooed man.

"Where are you going?" Professor asked.

"The big room," he growled. "I sleep on soft sofa."

"Put some wood on the fire."

"Da, da." Slobodan's voice, along with his footsteps, disappeared down the hall into the living room.

The pitter-patter of paws running toward us announced the return of Jid.

"It's stopped snowing," he said. "Sure is a lot of it. Looks awesome. I've never seen so much. It's as high as the woodshed roof." He stretched his arms up toward the ceiling. "Way taller than me."

Shoni placed her paws on my knee, her entire body wagging with her tail.

"Please, Professor, cut me loose. If the snow's as deep as Jid says it is, I'm not going anywhere."

"Why should I trust you?" He lifted the puppy onto my lap.

Shoni slathered my face with moist kisses, punctuated by a nibble or two. Ski-jump noses and fleshy earlobes were her snack of choice.

"I promise I won't try to escape, if you promise you won't harm us. Ouch, Shoni, that hurts." I strained to move my face away from her pinprick puppy teeth.

Jid took her away. "We won't do anything. We won't even tell Will."

Professor whirled around. "Who's Will?"

"He's a friend." I avoided eye contact with the boy.

"Do you mean Will Decontie?" Larry asked. "He still the police chief?"

"Police chief?"

"Yeah, the Migiskan Tribal Police," Larry continued.

Larry, shut up, I screamed to myself.

"Is this a police force associated with your reserve?"

"Yup."

"Why didn't you mention this when we were going over the pros and cons of this location?"

"Sorry, Professor. I didn't think of them. The force is so small, only two or three cops. If they couldn't handle a bunch of bad apple kids on the rez, like me and my buddies, I figured no way they could handle some escaped cons."

"They can always call in support. So how close is their station?"

"About a ten-kilometre drive from here," I answered, increasing the distance.

"Red, why didn't you tell me about them?"

"Like Larry, I didn't think they mattered. Besides, they just handle reserve policing. This place is outside their jurisdiction."

"So now you're telling me we've got cops on our fucking doorstep."

"Slow down. Look outside. The cops aren't going anywhere in this stuff. It doesn't matter whether they're fifty kilometres away or ten. They won't be coming here any time soon. Besides, they would have to know that you guys are here. Without a phone — you broke it, remember — I sure couldn't tell them. So unless one of you guys did, I don't think they'll be landing on my doorstep."

"I was going to cut you free," he sneered. "But now that I know that you purposefully kept this information from me, I'm going to keep you tied up."

He walked out of the room, shouting, "Slobo, what time is Jo coming?"

"Don't worry about him," Larry said. "He gets mad fast but calms down just as quick."

"Can you untie me? My hands and arms are really hurting."

He shook his head vigorously. "Sorry. Professor'd kill me."

Jid had been standing behind my chair while we'd been talking. I could feel his hands working away at the ropes around my wrists.

To try to distract Larry, I asked, "How are you feeling? Any better?"

"I suppose, but my gut hurts like hell."

"You need to see a doctor. If infection sets in, it could turn out very badly for you. Is there any way you could convince Professor to give yourselves up so you can get to a hospital?"

"You gotta be kidding. You know what'll happen to us if we get caught? Three guards are dead 'cause of us."

"But you didn't kill them, did you?"

"No."

"Did Professor?"

"I don't think so. But it all happened so fast, I lost track of what was going on, and then I got hit."

"If you turned yourselves in, chances are the authorities would be easier on you than if you were captured."

He remained silent. He kept moving his eyes in the direction Professor had taken and then back to me. I felt that he was wavering.

"Don't you think it's better to be alive behind bars than dead?"

"But Professor's gotta job to do. That's why they planned the escape."

"What job?"

"Can't tell you." His eyes shifted to where his hands had been picking away at the loose blanket thread.

"Who are 'they'?"

"Look, I said too much already. Don't let on to Professor that I told you, okay?"

"If you were in the hospital, they would give you methadone." I wasn't going to give up, not yet.

"Yeah, but Slobodan said Jo's bringing smack." He wiped his nose with his sleeve, closed his eyes, and pulled the blanket over his face. The discussion was over.

THIRTY-FIVE

I wiggled my fingers. They moved. I could even slide my
wrists up and down.

"Thanks, Jid," I whispered into his ear. "Feels good,
but that's enough. If you loosen them further, Professor
might notice."

Relief. My hands tingled with the spreading return of
sensation.

"The guy who talks funny scares me," he said.

"Me too. Stay close to Professor. He'll make sure
Slobodan doesn't hurt you."

He hesitated. "I guess."

"What are you two whispering about?" Larry suddenly spoke up, causing Jid to jump away from me. He
landed on Shoni's tail. She yelped. Lifting her up, he
hastened back to his armchair.

"We were talking about Slobodan. He really scares us."
I tested my hands and felt with some aggressive tugging
they would eventually slip loose.

"Nope, you don't want to mess with him. He ain't
called Tiger for nothing. Says he was mixed up in some
war back home. Did a lot of killing. I hear he got into

plenty of fights at Millhaven. Spent a lot of time in solitary."

"I thought you escaped from another prison."

"Yeah, Joyceville. I guess he cleaned up his act and got transferred to medium. He's quick with the fists when the hacks ain't looking. Most of us stay clear of him."

"He couldn't have cleaned up that much if he was dealing heroin."

"Yeah, well, you know how it goes. A lot of things the hacks don't know about."

"How long is he in for?"

"Came in a couple of years ago. He's a lifer, like me. He's got a ways to go before he comes up for parole."

"Sounds like a good reason to escape."

"Yeah, but he didn't escape for that."

"What other reason would he have?"

"Lots." He flicked his eyes in the direction of the living room to the murmur of voices. "But I can't tell you. Professor'd get mad."

"Fine. Tell me what you know about the Serb?"

"Not much. He's an enforcer for the Devils."

"Like the bikers on TV?" Jid piped up. "Does he shoot people, stick their feet in cement, and throw them into the river so no one can find their bodies?"

"They must've found one body, otherwise he wouldn't have ended up in jail," I quipped.

"Professor says someone snitched on Tiger. It's why he wanted to escape. Wants to waste the guy."

"Does the man live around here? Is that your reason for coming to this area?"

Larry glanced again toward the voices, which had raised a decibel. "I don't know where the snitch lives. Probably Montreal. Tiger's from there."

"So you have another reason for coming here?"

"Un-hunh," he grunted, keeping his lips firmly closed. He wasn't about to divulge anything more.

"Man, I gotta pee." Larry carefully pushed himself into a seated position and then inched his legs around and onto the floor. He held his stomach as if worried its contents might spill out. "Jeez, that hurts."

"Jid, he needs the bedpan. Can you get it?"

"Nah, I don't want to use that. I'm feeling all cramped inside. I need to stretch my legs. Can you help me up, kid?"

Jid moved over to the sofa and stood in front of the injured man.

"I'm not sure you can manage the stairs," I said. "They're pretty steep."

"Sure I can, eh, kid?" With one hand clinging to Jid's arm, he struggled to stand up but barely lifted off the couch before collapsing in pain.

"Jid, you better get the bedpan."

"No, I'm gonna do this. Professor's always telling me I'm too quick to give in. I need to stick with it, so this time I'm gonna." He braced himself. "Turn around, Jid. That's it. Don't move while I put my hands on your shoulders."

He grunted and groaned while he eased himself upward into a standing position. Despite the pull of the man's weight, the boy remained firm.

"Ahhhh, there I done it." He smiled broadly at his achievement. Clutching his abdomen, he straightened up as best he could. "Hurts, but it's a good hurt. Come on. Let's try walking."

Gripping Jid's shoulder, he took a couple of trial steps. "There, that ain't so bad. A strong hockey player like you can get me up those stairs, eh?"

"I guess." Though the look on Jid's face would suggest otherwise.

"You should get Professor to help you," I advised.

"Nah, Jid and me can do it, eh? We'll show those two jerks what a couple of pipsqueaks can do."

Despite the age difference, the injured man was almost as slight as the boy and little more than a head taller.

The two of them shuffled past me toward the door. "I don't think a fall would do you any good. Be careful."

"We're good," he replied before they turned, albeit a bit shakily, toward the stairs.

Within seconds of hearing their first tentative footsteps on the wooden stairs, the tattooed man strode past the open door toward them. "You should've called me, P'tit Chief." This was immediately followed by a much firmer tread.

Jid returned, rubbing his shoulder. "I could've done it."

"I know, and Larry thought so too, but Professor's his special buddy. It's good you let him take over."

"Didn't give me much choice. He pushed me away. Almost made me fall."

"Did he hurt you?"

"Nah, not really. My shoulder's a little sore where he shoved me. He's pretty strong, isn't he? Maybe he lifts weights. If I did, do you think my muscles would get bigger?" He lifted his arms in strongman stance and tried to make his biceps rise a little higher. "Make me a better hockey player."

"Perhaps, but there's one thing you have over the bigger players, and that's speed. I'd practise skating if I were you. Become like Wayne Gretzky."

"Yah, that's what Shome tells me to do." Jid squeezed each of his biceps in turn. "Not very big, are they? I gotta do something."

"You could eat spinach, like Popeye."

"Who's he?"

"A cartoon character with big, bulging muscles who used to eat spinach to make them grow bigger."

"I hate spinach." He tested his biceps again. "If I had bigger muscles, I could fight these guys."

"I'm sure you'd get in a few good blows, but the best way to handle them is doing what we're doing. Nothing."

He shrugged. "I guess. I wish they'd go."

"Keep telling yourself they'll be gone in the morning."

"I sure wish Shome was here. He'd kick these guys out."

"And could get hurt in the process. To tell you the truth, I'm very glad he isn't here. They'd see him as too big a threat and would try to neutralize him."

"Like tying him to a chair?"

"Likely worse."

Jid gingerly touched his cheek where it was swollen and red. "I guess we kind of look the same, eh?"

I felt my own swollen face. "We could be bookends. Mine hurts a little. How about yours?"

"Not much. I get hurt worse playing hockey. Sure hope these guys go so I can play tonight."

"I hope so too." I felt the cold spread its tentacles down

my back and around my waist. "Could you make sure the blanket is completely wrapped around me?"

He tugged at my wrists and whispered, "The rope is really loose. I think you can get out of it now."

"Thanks. I'll stay like this until I need to be free. Okay?"

"But we can escape, right now." His face shone with renewed hope.

I hated to disappoint him. "It's not safe. They'd kill us before we had our snowshoes on."

Maybe we did have a chance if we tried now, while both men were occupied elsewhere. But I no longer had it in me to try another escape. I was too frightened of what they would do to us. As if to reinforce my cowardice, pain shot through the side of my face from the cheekbone to my chin. I winced. "Could you cover my hands with the blanket so they don't notice the ropes?"

I sensed his frustration as he wrapped the blanket around me, mummy style. "We'll do it later, when Professor and Slobodan are sound asleep, okay?

"Yah, sure." He didn't believe me.

He stomped over to the fireplace and threw a couple of logs onto the hot coals with more force than was needed. He stared at the renewed flame before turning back to me. "We're using up a lot of wood. I better get more."

"No, you stay here. Let them worry about it. Just make yourself comfortable, and when they return pretend you're asleep."

"Okay." He nestled into the chair's deep cushions and was tucking the blanket under his chin when he suddenly sat up. "Where's Shoni?"

He searched every dark corner in the room, peered in and under the chairs and sofa. He even lifted up Larry's blanket to see if she was taking advantage of its warmth. "I can't find her."

"Check in the kitchen. She might've returned to her crate."

As he walked to the doorway, Slobodan's face, lip curled, loomed through the darkness. "Lose something?"

From his upraised hand, he dangled a limp Shoni by the scruff of her neck.

THIRTY-SIX

"You killed my dog!" I cried out.

Grinning maliciously, he slowly waggled her lifeless body back and forth.

I tried to detect signs of life and saw none. My poor, poor innocent puppy. It took all my control not to burst my bounds and throttle the man. But I knew if I did, I would be dead, and where would that leave Jid?

"Auntie, she's not dead," the boy said in a low voice. "See, she's moving."

Her back twisted, as if she was trying to break free.

"You're hurting her." Jid reached up and tried to remove her.

But the man refused to let go, so it became a tug of war, with poor Shoni being the rope stretched between the two of them. When the boy realized what was happening, he stopped pulling but kept his hands around her so she didn't hang completely free.

"Let her go, you bastard." The words spilled out before I had a chance to think of the repercussions.

"Maybe I throw her in fire. She taste good, *ne?*" He hobbled over to the fireplace, removed the grate, and held her close to the licking flames.

Jid watched open-mouthed in horror, while I pleaded, "Please, please don't. She's just a little dog. She hasn't done anything to you."

"What you give me?" He locked his eyes onto my breasts and ran his tongue tauntingly over his lips.

My skin crawled with revulsion.

Shoni squealed and struggled to get loose.

"Set her free, please," I begged.

Continuing his grip on the puppy, he inched his eyes upward, over my breasts to my face and sneered, "I no like fat women."

He let go. Jid managed to catch her before she reached the stone hearth. Hugging her tightly against his chest, the boy scrambled to the chair furthest from the guffawing man.

"Please, leave the boy and dog alone," I said.

He continued to lock on to me with his pale, leering eyes.

Afraid to get into a standoff, I dropped my gaze and turned to Jid. "Is Shoni okay?"

"Just scared. She's really shaking, poor baby."

"Give her lots of pats from me."

He nodded and burrowed farther into the chair with the puppy.

The man remained standing with his backside close to the fire. I hoped it scalded him. Finally he muttered, "Too fat," and flung himself onto the spot where Larry had lain on sofa.

If all it took to keep him from mauling me was some excess body fat, I didn't mind being overweight. Though thanks to my husband's healthy cooking, I'd managed to get rid of a goodly amount of poundage. But over the past few months, with an extra cookie here and the odd piece of chocolate there, my jeans were beginning to feel snug. Lately I'd taken to wearing my old sweatpants because they felt so roomy and comfortable. But they also made me look fat. Right now, I was very thankful I was wearing them.

The biker wrapped the blanket around his shoulders. "Fuckin' cold. I hate this country."

So why don't you go back to Serbia? I thought. *We'd sure be better off without you.*

"I am not bad man," Slobodan declared.

Yeah, right.

"Just, how you say, pulling chain like monkey."

More like intimidation tactics 101. And it was working.

"I got girlfriend. I fuck you, she kill me."

So bring on the girlfriend. "I guess she'll be here soon."

"*Da.* Come in few hours."

And good riddance to all of you. "She'd better be using a snowmobile. She won't get in here otherwise."

"When road get ploughed?"

"Likely in the afternoon at the earliest."

"Good, we leave before guy plough road. Not good he see us. Not good for you."

It had never occurred to me to worry that Gerry would be in danger. A friend of Eric's, he'd been doing my road for the last few years and was usually very prompt in removing the snow. I would have to find a way to warn him. But it would be much better if these cons were nothing but a bad memory by the time he rumbled up to my house.

"Nice soft sofa." He ran his hand up and down the smooth, dark brown leather. "Not like in joint. We have cold hard plastic. I like nice things like these." He nudged the carpet with his foot. "Good carpet. Old, I think, from Persia. But no worry. You think I want to steal them? I don't steal. Not my job."

"So what is your job?"

"I make things happen."

"Is that why you escaped?"

"How you know?"

"Larry said you planned it."

He swore in Serbian. "Injun know nothing." He cracked one knuckle and then another.

Shoni, who'd been squirming for the last few minutes, slipped out from under the boy's arm and fell onto the carpet. Before Jid could catch her, she was scampering toward the biker. Annoyed or just plain mean, he aimed a kick at her head but fortunately connected with her rump. Nonetheless, it scared her enough to send her yelping back to her buddy.

"You meanie. Pick on someone your own size," Jid cried out.

"Kid, you got balls. You like my baby brother when he was little boy. I like you."

I hoped this liking morphed into not harming. "We're all tired. Why don't we try to get some sleep. Morning will be here soon."

I kept listening for sounds of the return of the other two. Surely they should be finished by now. But upstairs sounded as quiet as the rest of the house, while outside the deathly calm continued. If the storm really was over, I imagined the big push would be underway to clear the main roads. Maybe Gerry would be arriving sooner than anticipated. If so, I would have to be prepared.

Shoni continued to fuss. The boy was having a difficult time trying to contain her.

"I think you should put her back in her crate."

Glancing in the direction of the Serb, who for the moment seemed more interested in his fingernails than us, he nodded. "I guess."

As he passed in front of me, I motioned him closer and whispered. "Write 'Get police' on a piece of ..."

"What you talk about?" Slobodan cut in.

For a moment my mind went blank, then I said the first thing that entered it. "Sorry, I didn't want to disturb you. I was just giving him instructions about the puppy."

Before the boy moved to leave I mouthed "Window" and jerked my head in the direction of the front of the house, hoping he would understand. For a second incomprehension filled his eyes, and then the twinkle returned. He grinned and ran out of the den with the puppy safely in his arms.

Now all I had to do was to keep the Serbian occupied until Jid put the sign in place.

THIRTY-SEVEN

I hadn't exactly conversed with the man since he'd forced his way into my life, nor had I wanted to. But unable to move from the chair, talking was about the only thing I could think of to take his attention away from the boy. However, coming up with a topic that wouldn't hit one of his hot buttons was a challenge. He beat me to it.

He walked over to boxes of ornaments and pulled out a silver and purple glass ball. He returned to the sofa, where he watched it shimmer in the light from the oil lamp. "Pretty, like fancy woman."

"Do you have decorations like that in Serbia?" I asked.

"Not my house, but others, yes. In Serbia, Christmas come in January, not December like in Canada. We are Orthodox Church."

"Like the Russians."

"*Da*. We call Christmas Bozic. In good days was very special time for my family." His voice had a wistful under-current. "My mother very religious. She make big deal, make us follow Serbian traditions."

"We have many traditions too. They help make it a special time of year."

"You have Christmas tree. We have *badnjak*. Day before Bozic my father go very early in morning to forest to cut oak tree to make *badnjak*. Is very big log. Not small like those." He pointed to the remaining logs in the rack. "All night we watch *badnjak* burn and drink much wine. Mama say it bring good harvest and healthy children."

He smiled, the first genuine smile I'd seen spread across his face. Even his eyes were smiling. It almost made him seem like a normal human being.

"Your Christmas too short. We celebrate Bozic three days. Much visiting, much eating, much drinking. Mama spend many days cooking traditional food. My grandparents, uncles, aunts, cousins, they come. We eat *pecinica*, roast pig, not stupid bird. We pass *cesnica,* special bread, around table. Everyone get piece of *cesnica*. My sister and brother try to get piece with special coin. It bring luck for rest of year. Much laughing ..." His voice drifted off into a whisper as the memories returned.

I left him to his reverie until I heard a bang coming from the kitchen. It sounded as if Jid had dropped something. Worried Slobodan would notice, I said loudly, "I have many fond memories of my own childhood Christmases. When was the last time you celebrated such a big family Bozic, as you call it?"

"Long, long time. Not since a boy."

"Is that when you came to Canada?"

"No. I come later, when eighteen."

"How long have you been here?"

"Seventeen years."

"You were quite young. Did you come with your family?"

"*Ne*, I come alone."

"So why did you leave Serbia?"

"*Hrvati*," he spat out and slammed his hand, still holding the ornament onto the coffee table. The pieces ground into the wood and into his hand. He didn't seem to notice.

Though I had no idea what Hrvati meant, I decided it would be best to change to a more benign topic.

But before I had a chance, he continued, "I from Benkovac. After war, motherfucker Hrvati move in. No more Serbs live in Benkovac."

"Who are the Hrvati?"

"You English say Croats." He spat this out with even more venom. "My family live on farm many hundred years near Benkovac village. My grandfather, grandfather of my grandfather, way back many years. They grow grapes for the Veliki Vezir, the Sultan, you say in English. They make wine for the Hapsburg kings. It was beautiful. No more. War destroy farm, my family. No more Bozic."

"You must be talking about the Bosnian war."

"*Da*. War with Hrvati." He pushed up his sleeve and stabbed the tiger tattoo snarling on his bicep. "I am Arkan Tiger. I fight for mighty General Arkan. We kill many Hrvati."

"I think it took place in the early 1990s. You must've been very young to be fighting."

"Fifteen. My brother and me go to Arkan after motherfucker Hrvati kill my mother, rape my sister."

"I'm so sorry. That must've been very difficult for you." Hoping to turn his attention away from the dreadful memories and onto something that might reduce the tension in the room, I asked, "Did your brother come to Canada with you?"

"He dead too. Hrvati kill my father in massacre. Only my sister live. My baby brother die before the bad times."

"Does your sister still live in Serbia?"

"Adrijana go to New York City. She have son, husband, good life."

"How fortunate for you that she isn't far away. Do you get a chance to see her much?" The question was no sooner asked than I realized my mistake.

He chuckled. "In jail?"

"Sorry, I forgot. But why not? Prisoners are allowed visitors."

"I no tell her. I tell her I salesman. I travel much. No time to go to New York."

"She must mean a lot to you. When was the last time you saw her?"

"Three, four year. Before I go to jail."

"I imagine you haven't told her you're a member of the Black Devils either."

If the man could possibly look sheepish, he did. "In Canada she tell me forget bad time. She tell me do good. When I come to this big country, I try. In war I no can go to school. My uncle send me to a good school with priests."

"Did your uncle come at the same time as you to Canada?"

"No, he come before the war. He live many years in this country. He my sponsor. I live with him in Toronto."

"So what happened? Did you graduate?" I kept my ears peeled for the soft patter of Jid's approach.

"I try. But is very boring." He shrugged. "Maybe I too old. I like fighting. I am best Arkan Tiger." He waved his hand back and forth as if firing a machine gun. "Rat, tat, tat ... tat."

Though most of the flakes of broken ornament had fallen from his hand, I could see pinpricks of blood where a couple had become embedded in his palm. He ignored them.

"So what happened?"

"A motherfucker Hrvat. I see him in grocery store. He pretend he don't know me. But I know him. He rape my sister and kill my mother."

"So what did you do?"

"He have wife. I rape her. He have baby. I take baby and give to Serbian woman who can no have children because Hrvati rape her many times."

"But the child and the mother had nothing to do with the father's crimes."

"Baby born Hrvat. Now will be Serb."

"And the father, what did you do to him?"

"He no more." He cracked a knuckle.

"Is this why you were sent to prison?"

"Hah, for what? No one find body."

"But if the man killed your mother, why didn't you go to the police?"

"I do it Serbian way. Police do nothing. Is another country. They don't care."

"But it could be considered a war crime, and Canadian officials have arrested people for war crimes and sent them back to be tried in the country where the crimes were committed."

"Pffft. Take too long. Not always work. Serbian way more better."

Finally, I heard the quiet padding of Jid's moccasins coming from the kitchen. Unfortunately, the man heard them too. To distract him, I started rocking the chair from side to side and ended up knocking it over onto the floor. Lying on my side with the chair still attached, I felt as helpless as a beached whale. At least I'd had the wherewithal to keep my hands in the noose. Well, almost. When the chair was starting to keel over, my hand slid out to cushion my fall. With great reluctance, I forced it back into the ropes.

My ruse worked. I watched Jid slip past unnoticed while the biker hooted and slapped his thighs.

When he finally caught his breath, he said, "You stupid woman. I leave you so."

This suited me very nicely. I'd been dreading the feel of his hands as he hefted me upright. Knowing him, he would place them in the most intimate areas. But once Jid placed the sign in the window, he'd be returning, so I needed to distract Slobo again. I didn't want him discovering that the boy had been in the front of the house, otherwise he might be curious enough to investigate.

"Ouch!" I cried out. "I've hurt my arm. Please put the chair upright. I can't do it myself."

"You want my help?" He crossed his arms over his chest in a show of defiance.

"Please." I listened for Jid's approach and heard instead another sound, the slow lumbering of Larry and Professor coming down the stairs.

They were going to see the boy. I had to do something.

"Ouch!" I yelled loud enough for the other two men to hear. "My arm really hurts. I think I've broken it."

The Serb merely broadened his smirk and kept his arms fixed across his chest. "What you give me?"

Not again.

"Professor, you there? I need help getting up. I've fallen and hurt my arm."

I waited for sound of their quickening pace.

Instead I heard the boy running.

I should've known he'd come to my rescue.

"Hey kid, what are you doing?" Professor called out.

I was about to shout out an answer, when Jid replied, "Just putting more wood on the fireplace in the front room."

What a kid. Of course he'd come up with a plausible excuse.

THIRTY-EIGHT

Before I had a chance to respond, I was upright, sitting squarely in the seat of the chair with its legs once again firmly planted on the carpet.

"The ropes must've come loose in your fall," Professor said, untying my hands. He eyed me suspiciously from under his brow of snake heads.

I didn't bother to correct or confirm as I felt the rush of feeling flow back into my hands. My arms dropped to my sides with their sudden freedom. For a moment they hung uselessly like lead, and then the pain started. I breathed in deeply, hoping there was no lasting damage to my shoulders. As the ache slowly ebbed another took over, a sharp, throbbing twinge in the arm I'd landed on. Maybe I hadn't lied.

I gingerly touched my upper arm where the pain was most intense. I winced. That was all I needed. "Seriously, I think I might have broken my arm."

Jid's brow creased with worry. "You going to be okay, Auntie?"

Slobodan continued to sit with arms and legs splayed out on the sofa. His smirk grew more triumphant. "You get what deserve, bitch."

I steeled myself to move my arm. *Ouch*, but it moved. I flexed my fingers and carefully bent the arm a couple of times. No searing stabs of pain. "I think I'll be fine." I gently massaged where the throbbing felt the worst. "I don't think I've broken it, but I imagine I'm going to have a very big bruise." Another one to add to the one on my face. "Can you undo the ropes around my feet? I want to sit in something more comfortable."

I waited for Professor to stop the boy. Instead he stepped toward the Serbian and kicked the man's feet out from under him. "Get off the couch. Now!"

The Serbian howled, I wasn't sure whether from pain or from anger. Rubbing his sore foot, he planted his feet back on the floor and then crossed his arms in challenge.

I'd been too busy trying to save myself to notice Larry. I turned at the sound of a hoarse cough behind me to see him slumped into a leather chair, clutching his stomach. Drops of sweat beaded his forehead while his body shook uncontrollably.

"What's wrong, Larry?" I kicked off the loosened ropes and stood up before I realized my legs needed time to adjust to their newfound freedom. I only kept myself from falling by clinging to the back of the chair. When I had enough stability, I stumbled over to Larry while the professor and the biker continued glaring at each other.

"Let me look at your dressing to make sure it's okay."

"Nah, it's fine." He brushed my hand away. His teeth chattered. "Just need a hit, eh? Then I'll be okay."

"I still think I should look at it. You may have damaged something walking up and down those stairs."

"She's right, P'tit Chief," Professor interjected. "Lie down on the chesterfield and let her check you over."

He turned his attention back to the Serb. "Get your fat ass off that sofa."

Once again they were in a dangerous standoff, like a couple of dogs, one a Rottweiler, the other a Doberman, fighting over who was top dog. Would the biker toe the line again or would he finally retaliate?

As a precaution, I pulled Jid away from where he waited for the action to begin and shoved him behind Larry's chair. "Stay there, okay?"

The same glint of resistance flashed into his eyes that I saw lighting up Slobo's. "Look, Jid, I don't want you to get hurt, okay? One of us needs to come out of this alive. And it's more likely you than me."

Larry added in a muted voice, "Ya gotta stay outta sight, Jid. Hide out in another room. They'll forget about you soon enough."

"Good. Hide in Eric's office. They won't think to look there," I whispered.

"I'm not going to leave you, Auntie."

"You have to. If they forget about you, you'll be able to leave and go for help. Wait until they're quiet and go."

I didn't dare look at Larry's reaction, but for some reason I felt this would be fine with him. Maybe it was because Jid was just a boy with many years ahead of him, or perhaps it was because he came from the same community. Regardless, I felt confident that Larry wouldn't mention this to his lover.

However, before Jid could sneak away, the biker abruptly rose from the couch, and cursing in Serbian, placed his hands on the tattooed man's chest and shoved hard. But Professor was like granite and remained firmly fixed. I waited for the viper to strike. So did Slobodan. When nothing happened, the biker gave Professor another shove before heading out of the room, flinging more Serbian curses after him. His uneven footsteps echoed down the hall toward the living room. Only then did I notice the glint of a steel blade extending from Professor's hand. It wasn't Eric's hunting knife but the thin sharp boning knife he used to fillet fish. Professor was adding to his arsenal.

As quickly as the blade appeared, it disappeared.

"Kid, help me get Larry on the couch."

Slumped between the two of them, Larry put only nominal effort into walking and collapsed with several painful groans onto the sofa. Professor helped him stretch out his legs before saying, "I'll check your dressings before you get settled in."

When he was finished, he said, "Nothing to worry about. You're going to be like new in a couple of days." He kissed his friend on the forehead and smoothed the dishevelled hair before resuming his seat at the end of the sofa. So much for Jid disappearing into Eric's office.

Jid picked up Larry's blanket from the floor and draped it over his thin body.

Smiling weakly, Larry raised a trembling hand and ruffled the boy's hair. "Thanks, kid. *Kije-manido* is looking out for you. You're gonna be okay."

"Yeah, but are you gonna be okay?" Jid replied. "You don't look too hot."

"It's the horse, kid. It keeps calling. It ain't gonna let me go."

"You mean the drugs you take, the heroin?"

"Yah. I guess you kids know everything, even if you live in the bush. Don't you start down this road, kid, you hear? *Kije-manido* get mad."

"So why do you do drugs? Did *Kije-manido* get mad at you?"

"I guess the Creator gave up on me. I'm weak, kid. Can't say no. But I can see you're strong, got backbone. Don't let it get a hold of you." He stuck his hand into the neck of his T-shirt and pulled out the tiny leather pouch I'd seen earlier. "Here, take this." He lifted it from around his neck and held it out in the palm of his trembling hand. "My grandmother gave it to me to keep the spirits happy. But it ain't done me much good. I have a feelin' its medicine will work for you."

"No." Jid backed away. "It's yours. You need it for protection."

"Didn't give me much protection with this gunshot, eh? Take it. I want you to have it."

"You coulda got killed."

Larry chuckled. "Yah, I suppose there's that. Well, if you won't take it, I'll give you something from it."

"But you're not supposed to open it. It'll make the spirits mad."

"Won't make much difference. The spirits have been mad at me for a long time." Larry struggled to open it up, but his shaking made it almost impossible to release the thin leather drawstring.

"Let me help you," I said, picking up the delicate pouch.

"Should be a tiny blue stone with red lines through it. The girlfriend said it was an agate from the rez."

"But you can't take it out," Jid insisted. His face mirrored his distress.

"I suppose some elder drilled that crap into you, eh?"

"Kòkomis. But it's not crap."

"I'm sure your grandmother's a respected elder, but elders don't always get it right. She probably stayed put most of her life, so things didn't change much for her. But a man like me who's lived in many places picks up things as he goes along and gets rid of them too. My medicine shows this. I suppose you could call it a story of my life."

I thought of the disparate items Eric's amulet contained and realized they did tell the story of his life. The minuscule wood carving of an *odjik,* or fisher, his grandfather had made especially for him, which saved his life when I'd lost all hope of finding him alive. A sliver from the hockey stick that had scored his winning Stanley Cup goal. Or the fragile petals of the dried cardinal flower I'd laughingly placed in his hair what seemed a lifetime ago when we made love on a carpet of moss. I could still hear him whispering *Miskowàbigonens* into my ear, little red flower, his spirit name for me. Would I hear it again?

"Jid would be honoured to accept it." I removed the highly polished stone from the shaking hand and passed it to the boy.

Jid pulled his own amulet out through the loose neck of his T-shirt and slipped it over his head. His great-grandmother had made it. It was her way of keeping her much-loved only great-grandson safe. Though I'd seen her sew beads countless times on moccasins, I was amazed at her ability to create such intricate designs without the use of sight. Blinded by cataracts, which she refused to have removed, she'd managed to bring up the orphaned boy without any help. What a magnificent job she'd done.

He gently pried open the delicate deerskin pouch but hesitated as if not sure he should put the stone inside.

Larry held his breath as he waited to see what the boy would do.

Jid turned the agate over in his hand. "It's pretty. Looks like one I've got. Now I'll have two."

He continued to study it for a few more seconds before slipping it inside the amulet. At the same time he removed an item. He held it tightly in his fist. Smiling, he stretched his arm out toward the sick man. "This is for you." He opened his palm to reveal a fringe of dark brown fur. "It's from the moose I killed."

"Moose, eh? First kill?"

Jid beamed.

"Yeah, I remember my first moose too. I'll keep it safe." Larry struggled to place it inside his pouch but couldn't. So the boy did it for him and then slipped it back over the man's head.

"Nice amulet you got there," Larry said. "Your *kòko-mis* give it to you?"

"Yeah, when I was little."

"Mine too." Larry ran his fingers over the intricate beading. While a number of beads had disappeared over the years, the design of a beaver was still recognizable. It appeared very similar to the one on Jid's pouch.

The two of them continued to stare at each other as if sharing a secret moment. Then, Jid, as if embarrassed, walked away and sat down, but not where he'd sat before, in the armchair the farthest away, but in the one closest to the sofa.

Professor, who'd been silently watching the exchange, stood up. "I'm going to boil some water. I think a hot toddy will help with the pain, P'tit Chief."

The three of us said nothing as we listened to his footsteps retreat down the hall. The second they faded into the kitchen, Larry turned to Jid. "Quick, go, before he comes back."

The boy glanced at me as if seeking permission.

"Yes, go. Hide where I told you to, but be extra careful when you pass the living room. I think that's where Slobodan went. Wait until everyone is sound asleep. When you leave, take Shoni."

He started to protest.

"You have to. It's the only way to save all of us."

He wavered for another second before giving me a tight hug. He ran out of the room to Eric's office.

I walked over to the chair farthest away and angled it such that when Professor returned he would only see the back of my head. I snuggled deep down into it, covered myself completely with the blanket, and pretended that the boy was sound asleep beside me.

THIRTY-NINE

I didn't dare look up when I heard Professor return, in case he walked over to where I was scrunched up in the chair trying to make the blanket look like it was covering two people. From the tinkle of ice, it sounded as if he'd poured himself another drink, which surprised me given his ban on alcohol. He and Larry spoke, but at such a low volume it was impossible to hear what they were saying. The rest of the house was quiet. Hopefully Jid was safely hidden in Eric's office. And the Serbian, if he hadn't yet fallen asleep on the front room chesterfield, soon would be.

The sofa creaked. I tensed as footsteps padded across the carpet toward me. But they continued past. A log landed, and then another onto the fire, followed by the crackle of renewed flame. The footsteps returned to the sofa.

I snuggled farther into the chair. It smelled of Eric. This was his spot, where he relaxed, where he enjoyed his Lagavulin, where he read, usually one of the books from Aunt Aggie's library. He had set himself a goal of reading all the books on the shelves in this room and in the living room. I'd joked that he'd still be going through them when I finally wheeled him off to the old peoples' home.

He'd chuckled and said that it'd give him something to do, since I would've lost all my marbles by then.

I inhaled deeply. With it came the good times. The time we squeezed into this very chair, trying to keep warm during another power outage. We'd just finished a delicious cheese fondue in front of the blazing fire. The room was aglow with candlelight, for I had placed candles and tealights on every open flat surface in the dark room. Sergei lay curled at our feet, as close as he could get without being on our laps. By this time our beloved dog had slowed down considerably and was only interested in lying down with us in close proximity. A few months later we had to make the terrible decision to have him put down.

But that was in the future, and on this night we had been feeling good. We were celebrating our six-month anniversary. Eric had given me a dozen red roses. They were overlooking us from their pride of place on the mantel. I had given him a couple of his favourite Cuban cigars. He was itching for the weather to warm up so he could enjoy one outside on the porch. We were chattering and laughing, happy with life. And one thing led to another and we were sneaking upstairs to continue our celebration.

Or another time, when I was deep in the throes of alcohol withdrawal. Not a happy memory, some might think, but for me it was. It was the turning point. My whole body was consumed by the desire to taste the burning liquid. I was furious with Eric for removing every single bottle from the house. I was yelling and crying at the same time. Punching, kicking him, the furniture, and anything else in the way. He didn't flinch. He sat calmly in his chair, talking softly to me as if he were discussing the weather. Gradually his serenity penetrated, and I slowly quieted down.

When the tantrum was finally over, he wrapped his arms around me and held me close. He told me how much he loved me, how much he admired my strength to overcome the addiction and what a wonderful new life awaited me. I believed him. From that moment, I never looked back. Sure, there were times when I wanted a drink so badly, I could taste it — there still were, but I never gave in and never would. He was right. My life was so much better without alcohol. I couldn't have done it without Eric, my rock, my staff.

When he first took notice of me, I was thrilled and totally amazed that this embodiment of a catch would be interested in fat, boring me. Then I did what I always do in relationships, started pushing him away with my obstreperous behaviour. The drinking didn't help either.

Some fancy psychologist my mother made me go to after my first husband left me said that I acted this way out of fear of getting too close to someone. She said it was like a self-fulfilling prophecy. I was so afraid of being hurt that whenever I felt someone was getting too near, I shoved them away and of course ended up getting hurt. Because, as I grew up telling myself, I always got hurt. She thought this fear likely resulted from my not having dealt completely with the loss of my father at a young age or the death of my baby brother. At the time I knew she was right, but I didn't want to hear it, so I ended up hiding in a fog of alcohol.

Then Eric came along. Miraculously, no matter what I threw at him, he refused to be pushed away, although I had come close. And now I'd gone and done it again. I'd pushed him away, maybe for the last time. And for what?

Some petty jealousy. How could I be so incredibly stupid as to jeopardize everything that was good in my life? If I made it out of this horror alive, I vowed I would do everything I could to keep him.

I hunkered down even farther into the chair. The warmth against my face made me realize that I should've given Jid a blanket. Eric's office would be a refrigerator. There was a blanket in the room, the red and black ceremonial blanket, a gift from a Haida friend. But the boy likely wouldn't see it neatly folded on a shelf.

I felt very fortunate to have Jid in my life. He was one terrific kid and seemed to be taking this terrible situation in stride. I prayed that this time he would finally manage to escape. With the storm over, it should be a straightforward snowshoe down the Three Deer Point Road to the main road. And if the gods were with us, it would be cleared and help would be a simple matter of flagging the next vehicle to come along.

The sofa creaked again. I waited for the sound of Professor's approach but instead heard more creaking and the barely audible clink of a glass being placed on a table. Maybe the man was settling in for some sleep. I was feeling that way myself even if my stomach was churning with nerves.

It had been a long night and was far from over. Perhaps a few hours' rest would help fortify me for what was to come. However, being crunched up in an armchair, no matter how commodious, wasn't exactly conducive to sleep. Despite the cramps in my legs, I didn't dare change my position. The tattooed man needed to be satisfied that the two of us were fast asleep so he would feel confident enough to drift off himself. Only then could Jid leave.

FORTY

I felt myself sliding into sleep when Larry's voice broke through and brought me back to reality. "Professor, what do ya think of the boy? A good kid, eh?"

Damnit, Larry, why did you have to mention Jid, when we were trying to get Professor to forget about him?

"Reminds me of when I was that old," Larry continued. "The rez is a great place for a kid to grow up. Lots of freedom. Not like growing up in a city, eh? I spent a lot of time hunting and fishing with my uncles. Even when I was supposed to be in school." He laughed. "Caught me a whopping big muskie one summer. We gorged on it for days."

"No doubt as exciting as your first moose."

"That was one hell of a bull moose, eh? Even my Uncle Jimmy was impressed. Had a spread a good five feet wide. And I was only twelve years old."

"I thought you said the antlers were four feet across."

"Yah, well. Four, five. What's it matter? They were big. You know, that rack was almost as wide as I was tall." He laughed. "My uncle's big gun sure had a hell of a kick to it. Landed on my backside right into the bushes. If I hadn't shot that bull dead on, he probably woulda runned me over." His laugh was easy, with none of the earlier strain I'd heard in his voice.

I took this as a sign that the pain was lessening. But I wished he'd stop talking so Professor could fall asleep and Jid could escape.

"I bet I was the same age as this kid. He's killed his first moose too. He was telling me about it. He's the kind of kid a father'd be proud of. I wonder if he's passed through his first sweat. I'd sure love to guide him through it."

Eric was already talking to Jid about guiding him on his first sweat ceremony. I understood it was meant to be the boy's spiritual initiation into Algonquin manhood, though Eric didn't explicitly call it that. He was hoping to do it this summer, after Jid turned thirteen. He'd asked me if he could build the sweat lodge on the shore of an isolated cove along the Three Deer Point shoreline. They were even talking about Jid doing a vision quest. But that was all I knew. This wasn't something discussed in front of women.

"Professor, did I ever tell you what they did in the old days?"

"No, but I have read about it. It's called the Wysoccan Ceremony."

"Yeah, that's the name. I always forget it. Did you know the stuff can kill ya? In the old days not all the guys made it through. I guess only the real warriors made it."

"I believe Wysoccan was derived from jimson weed, which is considered poisonous. It's a powerful hallucinogenic. Administered over many days, it was meant to wipe out childhood memories and give these young men a clean slate into adulthood."

"So it was a kinda drug?"

"Yes, a bit like the psilocybin mushrooms the Aztec and Mayans used, or *lophophora williamsii*, otherwise known as peyote, which is made from a type of cactus that the Native American Church uses."

"Guess that's why I like drugs so much, eh? But shit, heroin sure didn't turn me into a warrior."

"It will if you survive withdrawal without giving in. Do you know if your grandfather went through this ceremony?"

"Nah, the priests had stopped it by then. But I remember him talking about the terrible time his *mishomis* had when it almost killed him. The experience made him a true warrior looked up to by everyone in the clan. He became chief when he was still a young man. They say he was one of the great ones."

"You have the makings of a chief in you too. That's why I call you my P'tit Chief."

I heard rustling as if from fabric rubbing against fabric, followed by what sounded like a kiss, several, in fact. Embarrassed, I tried to block my ears to this intimate moment.

After a few minutes, Professor said, "You look and sound much better. I think you're going to make it. You had me worried there for awhile."

"Yeah, but I still got the shakes. I feel like I can handle 'em now."

"Good for you. I know you can lick this."

"Professor, about the kid. You ain't gonna do nothing to him, eh?"

"What do you think I should do?"

"He's a good kid. If I had one of my own, I'd want a Little Squirrel just like him."

"But he can identify us."

"I bet I could get him to say nothing about us."

"And if he does? He could screw this job up royally. And you know how important it is that I do it. I need the Devils as much as they need me."

"This is going to be your last one, eh? You promised."

"Yes, I promised."

By this time I had stopped breathing. Although it might help to explain the bizarre relationship between the Serb and the tattooed man, it certainly brought home the precarious position Jid and I were in.

"What if we stash the two of them away until after the job is done?"

"I suppose you want the woman also."

"Yah, she's good people too."

By now my heart was pounding so hard, I could barely hear.

"You know Slobo's not going to like it. But I'll see what I can do."

"Thanks, Professor. You got a big heart. That's why I love you so much."

More kissing.

"You see that Christmas tree decoration over there on the bookshelf. It's supposed to be a beaver with that long tail, though it don't look much like one. I had one just like it growing up. My *kòkomis* made it for me out of birch bark."

For a second I wasn't certain which decoration he was referring to, until I remembered Jid had brought it to put on the tree. Kòkomis had given it to him for his first Christmas tree. He'd hung the beaver on every tree since.

FORTY-ONE

I desperately tried to push Jid through the deep snow and into the hollow beneath the boughs of a spruce tree. Behind me I could hear the approaching stomp of snowshoes and the sound of laboured breathing. The boy finally clawed his way in and disappeared under the boughs.

"I'm in," Jid whispered. "Hurry. He's getting closer."

I attempted to move my feet. They were stuck. I struggled to lie on top of the snow and crawl my way into the tree well. Instead I sank farther into the drift. I strove to push myself through it, but it was like trying to punch through a cloud. My face, my nostrils, my eyes were covered in icy crystals. But I couldn't release my hands to clear my face.

The snow resonated with the sound of his approach.

A sudden blast ripped through the darkness. I clawed, thrashed, dug deeper into the snow, grasping on to whatever purchase I could find. But wait a minute. It had substance. It was warm. I fought to release myself from its suffocating grasp and found myself battling a wool blanket. And then I was fully conscious.

I stopped moving and listened. Was that explosion in

my dream or was it real? I heard whimpering. I cautiously raised my head above the back of the chair.

Larry was struggling to stand up. Professor was gone.

"Larry," I whispered. "What was that loud noise?"

The oil lamp had gone out. The remaining coals in the fireplace provided barely enough light to see Larry.

"A gun. Someone got shot."

"Where is Professor?"

"He went to talk to Tiger."

A chill raced through me.

Footsteps echoed down the hall toward us. I froze. It had better be the tattooed man. But I was terrified the uneven gait was telling me it was the Serbian.

A funnel of light illuminated the photos on the hall wall across from the den. I watched with trepidation its brilliance grow brighter. It flooded the doorway and blinded me. I looked away, unable to identify the man behind it.

I held my breath and prayed to whichever god cared to listen.

And knew none of them had when I heard the Serbian's gravelly voice. "Where the kid?"

Before I had a chance to come up with an answer, Larry cried out, "What have you done to Professor? Did you hurt him?"

Slobo crowed. "I kill the fucker."

Worse than my worst nightmare.

With my heart pounding, I buried myself under the blanket and slunk farther into the chair cushions, wishing I could disappear. I prayed with all the religious fervour I had in me that Jid had escaped.

My chair shuddered at the same time as I felt the whack against the side of it. The blanket was yanked away. I could feel the man's hot breath on my face. "What you do with boy?" Slobodan spat out.

I opened my eyes to two piercing orbs of blue inches from my face.

"He's gone," I whispered, hoping to prevent him from searching the house in case Jid was still here. I would do whatever was in my power to keep this fiend from finding the boy, even if it meant he would take it out on me.

"You motherfucker," Larry shouted as he flung his wiry weakness against the steel of the biker. The man batted him away as if he were a mosquito, tossing the injured man onto the floor. Larry let out a groan but managed to get back to his feet. Wincing more from anger than pain, he again flung himself against the man and was swatted away. He fell back onto the carpet, where he remained, clutching his stomach.

As the Serbian raised his leg to kick the downed man, I summoned my courage, jumped from the chair and flung myself at him. "Leave him alone!"

He kicked my feet out from under me. I tried desperately to avoid landing on Larry and almost succeeded, catching his leg before I could roll away. He grunted with pain.

I braced for the next kick. I let out a whooshing groan as it caught me in the ribs. *Thank God he's not wearing shoes* was all I could think as I fought to regain my breath. Then I remembered the cut. When his foot came toward me again, I grabbed and squeezed as hard as I could on the injured ball of his foot.

He howled and then lunged toward me. When I saw the mad fury in his eyes, I knew I'd gone too far. It was the same rage I'd seen in my ex's eyes when he threw me against the counter and broke my arm.

I scrambled to get beyond the man's grasp and failed. With both hands he seized my vest and wrenched it apart. I tried to fight off his hands. He smacked me hard across the face and then pulled at the neck of my sweater and ripped it. The sudden cold air on my breasts had me frantically trying to hide them. I shuddered at the lust filling his eyes as he stared down at my nakedness. I struggled to back away.

I thought I heard Larry shouting at him to stop, but the blood was rushing so loudly through my ears, I wasn't sure. While I attempted to cover myself up with my hands, I used my feet to shove and slide myself along the floor in an effort to put distance between us.

Suddenly something sharp cut into my thigh. The glass shard! I slipped it from my pocket and sliced my finger in the process. Good. It was sharp.

I scrambled to stand up as he lunged toward me again, knocking me to the floor. I stabbed at his face and felt it connect.

He roared in fury.

I raised my hand to strike again and was stopped by the cold edge of steel against my throat.

"Do that again, I kill you."

Blood poured down his cheek.

He banged my hand against the floor, forcing me to let go of the shard. Still holding the knife against my throat, he kicked it away.

His eyes bored into my breasts.

"I like woman with big tits."

He brushed his hand against them. I flinched and wished the floor would collapse beneath me and swallow me whole.

I tried to settle my spiking nerves. Tried to remember what a woman was supposed to do when being raped. Succumb or fight. But the knife took that decision away from me. Was I supposed to try to reason with him? But the manic intent in his eyes told me he was beyond reasoning.

"Don't move," he ordered, removing the knife from my throat. Eric's knife. Eric … if only you would walk through the door now. But it was a futile hope. Just as it was a futile hope that anyone else would walk through the door to stop him.

I tried to push the frayed end of my sweater over my breasts. The knife returned to my throat.

"Don't move. You hear."

I remained rigid as he flicked the ends of my clothing away to completely expose my breasts. He rubbed and kneaded them. Licked and sucked on the nipples. I tried to make myself as small as I could. Tried to thrust my mind to another dimension. Tried to pretend this wasn't happening.

I almost succeeded until I felt my jeans being pulled down over my thighs. He cut my underpants away and tossed them aside.

I didn't think I had ever felt so exposed, so helpless in my entire life. Not even when my ex attacked me.

He wrenched my legs apart.

"A real redhead." He guffawed. "Never had red pussy before."

I squeezed my eyes closed, but I couldn't block out the sound of the zipper coming open on his jeans. I tensed and girded myself, counting off the seconds before I would feel the thrust of his penetration.

I gasped when I felt the searing pain as he forced his hardness into me. Oh my god, it hurt.

"What in the hell you doing, you big fuck?" a female voice shouted.

FORTY-TWO

I lay with my eyes closed, sprawled out on the hard, cold floor, unable to move, unable to hide my shame. I felt only a pervasive numbness. My mind was a blank. I wanted to hide, to retreat, but I didn't know how. Maybe if I stayed here, it would all go away.

"Messing around on me, eh?" A female voice cut through the fog.

Who was this? I couldn't stay here. I had to do something. I breathed in deeply several times and willed myself to open my eyes.

A tall, muscular woman with a red tuque pulled down over her white-blond hair stood over the Serb. Tight pants and a red leather biker jacket only served to emphasize her curves. In one hand she dangled a snowmobile helmet. With the other she pointed a gun at my rapist's head.

It was his time to squirm. "*Sunce*, no woman good like you.... But it such long time without a woman...."

This was Jo.

Her timing couldn't have been better. But I didn't know whether to kiss her feet in thanks or cower back in fear. I inched away from the Serb. My hand touched the blanket. I snatched it up to cover myself.

He pushed the gun aside. "Give me kiss."

Puckering his lips, he lifted his face up toward her, but she turned her head away. "Who's the bitch?"

"She own house."

"I thought it was an old lady."

"She dead."

"What happened to your face?" She ran her fingers through the blood seeping from the wound, brought them to her lips, and sucked.

"The bitch cut me."

She stopped sucking and aimed the gun at me. "I could kill you for hurting my man."

Should I plead self-defence against being raped by her boyfriend? But her hard edge suggested she wouldn't care. I remained silent and wrapped the blanket tighter around my nakedness. My hands were trembling so much, I could barely hang on to it. I backed farther away.

Jo leaned over, grabbed his hair, and kissed him hard. He responded in kind. I glanced around, trying to make out Larry in the dark shadows of the room, but I didn't see him. I then realized it wasn't quite so dark. The greyness of dawn was creeping through the window.

The woman broke away. "You're still the best kisser I know, Tiger. It's sure been one hell of a long time."

"You fuck no other man, ne?" The kiss had recharged him.

Now it was her turn to look guilty. She brushed a long, silken tendril off her face and shrugged. "Like you said, you're the only man for me." She bent over, caressed his renewed hardness, and kissed it, and then she gave it a mighty pull.

He yelped.

"Where's the Viper?" she asked, straightening up. "We've got to get outta here."

Ignoring the question, he asked instead, "Where Freddie?" He pulled up his pants, fumbled to shove everything back inside, and zipped them out of sight.

I strove to quell my shaking, my whirling thoughts as I grappled with what had just happened.

"Freddie's waiting for us on the main road. The road's cleared now. But I had to use the Ski-Doo to get here. Fuck, there's a lot of snow out there. But if it's slowing us down, it'll be slowing the cops too."

"You see any?"

"Nah, not on the roads we were driving on, but the jailbreak's all over the news. I figure this side of Quebec will be crawling with cops soon. So we can't wait around."

"You change mind? I thought we stay until dark."

"Schedule has moved up. The boss heard the target was getting company later today, so it's gotta be done this morning."

I was too worried about my own situation to wonder what they were talking about. I'd managed to zip up my pants. But my skin crawled with the memory of him. I desperately wanted go upstairs and scrub him away.

Slobo pulled Jo to him. Once again they were pawing each other like rutting dogs. I took the opportunity to slide past them and into the darkness of the hall. I was almost at the stairs when the woman yelled, "Bitch, get back here."

I turned around to see her outline blocking the grey light seeping through the doorway.

"What's with all this fucking darkness?" she said, coming up to me. Her pistol hung loosely at her side. "Where's the damn light switch?"

"The power's out."

"Fuck, just what I need. Get back in here where I can see you."

"Please, I want to go upstairs to change." I let the blanket fall to one side so she could see my ripped clothes.

"Jeez, what did you do?"

I didn't respond.

"He do that?"

I shrugged.

"Sure is one horny bastard, ain't he?" She grinned. "Okay, up you go ... and take your time, eh?" She winked. She started to head back into the den and then stopped and turned back to me. "Look, I'm sorry. He can get a bit rough. I'll make sure it don't happen again."

Before she could change her mind, I scooted upstairs. But instead of going into the washroom, I ran down the hall to my bedroom and crawled into bed and under the duvet. I shook from head to foot. All I could see was his leering face coming toward me. All I could feel were his rough, scaly hands kneading and pawing me. All I could hear was the sound of his zipper opening, the silence of waiting. His licking, his sucking, his saliva all over me. The stabbing, the scraping. I tried to rub him away, but I couldn't. My nostrils filled with the stench of his lust. My whole body cried out with pain.

I moved over to Eric's side of the bed and breathed in his scent to drown out the stench and failed.

"Oh Eric, my dear sweet Eric. I want you to hold me and never let go."

I clung to his pillow. I tried to conjure up images of his dimpled smile, his gentle touch, his soft caresses, and failed.

Would Eric want to touch me now?

Would he think I was damaged goods?

Why, oh why did this happen to me?

Eric, where are you when I need you?

Why didn't you save me?

Why aren't you here now?

I punched and pounded the pillow. I threw it on the floor and stomped on it. Flung it back on the bed and pounded it and pounded it and pounded it, until I collapsed in a flood of tears.

FORTY-THREE

I felt more than heard a presence in the room. I stopped crying, cowered farther under the duvet, and braced for the attack. When it didn't happen, I cautiously poked my head out, praying I was wrong, that there was no one in the room. At first I didn't see anyone in the diffuse dawn light, but then I realized someone was lurking in the shadows just inside the door. It was still too dark to tell who waited there. However, I didn't sense a threat or the sexual danger of the biker. Rather, I sensed fear and indecision.

"Come here, Jid," I whispered.

He ran to the bed, jumped in beside me, and clung to me. "I was so scared. I didn't know what to do. When I heard the gun go off, I thought they'd shot you. I thought you were dead."

His body shook.

I wrapped him in the duvet and brushed the tears from his cheeks. "As you can see, I am very much alive. It was Professor who was shot."

I wondered if he'd heard the rape. I didn't think I'd screamed or cried out. Hopefully he knew nothing about it.

"Yeah, I know. When I finally left the office, I heard Larry crying in the front room, so I went and looked."

"Is Professor dead?"

"No, but I think he's hurt bad."

At least the man was alive, but likely not in a condition to control the biker. There was no one to protect us now.

"Who's that lady?" Jid asked.

"Jo, the biker's girlfriend." Maybe she would keep her boyfriend from harming us. But despite her sympathy, I had a feeling she wouldn't intervene. "What are they doing?"

"They're in the kitchen yelling at each other. She sounds real mad at him."

"Good, maybe they'll be too busy to think of us." Jid's trembling was starting to subside. "You're not supposed to be here. Why didn't you leave?"

"I tried to. I waited until it was real quiet, like you told me. But just as I was leaving Shome's office, Professor came down the hall. I ducked back inside. Then I heard the gun. It really scared me. I was so sure you were dead. I didn't know what to do."

"Why didn't you stay in the office?"

"I started to think maybe you weren't dead but were hurt real bad. I thought I'd better take care of you. I figured those guys wouldn't help you. Larry might, but not the other guys. Well, maybe Professor, but not that really bad guy."

I hugged him closer. "Thank you, Jid. You're the best kid in the world." I felt him squirm from embarrassment. I would never forgive myself if something happened to him. "Do you think there is any chance we can escape right now?"

We had to keep trying.

"I don't think so. Like I said, they're in the kitchen."

"That rules out the back door, and the tree is blocking the front door, but there is the dining room door. Or better yet, we could go out one of these windows." I pointed to the two large sash windows overlooking the lake. "We could climb out onto the verandah roof and jump down into the soft snow."

"What about our snowshoes and jackets?"

"Lots of warm clothes up here. We can make our way around to the back porch for the snowshoes."

"What about Shoni?"

My dear sweet, little puppy. I hated to do it, but I had no choice. "I'm afraid we'll have to leave her behind. But they won't hurt her."

"You sure?"

Not really, not with that demonic biker. *I'm sorry, Shoni, Jid's life is more important.* "Professor will keep her safe. Now, off you go to your room and put on as much warm clothing as you can. And not a sound, okay?"

I waited until he'd left before leaving the bed. I'd been afraid he would see my torn clothes. My only desire now was to wash the horror away. Clutching clean underwear, jeans, and a top, I tiptoed to the bathroom, filled the sink from the spare water container and scrubbed and scrubbed and scrubbed the touch of his hands, his tongue, his penis away. I didn't care if the water was freezing cold. I wanted him gone.

I was so intent on rubbing away the last vestiges of the monster that I almost missed the quiet tap on the door. "Auntie, you better hurry. I hear noise coming from downstairs. They might be looking for us," Jid warned.

I hastily dried myself, slipped on the clean clothes, and threw every single item of the contaminated clothing into the garbage. I'd burn them later.

The two of us scurried back into my room and closed the door softly behind us, but not before I too noticed the increased sound of activity downstairs. I couldn't make out what they were saying, but it was obvious Jo and the Serb were standing close to the bottom of the stairs. We had to leave now.

I rummaged through my drawers and was very glad to discover a down-filled sweater tucked away in a corner. I hastily donned it and added an Icelandic wool pullover. Unfortunately, my mitts and gloves were at the back door, but socks would do in a pinch. I tossed Jid a pair. "For your hands."

Nodding, he tucked them into his jeans pocket.

Boots were another problem. But I had a pair of trail shoes in my cupboard. I found another pair of wool socks and pulled them over the shoes and up over the bottom of my jeans in an attempt to keep the snow at bay.

"Are those worn-out runners all you have?" His red sock poked through a hole in the toe.

"Yah, my boots and the new kicks Shome gave me are downstairs."

"Put a pair of Eric's heavy wool socks over them and tuck them into your jeans like I've done. Now help me get this window up."

Although Aunt Aggie had replaced the original windows with thermal-paned ones, that was a good thirty years ago. Over time the sliders had become warped. It usually needed Eric's strength to wrench them upward.

For once, the gods were smiling down on us. With minimal strain, Jid and I managed to slide up the window closest to the front of the house and high enough for me to squeeze through. The air coming from outside felt only slightly colder than it did inside, so we should be okay with our makeshift winter clothing. The snow rising above the window ledge spilled onto the floor.

I heard someone tramping up the stairs.

"Quick. You go first," I whispered.

Jid scrambled through the opening and sank up to his knees in the white stuff. I followed and found myself floundering too. It was impossible to tell where the edge of the roof was. I closed the window behind me in an attempt to throw them off, although the snow on the floor would give us away.

"Wait until I'm on the ground before you jump down, okay?"

I half crawled, half walked to where I thought the edge should be and guessed wrong. Without warning, my arm punched through to nothing and I was tumbling head first to the whiteness below. I managed to flatten myself out and landed body deep with a face plant into the cold froth. Fortunately, it *was* like landing in a cloud.

Sputtering out ice crystals, I struggled to stand up, only to realize I was in full view of the living room windows. Although I could see the faint glow of the fire, it was too dark to tell if anyone was looking my way.

"Jid," I called out softly. "Follow my route, but come feet first."

That was something I should've done. Since the ground floor of this side of the house was all windows, there was nothing I could do to prevent Jid from being seen. I could only hope that Larry was too busy helping his lover.

A minute later the boy was sinking into the drifts beside me. I helped him to his feet. With the snow thigh-high for him and knee-high for me, it was going to be impossible to move quickly. Fortunately, it was like fluff, so we should be able to wade through it as if it were water.

"Let's get the snowshoes."

FORTY-FOUR

I had a decision to make. We could stay on this side of the house and go around the back to reach the porch, which was opposite where we were standing, or we could get to it via the front of the house. While the back route would be shorter, it would put us in full view of the living room and kitchen windows. Larry and Professor were in the living room. The risk was too high that Slobo and his girlfriend would end up back in the kitchen and would see us.

I took the front route, though we did have to keep our heads below the height of the verandah railing as we passed the few living room windows that faced the front. Fortunately, the collapsed roof and broken tree blocked most of them.

It was one sweaty and very slow slog, much slower than anticipated. I was tempted to remove the Icelandic sweater by the time we pushed our way up and over the trunk of the downed pine, but I didn't dare in case it slowed us even more. I'd never encountered so much snow in one dump. Everything in sight seemed to be choking under a suffocating layer of meringue. Fir trees, bushes, the woodshed, and other outbuildings had been turned into shapeless white blobs. The only thing identifying my truck was a corner of the rear window, where the wind had whipped away the snow.

Although the snow had stopped, heavy, dense cloud threatened more. I hoped it would hold off until we'd reached safety. My watch said it was close to eight-thirty, late enough to expect some traffic on the main road, traffic that could whisk Jid and me away to the safety of the Migiskan police detachment.

"I can't see my sign very well." Jid pointed to where the window in Eric's office was partially obscured by the cave-in. I could just make out the words GET POLICE printed in large red letters on a piece of paper taped to the most visible corner.

"Doesn't matter. We won't need it. Can you walk faster?"

"I'll try. But it's hard." Despite the advantage of my track, he still had to force his way through. "You know, I don't think the snowshoes are gonna work. They'll sink in this stuff. It's way too soft."

"I was wondering the same thing."

Since Migiskan Road was already cleared, Gerry could be on his way. When Eric was away, he made a point of ploughing my road before most of his other customers.

"Let's forget the snowshoes and take advantage of the Ski-Doo track." I pointed to the trench threading its way down the middle of the driveway. "The walking will be easier, and we might run into Gerry."

"Or maybe we steal the Ski-Doo?" Jid raised his eyebrows in question.

"Why didn't I think of that? But I don't know how to drive one." I wasn't a big fan of snowmobiles. Too noisy and smelly for my liking.

"I do. My uncle lets me drive his."

"Okay, you're on. They won't be able to come after us, either."

We'd rounded the corner of the house and were looking at the snowmobile parked a short distance from the back porch. It looked to be a powerful machine.

"Wow, it's an Arctic Cat. Cool." Jid's eyes were bright with awe.

"Does that mean it will get us out of here quickly?"

"Yah. It can go 110 klicks."

"But the key'll be inside with Jo."

"My uncle always leaves his in the ignition. But if it's not there, I can hotwire it."

Though I didn't approve, this rather shady skill had proved a lifesaver last summer when I lost my truck keys while we were canoeing on a nearby river. "Let's pick up our pace. I'm worried they'll discover we're gone soon."

We clawed our way along the side of the house, careful to duck our heads below the window ledges. I wasn't worried about being seen through the first set of windows. It was unlikely any of these thugs had wandered into Eric's office. But the glow coming from the den window set my teeth on edge, particularly when it darkened for a second as if someone had walked past the window. It was about the size of the biker.

At the thought of the biker, the images of the rape came flooding back. I stopped. My breath came in short, gasping pants as the icy chill of fear rolled over me. Unable to push a foot forward through the snow, I watched helplessly as Jid moved away.

Realizing I was no longer behind him, he turned around short of the den window. He waved me frantically forward. "Come on, Auntie, we gotta go."

"You go ahead." The shadow blackened the window again. "No, come back." Terrified Slobo would see us, I tried to back up but found myself paralyzed, unable to move forward or backward.

"Auntie, we've gotta get the Ski-Doo."

But I no longer saw the machine or the boy. Instead I saw the man's lusting face leaning over me, his mouth open, tongue ready. My nostrils filled with his reeking breath. My breasts cringed from the roughness of his hands. I fought to push him away and found myself punching snow.

"Auntie, Auntie, what's wrong?" came a voice through what seemed like the other end of a tunnel. Then the tunnel disappeared. I was lying on my back. Instead of a rapist's face, I was looking into the innocence of youth. Jid's eyes were wide with alarm.

"Auntie, you okay?" I felt his hand search out mine.

"Yeah, I'm fine, just give me a minute, okay?"

I closed my eyes, and when I opened them I was looking into Slobo's gloating face. This time I knew he was real.

I screamed.

FORTY-FIVE

Every cell in my body recoiled with the memory of the man's brutality, while my mind screamed, *Get out of here!*

Half-sitting, half-lying, I thrashed at the snow, desperate to back as far away from the psycho as I could.

"Don't hurt me," I pleaded.

I kicked, punched, clawed at the snow. Panic consumed me. All thought of Jid vanished. I flailed. I lashed. I scratched. But I only buried myself deeper into the coldness.

I gave up. "Please don't hurt me."

I gulped in mouthfuls of air. My chest pounded. My body shook. Tears slid down my cheeks. I tried to wipe them away and only succeeded in covering my face with more snow.

I waited, not sure what I would do if he touched me.

Instead I heard him growl, "Get up, bitch."

I lay still and kept my eyes clamped shut.

"Now!"

I heard someone swishing through the snow toward me. I girded myself but remained where I lay, unable to move.

"Auntie, you okay?"

I cleared the snow from my eyes and looked up to see the man standing several metres away, his legs rooted in the snow, his arms held tensely at his side. The cut where I'd sliced him was an angry red against the pallor of his cheek. He touched it and sneered. He raised his revolver and aimed it directly at my head.

"I shoot you and then boy."

Midway between us stood Jid, frozen in midstride, his face a mirror of fear.

I was too paralyzed to try to save him. Instead I closed my eyes and whispered to myself, "Goodbye, my son, if only you were. Goodbye my love, my one and only. I'm sorry. I've failed you both." I held my breath and waited.

As if from the bottom of a barrel came a voice. "Tiger, honey, what are you doing out there?"

"These two escape. I shoot them."

I waited for what seemed like an eternity.

"Nah, don't," came the reply. "Bring them inside. They still might come in handy as hostages."

I took a deep breath and slowly opened my eyes to stare straight into the barrel of Slobo's gun. For one heart-stopping moment I thought he was going to ignore his girlfriend. Then he slowly lowered it.

"Get inside!" he yelled. He punctuated it with a shot fired into the air. The sudden bang cut the stillness like a knife, causing an overhang of snow to drop from the woodshed roof.

The sound brought Jo back onto the porch. I could see from her expression that she was expecting to see us lying bleeding in the snow. I felt a frisson of hope when I saw her visibly relax. "Tiger, I want them inside, now."

My legs were shaking so much, I thought I would fall, but I managed to stay upright and make it to Jid, who clung to me as if his life depended on it. Tears streamed down his face.

"There, there, it's okay." I patted his hair and kissed his forehead. "Just keep telling yourself we're going to make it." I held him close.

My bare hands were so cold, I could barely feel them. I'd lost the sock mittens in my panic. I could also feel the icy prickle of melting snow slithering down my back. A convulsive shudder ran through me.

"Move," Slobo shouted.

Hanging on to each other, we pushed through the snowdrifts toward the porch stairs. But the Serbian refused to budge from where he blocked our path, as if daring us to come near him. We detoured to the Ski-Doo track.

The man sneered, "Bitch, I get you later."

His girlfriend eyed me intently from the top of the stairs.

Passing the Ski-Doo, I noticed that the key was in the ignition. I nudged the boy to ensure he saw it too. Maybe by some miracle he would be able to escape.

Funny thing, hope. Even when it looked as if all was lost, it continued to percolate. I took this as a sign that I had not completely given up.

We clambered up the steps to the porch. While brushing the snow off our clothes, I thought I heard a distant rumble that added to my hope. A noise I'd heard many times before. The sound of Gerry's snowplough coming up my road. I couldn't tell how far away he was, but I felt confident that within a few minutes he would be within view. Which raised a whole new worry. What would these guys do when they saw Gerry?

Jid glanced in the direction of the driveway. He heard it too.

Anxious to get these killers inside before the truck appeared, I called out, my voice shaking, "You guys must be hungry. Let's go inside and I'll make breakfast."

Slobo grunted in response and made his way towards the porch. To cover up the sound of the plough, I stomped my feet on the boards as if trying to get rid of the snow. Jid did likewise. But the minute the man's foot touched the bottom step, I shoved Jid in front of me, past Jo and into the kitchen, putting as much distance as I could between the monster and us.

We both slipped and slid on the floor, barely able to remain upright with the wet socks covering our shoes.

The puppy whined and scratched at the door to her crate.

"Shoni's glad to see us," Jid whispered. "I didn't think I was going to see her again."

The poor kid. No child should come so close to death. But his trembling was diminishing, and he was talking. He was going to be okay.

He lifted Shoni out of the cage, clutched her to his chest, and buried his face in her fur. A puppy. The perfect remedy. Just what he needed.

For a moment she was quiet, glad to be with her buddy, but then she started struggling and whining again.

"She's gotta go," he whispered. "Do you think they will let me put her out?"

"Let me do it." I held the puppy close and started toward the back door.

"Stop right there," Jo ordered when I tried to pass. "What do you think you're doing?"

"The dog has to go the bathroom."

"You think I'm stupid enough to let you go outside?"

Before I could react, she pulled Shoni from my hands and threw her at her boyfriend as he was coming through the outside door. He fumbled with the wriggling body but managed to hang on. It was too much for the poor dog. She released a watery stream. Cursing loudly in Serbian, he dropped her and kicked her away. Whimpering, she scampered across the floor back to me.

I picked her up and held her close. Her entire body quivered as much as I was quivering.

"Stupid dog," Slobo growled, coming into the kitchen. "Do again, I kill her." The entire front of his jeans were soaked. "You got husband. Get me clean jeans."

I wasn't sure whether they would fit, but I wasn't about to ignore his order. Holding the puppy with one hand and Jid's hand with the other, I made for the hall. I wasn't going to leave either alone with these people, if you could call them people.

"Stop," Jo yelled. "You're not going anywhere. You're staying right here, where I can see you. Send the boy."

"Do another sign," I mouthed as he let go of my hand. I jerked my head in the direction of upstairs, hoping he would understand.

"Get back into the kitchen," Jo ordered.

I could just make out the faint growl of the snow-plough. I'd forgotten that the sound carried through the walls, though it could be mistaken for the wind. If they did recognize the noise, hopefully they would decide to remain hidden and let the plough continue on its business.

So far neither of them were paying attention to the growing rumble. They were more interested in pawing each other.

I put Shoni back inside her cage. I could hear the blade scraping the snow off the road. Gerry was almost here.

Jo cocked her head in the direction of the noise and then dismissed it. "Where's the kid? He should be back by now."

"Jid," I called out, walking toward the hall. Maybe I could sprint upstairs.

"Get back here, or I finish what Tiger started."

I turned to see Jo's pistol pointed straight at me. She walked toward me. "Hey kid, you better still be up there. Where are the jeans?"

I heard running from the front of the house, then Jid called out, "I got 'em." He raced down the stairs a little too fast and almost slipped in his stocking-covered shoes, but he managed to remain upright with the jeans still clenched firmly in his hand.

There was no mistaking the whine of the truck's engine now.

"Hey, Jo. You better come here. Someone come," the Serbian yelled from the kitchen.

"Fuck! In the kitchen. Both of you," Jo hissed. "Is it the cops?" she shouted at Slobo.

If only it were.

"I see only big truck," he answered from his position by the pantry window.

"It's the snowplough," I said.

"Good. We can use the road," Jo replied. "Will he want to see you?"

I shook my head. Usually he was in too much of a hurry to stop, but this time he might when he saw the damaged porch. Knowing Eric was away, he would want to check up on me. If he did, I feared they would kill him, and there was nothing I could do to warn him.

"Tiger, stay in the kitchen with them and keep your gun on them. They try to do anything, shoot. I'm going up front to make sure this guy stays in his truck." She headed up the hall toward the front door with her own gun ready.

I panicked, horrified of being left alone with my rapist. I started to run after her and found myself being wrenched backward. I slipped, lost my balance, and fell to the floor. I looked up into the muzzle of his gun.

"No move," came the order.

The house descended into a deathly stillness as we waited. The only sounds were the scraping of the plough along the drive, the whining of the truck's laboured engine, and my pounding heart.

I prayed that Jo wouldn't notice Jid's sign. I prayed that Gerry would see it and head back down the road without letting on. I stopped breathing and waited for the sound of the truck's retreat.

Instead the silence was shattered by loud, hooting shrieks.

FORTY-SIX

I took me a few seconds to realize it was laughter coming from the front of the house.

Before I could react, Slobo yanked me from the floor, almost tugging my arm out of its socket, and pulled me behind him as he marched down the hall toward Jo's chortling. I heard Jid scramble to keep up.

"What going on?" the Serb shouted.

"You wouldn't believe who's here," came the woman's husky voice from Eric's office.

She was standing at the window, her head angled to enable her to see under the partially collapsed roof. I tried not to stare at the white wedge of Jid's message dangling above her head.

Dropping my hand, Slobo moved in beside her, blocking my view. I stepped back and almost collided with the boy standing next to Eric's desk. He arched his eyebrows in question as a voice behind us asked, "What's going on?"

I turned to see Larry limping into the room.

"I've no idea," I said. "How badly hurt is Professor?"

"He'll be okay. It's just a flesh wound, though it knocked him out cold."

For some strange reason I felt comfort in the news. Despite the tattooed man's threatening appearance, I'd grown to like him.

"Hey, Jo, Tiger, who's out there? Can't be the police, else you'd be shooting."

"Bébé Jean and Freddie," Jo answered, standing back from the window. "Tiger, tell them to come in the back. Only way to get into this fucking house."

More of them. Just what we needed.

The Serbian flung open the window and shouted.

I caught a glimpse of a silver pickup with a tall blond man in a black leather jacket standing beside it. My heart sank when I saw the second man in a down jacket pulling Gerry from the cab with a pistol pointed at his chest.

"Tiger, let's get these two back to the kitchen." Jo motioned with her gun for Jid and me to move. Locking her eyes with mine, she continued, "Keep your fucking hands off my man."

So much for female sympathy.

I pushed the boy in front and followed him out of the office and into the hallway with Jo breathing down my neck.

"It's so damn dark. When's the power coming back on?" Not waiting for an answer, she continued, "Jesus, how can you live in such a hole? Give me a city anytime."

I was about to ask who the two men were when Professor called out as we were passing the archway into the living room. "Jo, can you come here a minute?"

The woman signalled for us to go into the room with her while Slobo continued on down the hall. In the low morning light, I could make out the tattooed man's darker shape sitting in one of the light yellow wingback chairs next to the stone fireplace. He was rubbing his head. The fire had burned down to a few ineffective coals.

"It's just as fucking cold in here," Jo exclaimed.

"I'll put more wood on the fire." I started to walk over to the dark corner where the woodbox was located.

"You stay right where I can see you. The boy can do it."

"Don't worry about Red. She's won't do anything," Professor said. His voice sounded weak. "Apart from trying to escape once, she's been good. She saved Larry's life."

"If she's what you call good, I hate to see what you call trouble. She just tried another escape. And look what I found in the window." She held up Jid's note. "Still think she can be trusted?" She ripped it into several pieces and let them flutter to the floor. "Tiger has shot people for less reason."

Jid watched, horrified.

"Look, Red, promise me you'll be good. It'll make things easier for you and the boy."

"Sure," I said, not believing him.

"We're going to have to do something about them," Jo said. "And we have another problem. The boys have the driver. Why didn't they just put a bullet in his head and dump his body in this fucking snow and save us a lot of trouble?"

I felt a sudden chill as I watched the log slip from Jid's hand onto the floor. He stared back at me in alarm. I went over and placed my arm around him. We'd only had a delay in our execution.

Professor merely grunted in acknowledgement, causing my heart to sink further. "What driver?" he asked.

"The snowplough. The boys followed it up the road. We need to sit down and plan what we do next. I hate this fucking snow. It's made a mess of things."

"Yes, but remember if we can't move, neither can the police. Any sign of them?"

"Not that we saw. The radio said the pigs are looking all over Ontario for you." An expanse of white teeth spread across her face, but I wouldn't call it a smile. "It was brilliant of you to suggest they ditch the getaway car in the opposite direction. The pigs are scrambling to catch you at the U.S. border."

"What about the target. Is he still there?"

"As far as we know. Snowed in, like us."

I shrank at the word "target," particularly when they both glanced at me. I pretended to examine a thread dangling from my sweater. If this meant what I thought it meant, all the more reason for killing us.

"You guys want to talk. We'll get out of your way, okay?" I propelled Jid out of the room before they had a chance to stop us.

I could hear voices echoing from the kitchen. I didn't want to join them and was debating detouring into the den when I heard Gerry ask, "Where's Meg?"

"Who in the hell's Meg?" answered a raspy tenor voice.

"What have you done with her?" Gerry persisted.

I had better let him know we were alive, so I continued past the den and into the kitchen. Two sets of cold, inquiring eyes stared back at me.

"Good, there you are," Gerry said, standing against the counter, rubbing a shoulder.

He'd pulled off his wool toque to reveal his bristly brush cut and was in the process of unzipping the bulky work jacket that looked old enough to have belonged to his trapper father. Though a gun was no longer pointed at him, the blond guy standing beside him still held one in his hand, while the other had slipped his into his belt.

"You've got the boy too," Gerry continued. "Claire said she thought he was visiting."

Claire was Gerry's wife and prided herself in knowing everyone's business on the reserve.

"Who are these guys?" He jerked his head in the direction of the three men.

The blond one with his unkempt hair and unshaven face and his black leather jacket with Black Devils patches on full display could've been a carbon copy of Slobodan, while the other, in his red down-filled jacket, neatly trimmed salt-and-pepper hair, and businessman's paunch, had an air of respectability about him. The gun said otherwise.

Slobo had taken up one of the chairs at the table, in front of a bowl brimming with Eric's homemade granola. With his mouth half full, he yelled, "Shut up!"

Gerry clamped his mouth shut, started to open it, then, seeing the ferocity reflected on the Serbian's face, closed it again and kept it that way.

"Good you guys made it," Slobo continued.

"It looks like life in the clink treat you good, Tiger." The biker patted his flat stomach, where the Serb's was bulging over his buckle. "Perhaps you should have stayed inside." He spoke with a slight French accent. Likely he was Bébé Jean, although at more than six feet he could hardly be called a baby.

"Food is shit. But lots of it." Slobo spooned more cereal into his mouth. "You see cops?"

"Not a one. They are too busy looking for you along the border."

"Hey, are you the guys that —" Gerry stopped when he saw my glare.

"So what happen now?" the Quebecer asked.

"It's up to Jo," said the other man. "It's her gig."

At that point, the woman, with Larry and Professor following unsteadily behind, walked into the heat of the kitchen.

FORTY-SEVEN

Blood oozed from what looked to be a severed head of a snake on the top of the tattooed man's head. I didn't see any other bullet wounds, but he was rubbing an egg-size lump at the back of his head.

The Serbian stopped eating. Removing his hands from the table, he straightened up against the back of his chair in anticipation of a confrontation. Professor walked over to the table and took the chair across from him but refused to acknowledge the challenge with so much as a glance. Despite the man's weakened condition, I could sense his inner power and strength.

Slamming the chair against the wall behind him, Slobo stood up and joined the other two men.

Clutching his stomach, Larry shuffled into the kitchen. Instead of taking up a chair next to his protector, he continued across the kitchen to Jo, who was rubbing her hands over the heat of the woodstove.

He mumbled nervously, "You got my stuff?"

"What are you talking about?" She continued rubbing her hands.

"Stuff. You know, stuff." His voice rose an octave.

"Tiger said you were bringing some."

"You talking about heroin? You an addict?" She faced him, not bothering to hide her contempt.

The two newcomers, who'd been ignoring the injured man, now regarded him with interest. I thought I detected sympathy in the eyes of the respectable-looking man, but the blond biker curled his lip in derision.

Larry squirmed with embarrassment. "I really need some."

"Sorry. Tiger didn't mention it. You'd better not crap out on us and do something stupid. We can't afford it." She turned her back on him and resumed warming her hands.

For a moment I thought Larry was going to lose it, but he managed to keep himself together, dragged his feet back to where his lover was sitting, and took the chair next to him.

Professor placed his arm around Larry's trembling body and said softly, "It's for the best, P'tit Chief. You're going to make it. You'll be a much better man for it." He kissed him gently on the forehead.

The blond man looked away while the other stranger watched with interest, which made me wonder about his inclinations. After a few seconds he said, "Hell, what happened to you, Viper? Nothing wrong with you when I hauled you out of the van yesterday."

So he was involved in the escape. Not so respectable after all.

Professor jerked his head toward the Serbian. "One of your upstanding members. My price has just gone up."

"You bastard," the man growled. "Wait till the boss hears about this." He punched Slobo in the jaw, knocking his head sideways.

Before the Serb could respond, Jo was yelling, "Stop!" She slipped between the two men. "Fighting isn't going to get us anywhere. Tiger will pay the increase."

From the surprised look on her boyfriend's face, I could tell he hadn't anticipated this outcome. But he didn't attempt to contest it.

"Look, guys, Viper has said he is up to the job, so we need to finalize our plan," she continued.

"*D'accord*," the Quebecer agreed, while the other man said, "It's your show, sweetheart."

Jo shot back, "The name's Josephine. I'm not your sweetheart, never have been, and never will be. Are you going to work with us, or do I tell the boss?"

The man drummed his fingers on the counter. Finally, he nodded. "Yah, I'm in."

"Good. First we need food. You," she said, pointing at me, "your kitchen, you cook."

"Sure." Now was not the time to tell her I didn't cook.

"You, driver, help her."

Good. Gerry liked to brag that his fried eggs were the best on the rez.

"Jean, Viper, Freddie, you come with me. Larry and Tiger, you stay here."

"But *sunce*, you need me." Slobo pushed away from the counter and walked over to his girlfriend.

"Tiger, honey, remember what we discussed. It's better you stay out of this."

"But I more better than that faggot," he spat out.

"I know you are, honey, but not this time. He is the man we need for this operation. Besides, I want you to guard these three. They try to escape, I give you permission to shoot them. We're too close to completing the job to have them ruin it."

"Better we kill them now."

"Not yet. We might need them." She ran her fingers up and down his thigh and then squeezed hard. He yelped. "When we no longer need them, I'll give you the honours."

Before the full implication could sink in, she was demanding breakfast be on the table by the time they returned. There wasn't an "or else." It had already been said.

I watched her stride out the kitchen door without a single flick of her eyes in my direction. The three men followed. I listened to their boots clomping in unison down the hall like a death knell, until it stopped when they went into the den.

Larry remained seated at the table, appearing not the least upset at being left out of the action. The biker resumed his chair across from him and placed his revolver in full view on the table. Crossing his arms across his chest, he leaned back, balancing the chair on its back legs. Gloating was the only expression I could use to describe the expression on his face.

"You heard her. Make food," he rasped. "I starving."

Larry raised himself from the chair. "I'm cold. I'm going to sit by the stove. Jid, do you want to join me?"

The boy hesitated, uncertain. I gave him a little push in the injured man's direction. I had a sense that Larry would do what he could to protect a fellow Algonquin, especially one young enough to be his son.

I watched the boy drag a chair to where Larry sat in Aunt Aggie's rocking chair. His movements were that of an old man. His youthful exuberance was gone. He was as terrified as I was.

"You better know how to fry eggs," I said, turning to Gerry. "I always break the yolks. Given the mood these guys are in, I don't fancy giving them another excuse."

Gerry appeared equally stunned. "Do you really think they'll kill us?" he whispered. "I tell you, I was sure scared when they stopped my truck and waved guns in my face. I didn't know whether I was going to make it to your house in one piece. But I was sure hoping you wouldn't be here. I didn't want to get you into trouble. So how long have they been here? Who in the hell are these guys?"

"Shut your mouth," Slobo shouted. "Get to work."

Gerry backed up, almost knocking over the garbage can behind him. He looked as if he were about to open his mouth to say something but then clamped it firmly shut.

I motioned for him to follow me into the pantry to get the eggs. Luckily, I had three dozen of them in anticipation of the Christmas crowd. While I passed Gerry a carton, I whispered, "Did you hear anything about a prison escape?"

"Yeah, the radio and TV were full of it." His dark brown eyes opened wide. "Oh my god, they really are those guys."

"Yup."

"Holy shit. They said all the guards were killed."

"I know. Did you see any sign of police anywhere?"

"Nope. Decontie and I were talking about it just before I started my run. He was happy that with all this damn snow, they were nowhere near here. He asked me to check on you to make sure you were okay. I guess not, eh?"

"He didn't happen to mention a strange phone call from me yesterday?" I had to ask, though I knew the answer.

"Nope, nothing. So what do we do now?"

Hearing the sound of approaching footsteps, I said, "Make breakfast."

And I almost collided with Slobodan as he crossed the threshold of the pantry. In my panic, I backed into the Christmas tree. "Ouch!" I cried out but didn't dare move away from the tree.

"What you doing?"

"Getting eggs." I held a carton up to show him. "How many eggs do you think people will want?"

"Fuck, I don't know. I eat four with plenty bacon."

I had little over a half pound remaining in the fridge, so bacon was going to be a problem. But maybe there was some other kind of meat we could use. Bread was also in short supply, but there were half a dozen stale muffins in the bread box. There were nine to feed, including myself. My stomach was in too much turmoil to hold anything. I doubted Larry was up to eating, and Gerry likely already had breakfast. So it was really the four men and the woman we had to worry about. I could fill Jid up with cereal.

Removing enough plates from a shelf, I spied a box tucked away in the corner of another shelf.

Shoving it into my pocket, I headed back into the kitchen and said to Gerry, "We'll have scrambled eggs instead."

FORTY-EIGHT

By the time Jo and her escort were tramping onto the kitchen linoleum, Gerry and I were placing platters of eggs and bacon on the table, including the ham Gerry had fried up after finding a tin in the cupboard. Jid was removing the last piece of toast from the stovetop toaster. He added it to the rest of the toast and put the basket beside the jar of blueberry jam and peanut butter. We were ready.

Without a word, the men took up seats at the table and began piling eggs, bacon, and ham onto their plates.

Jo was more circumspect. After taking a seat beside her lover, she surveyed the eggs and said, "I thought we were having fried."

While Gerry struggled for an answer, I replied, "You wanted breakfast in a hurry. Scrambled eggs are faster to make than fried. Here's some hot salsa to go with them."

Satisfied with my answer, she spooned a healthy portion onto her plate and doused it with the salsa.

Gerry and I tried not to watch too closely.

"Aren't you eating?" she asked.

"I've already had my breakfast," Gerry rushed to answer.

He was standing by the stove watching over the percolating coffee to ensure it didn't boil over.

"I'm not hungry," I replied.

Jo was acting a bit too suspicious for my liking. I placed a spare chair at the opposite end of the table from her and her rapist boyfriend and spooned a small amount of eggs and ham onto a plate. I figured a mouthful or two wouldn't hurt.

The fluffy eggs looked innocent enough. I hoped these killers thought so too. Though Gerry had fried them up in the heavy cast-iron pan, I'd prepared them. I didn't want him having the responsibility of adding the poison. I'd tossed in the entire contents of the box of mouse poison I'd found in the pantry. I doubted there was anywhere near enough to kill anyone, but it might leave them feeling miserable.

To help disguise any bad flavour, I added fried onions and red pepper. Because the box described it as being cheese-flavoured, I tossed in lots of grated cheddar. It smelled delicious. The men seemed to think so too, for they were shovelling it down their throats. They didn't seem to mind the odd piece of grit. Gerry and I hadn't come up with a way to disguise that. If anyone asked, I was going to say that it was the spices, a special salsa mix added to give them oomph.

I'd given Jid a bowl of Eric's homemade granola, one of his favourites, and told him not to eat any eggs because there weren't enough to go around.

Gerry had distracted Slobo while I poured the tiny granules into the eggs. But as I'd walked to the cookstove to throw the box into the firebox, I'd noticed Larry watching. I thought he was going to say something. Instead he merely shrugged and turned back to flipping the pages of one of Eric's hockey magazines. When Larry suggested Professor should try some granola, I knew that he had seen me. I set the bag on the table with a container of raspberry yoghurt and several bowls.

Jo, as if taking a cue from the tattooed man, set her partially eaten eggs aside and poured herself a big bowl of granola. "Much better for you than cholesterol-ridden eggs, eh, Viper?"

She kept her eyes on me the entire time. But if she suspected, why didn't she warn her men?

I was doing my best to avoid staring at the eggs, as was Gerry, although I caught him sneaking a peek or two. I managed to swallow a couple of mouthfuls then surreptitiously slid the rest into my napkin.

"*Délicieux*. Usually I am not a fan of eggs," Jean said, placing his fork on his empty plate. "I have had sufficient."

"Good," Slobo said. "More for me." He shovelled another large portion of eggs onto his plate and doused it with salsa.

Eat up, eat up, was my only thought. *I hope you bleed to death.*

"Bet you don't get good food like this in the slammer, eh, Tiger?" Freddie said with his mouth half full of egg. "Better than the wife's. But don't tell her I said that."

If I had expected an immediate reaction, it wasn't happening. Though the three men had devoured enough eggs for eight, they didn't appear the least affected.

This must have satisfied Jo. "You can't be too healthy," she muttered and finished the eggs on her plate and then helped herself to the remaining ones on the platter. "They smell too good." She raised a forkful to Gerry and me. "Compliments to the chefs."

I chuckled inwardly. It was the first time anyone had ever complimented my cooking. Perhaps it would become known as Meg's killer dish. I noticed Gerry couldn't stop a grin from spreading across his lips.

"Okay, guys," Jo said, slamming down her knife and fork beside her empty plate. She looked at her watch. "We leave in an hour."

Our smiles vanished.

"But we have enough time for another cup of coffee." She brought the coffee pot from the stove and poured herself a mug full. "Good stuff. Anyone else?"

Professor set his empty mug in front of her. "I could do with some more fuel to steady my aim."

I thought I heard an intake of breath from Freddie as Jo stopped pouring. Her ice-blue eyes seemed to bore right through the tattooed man's piercing amber ones.

"What does it matter?" He shrugged, training his eyes on me. "Pour the coffee, Jo. I need it after what your man did to me." He touched the wound on the top of his head. "Another half inch and you would be having a lot of explaining to do."

Slobo smirked while Jo glanced briefly in my direction and Gerry's before continuing with the pouring.

Though my mind was a whirl of questions, I pretended I hadn't noticed this byplay and concentrated on removing the dirty dishes from the table.

"Aim" only meant one thing to me. Pointing a gun at something or someone. I didn't think Professor was going hunting, at least not animals. I assumed it was what was taking place in an hour's time. The location must be close by, which would explain their reason for choosing my house as their base of operations. But more importantly, who was their target?

Gerry seemed oblivious as he concentrated on picking through the woodpile for the perfect log to the throw into the firebox. It seemed a rather useless exercise, since we'd finished cooking. He filled the copper kettle with water from the jug and placed it on the hot burner.

"For the dishes," he said.

Needless to say, washing up was the furthest from my mind. Besides, clean dishes weren't going to help us in an hour's time.

FORTY-NINE

I didn't want to sit around for an hour waiting for them to kill us. Correction. Forty-eight minutes. Twelve minutes had passed since Jo announced they were leaving. Gerry, focused on washing the dishes, didn't seem concerned, but perhaps this was his way of dealing with the threat.

Gerry's arrival was giving me a newfound courage. No one had moved the snowmobile, nor had I seen anyone remove the keys. Three people plus the puppy would be a very tight squeeze, but we could do it.

Only Larry and Slobo remained in the kitchen. The rest had returned to the den, ostensibly to finish planning the operation, or should I say "hit," for I was convinced that a hit was about to take place, with Professor as the assassin.

Another reason for leaving. Not only would we save ourselves, but we would stop someone else from being murdered.

We were three against two. Actually one, since I didn't think Larry would prevent us from fleeing. We just might be able to do it. We just needed to find a way to neutralize the Serb.

His eyes hadn't strayed from Gerry or me since the others had left the room. He continued to sit with his revolver in full view on the table within easy reach of his hand. His fingers would creep toward the gun, touch it, and then back off, almost as if he were itching to use it. Only now did I realize the revolver was the one Professor had taken from him earlier. He must've bullied Larry into giving it back.

Jid had rejoined Larry next to the woodstove. They were caught up in a discussion about life on the rez. The man was regaling the boy about his many exploits as a child growing up on the rez. Several of his partners in mischief were familiar names to me, as they would be to Jid, who seemed to be getting a kick out of learning that the adults in his life weren't quite the upstanding citizens they pretended to be. It was good that Jid was being distracted from worrying about what would happen forty-three minutes from now. Perhaps that was Larry's intention.

The two of them, sitting with their heads close together, could almost be two peas in a pod. Both were small of stature, with the same rich dark brown hair, although Jid's hair had a slight curl to it, whereas Larry's was poker-straight. They had the same slightly lopsided smile. Then Larry did something that made me sit up, a gesture I had seen Jid make many times. An odd movement of his palm, brushing his forehead as if trying to wipe out a memory or a thought. He would do it with his eyes closed. With a chill, I watched Larry make the exact same gesture, right down to the closing of his eyes.

Surely it couldn't be. But yes, it could.

I was about to ask Larry if he had spent time at Migiskan in the months leading up to his incarceration, when, as if suspecting the gist of my thoughts, he raised his eyes, and staring directly into mine, he shook his head. So he suspected too, but he didn't want the boy knowing that he could be his father.

It was within the realm of possibility. It sounded as if Larry had gone to jail months, not years before Jid was born. No one talked about Jid's father except to say that he was in prison. Nor was a name ever mentioned. The boy's only living relative was the aunt he lived with, the older sister of his long-dead mother.

I didn't know which side of the family his beloved *kòkomis* was from, but I'd always suspected his mother's side, since she would talk about the boy's mother but never his father. But that was only a supposition on my part. She could have just as easily been the grandmother of Jid's father. Upset at his having killed a man, she might have refused to talk about him. Though surely she would've told Jid something, for with his inquisitive mind, he would've asked. Yet I'd never heard the boy say a single word about his father, and respecting his privacy, I'd never asked.

I wondered about the boy's reaction should Larry, the escaped convict, drug addict, and convicted killer, turn out to be his father. Had he built up in his own mind the image of the perfect dad, as fatherless children often do? Did he base this image on Eric, his hero? Sadly, there was little similarity between the two men. Eric was everything Larry wasn't: responsible, honourable, loyal, caring, respectful, strong of mind and body.

Perhaps Larry sensed this and decided to keep the boy's dreams alive.

Shoni was scampering after a ball Jid had rolled across the floor, while Gerry continued to clatter away at the sink. Jid crawled after the puppy and rolled onto his back to let the furball climb over him. For the moment, squeals of laughter banished the danger. Even Slobo was grinning, if you could call a smirk a grin.

But the expression on Larry's face almost broke my heart. It spoke of a man's unrequited love for a son. Larry knew the truth. Either he had sensed it or realized it from something Jid had said. I felt a huge burden slide off my shoulders. Larry would do whatever he could to protect his son. Maybe he would help provide a commotion so his son could escape.

If they kept to Jo's schedule, they would be leaving in fifteen minutes. The low murmur drifting from the den told me they were still caught up in their planning and likely wouldn't be returning to the kitchen for some minutes yet.

Standing with the Serbian facing away from me, I tried to catch Larry's eye. When I did, I nodded toward the gun and motioned for him to take it. I turned my eyes on Jid and waved my hand toward the pantry, praying Larry would rightly interpret. With a barely perceptible nod, the injured man pushed himself out of the rocker and shuffled as fast as he could to the kitchen table.

Gerry had finished the dishes and was emptying the garbage from under the sink. It looked as if he was preparing to take it to the pantry. I was amazed by his tidiness, given the situation. But he was exactly where I wanted him to be. He would be able to take Jid and run for it. He would know how to drive a snowmobile and could get the boy away faster than I could. Besides, someone had to help Larry prevent Slobodan from going after them.

Nodding at Larry that it was time, I picked up the kettle and was walking over to pour boiling water onto Slobo's lap when I heard a bang. I looked up in time to see Gerry gone, with the back door closing behind him.

Cursing loudly in Serbian, Slobo reached for his gun. He snapped it up just as Larry's hand was about to touch the grip. Casting a puzzled backward glance at Larry, he ran toward the pantry. Jid scrambled to get out of his way. The man flung open the back door. I could see Gerry running toward the Ski-Doo.

He fired his gun, once, twice, three times.

Jo and the others rushed into the kitchen.

"What's going on?" she yelled.

Slobo sauntered back into the room, his gun tucked into his belt. "Guy try to escape. I stop him."

FIFTY

In a daze, I brushed past the biker and out onto the porch. Gerry lay crumpled face down in the snow a short distance from the snowmobile. I could see blood oozing through the back of his bulky jacket.

"Gerry, Gerry," I called out as I sped down the stairs. "Say something … please…."

He wasn't moving.

"Dear God, let him be alive." I knelt in the snow beside him. "Can you hear me?"

I detected movement in his chest. But I hesitated shifting him onto his back, afraid that I would hurt him further.

"*Le neige*. He cannot breathe," a male voice said behind me. I recognized the French accent of Bébé Jean. "Hold his shoulders and roll him over carefully."

I rotated his upper body as gently as I could while the blond biker turned his lower body over.

Gerry groaned.

I brushed the crystals from his nostrils and off his face and realized the snow's colour was more pink than white.

"Gerry, talk to me."

Blood trickled from the side of his mouth.

He groaned again. His lips started to move. At first no sound, then barely a whisper. I placed my ear next to his mouth. "I'm so sorry. I blew it. I ... I thought I could ... m ... make a run for the ... p ... police." He stopped and gasped a few shallow breaths before continuing. "P ... p ... please tell Claire and the girls ... I ..." A deep shudder ran through his body. I waited for him to continue before realizing it wasn't going to happen. He'd stopped breathing.

"Yes, Gerry, I'll tell Claire and your daughters that you love them," I finished for him, my eyes brimming with tears. I kept my head down and paid respect to his passing. I wished I had some tobacco to sprinkle around him or some smudge to cleanse his spirit. Hopefully the Creator would overlook the omission and help him on his way to wherever he was going.

Then the anger started to boil over.

"Monster!" I yelled at Slobo. "Murderer!"

He stood on the edge of the porch, his face a mask of indifference. A short distance away stood Jo, her fists clenched, her mouth a line of suppressed anger. I didn't know whether this was directed at me or at Gerry's killer. Through the pantry window I caught a glimpse of Professor's tattooed head and the short-cropped haircut of Freddie. Neither seemed overly concerned about the killing. It was business as usual.

Thankfully, I didn't see Jid or Larry. I hoped he was shielding the boy from the violent death of a man the boy had known his entire life.

"You coward." I raised my clenched fist at the Serb. "How dare you shoot an unarmed man in the back." I jumped up and almost collided with Jean.

I started to run toward my friend's murderer with

every intention of doing as much damage as I could. But Jean held me back.

"*Non, restez tranquille*," he said quietly. "*Trop dangereuse.* Stay still, it's too dangerous." Then in a louder voice, "*Cette petite madame* wants to kill you. Do I let her go?" He chuckled as I struggled to break free.

"Stop it. We don't have time for such nonsense," Jo shouted back. "Bring her into the house."

He began pulling me toward the stairs. I dug in. "What about Gerry? We can't leave him like that."

"He is dead. Nothing can happen to him now."

"But it isn't respectful."

"Freddie," he shouted. "Can you find a blanket or *quelque chose comme ça* to cover the body?"

"I didn't know you were such a softy, Bébé." Jo laughed. "Afraid of a little blood, eh?"

He grinned. "I don't like looking them in the eyes."

Disgusted by the banter, I shook my arm free from his grasp and put as much distance as I could from the man, from all of them. I didn't know what to do. Stay outside. Go inside. I didn't care if they shot me too.

Gerry wasn't hurting anyone. Why couldn't the monster have just shot him in the leg? That's all he had to do to keep him from escaping. Poor Claire. She was going to be devastated. With her mother dying less than a month ago, this was going to be very hard on her, on the girls. *Damn you, Gerry, why couldn't you have just stayed in the kitchen? Why did you have to try to be a hero?*

The man in the down jacket came out onto the porch holding one of the red Hudson's Bay blankets from the den. Before anyone else could take it, I ran up to him and yanked it out of his hands. No way were any of these bastards going to get near Gerry.

Gerry's face wore a mask of calm. At least he hadn't been in pain. But his eyes seemed to be asking, "Why me?" I closed them and mumbled a few prayers to whichever gods were listening, though after this senseless shooting I didn't think any were. I gently draped the blanket over him. The snow around his body had taken on a reddish hue. I covered it too. I continued to stand, head bowed, beside him. I didn't want to leave him alone to the bleak winter day.

"Get her inside, Bébé," Jo yelled. "We haven't got all day." The back door slammed shut.

I heard the shuffle of snow behind me.

"Don't you dare touch me," I hissed and stomped back to the house without looking back.

The show was over. Those who'd been standing on the porch had returned inside. Those at the window had turned away. Killing someone was as important as going to the bathroom.

I strode into the kitchen, intent on doing what I could to save Jid. I needed to know that Larry was going to protect his son. And most importantly that he had his lover's backing. While Larry might not have any standing with this gang, Professor did. Despite not being a member of the Black Devils, he held some kind of a position within their criminal ranks that forced them to pay attention to him.

But Jid was no longer in the kitchen. Nor was Larry.

"What have you done with them?" I shouted, panicking.

Slobo had taken over the rocking chair Larry had established as his own. He was more intent on examining his revolver than answering my question.

Jo glanced at me briefly before returning to berate her boyfriend. "You've fucked us up royally. How do you plan to get us there?"

"We use fucking GPS. Your fancy phone, *ne?*" the Serb replied.

Shoni's cage was empty.

"It doesn't fucking work. That's what the damn driver was all about," Freddie said.

"I not know. I not part of your stupid plan, *ne?*"

"What have you done to them?" I yelled again. I made for the kitchen door but was blocked by Jo.

"Where is Lake Robinson?" At about the same height, she peered straight into my eyes.

"What have you done with the boy?" I retorted.

"You tell us where this Lake Robinson is, and I'll tell you where the boy is," Jo replied.

I should've given some thought to the reason behind the question, but with Jid uppermost in my mind, I didn't. "Not far from here. About five k."

"Do you know the road?"

"Yes. Now tell me what you've done with Jid."

I was tired of her runaround. Rather than waiting for her to answer, I pushed her aside and sped into the hall. I assumed Jid was in the den. Or at least I hoped he was.

"Stop," Jo ordered.

I continued walking.

"Or I'll shoot."

I wouldn't be able to protect Jid if I were dead. I stopped in midstride and whirled around to find myself once more staring into the barrel of a gun.

FIFTY-ONE

"Get your boots on," Jo ordered.

"What for? My feet are already wet." Outside I hadn't noticed the snow filling my moccasins. Now I did.

A pitter-patter came running down the hall and crashed into my legs. I bent down to pick up Shoni.

"Were you with Jid?' I asked. She replied with slobbery kisses.

"Get rid of the dog," Jo demanded.

"I want to know what you've done with the boy." I placed Shoni on the ground by my feet. She whimpered and pawed my legs, wanting to be lifted back up.

"Go find Jid," I whispered.

But she merely stared at me with her liquid brown eyes, beseeching me to hold her. I gave in.

"Tiger, honey, do something about the damn animal," Jo insisted.

The man didn't hesitate to do his girlfriend's bidding. He snatched her out of my hands before I could resist. I assumed he was putting her into her crate, but he limped past it to the back door, flung it open, and tossed her outside before I could cry out, "Stop."

Grinning, he replied. "Piece of shit. Hate dogs."

Jo shrugged. "That's my honey."

"She'll freeze to death out there," I implored. I started toward the back door, intent on rescuing her.

"Stop. Don't move another step."

I stopped when I felt her gun jammed into my ribs.

"Get back to where you were. You don't move unless I tell you."

"Please, let me bring her back in. She'll die out there."

"Can't stand ankle biters. Give me a dog with a good snarl in him anytime, like a Rottweiler, a Doberman, or a tiger." She growled. "Come here, big guy, and give me a kiss."

They entangled themselves and rubbed against each other as if they had all the privacy of a bedroom and not a kitchen filled with people.

Freddie spoke up, his voice somewhat hoarse, "Look, Jo, we've got to get moving. We're running out of time."

She broke away from her man. Rubbing her fingers along his jaw, she said, "We'll have plenty of time for playing afterward." She gave him one last lingering kiss and then turned back to me. "You, get your boots and coat on now. We're leaving in five. Freddie, start loading the snowmobile into the truck." She yelled, "Viper, we're leaving! You got all you need?"

"I'm not going anywhere," I said.

She pointed her gun back at me. "This says you are."

"I'm not leaving without Jid."

"He stays."

"He's okay," Professor said, coming up behind me. "He's with Larry. Just do as you're told, and he'll be fine."

"How do I know he's still alive?" I snapped back, and then started shouting, "Jid, where are you? I want to see you."

"In the den," the boy called back. I didn't sense any fear in his voice. "I'm helping Larry with something. Is Gerry okay?"

Good. He didn't know. Not yet. I took a deep breath. "Yeah … yeah, he's fine. Look, I'm going be gone for a while. You take care of yourself, okay? Stay with Larry."

I searched Jo's eyes to help allay my fears but saw only intransigent determination. Bébé Jean turned away when I tried to read his thoughts. I didn't bother with Slobo. He wouldn't hesitate to kill a child. I didn't get a good feeling from Freddie either.

Though I hadn't expected to see blood seeping out of every orifice, as it does with mice, I had expected to see these men show some visible reaction to the poison. But there was none, not even a nosebleed. Maybe the poison was too old.

My last hope was with Larry and the tattooed man.

"Jid's going to be okay, isn't he?" I asked. "No one is going to hurt him."

"Larry will keep him safe. That's right, isn't it, Slobo," Professor said.

The Serb had the audacity to grin, which quickly vanished under Professor's penetrating glare.

"No touch boy." He held his hand away from his gun.

This only managed to ramp up my apprehension, particularly when I realized he was staying behind. For a few minutes, I thought there would be a neutralizing influence when it looked as if Bébé Jean was staying also. After he helped with Gerry, I'd decided that he was less bloodthirsty than the others. But that changed when he told Jo that he was going with them.

"Now that the driver is dead, you need someone to drive his snowplough. I can do it."

"Good, but that means Freddie, you'll have to stay behind. You okay with that?"

"No, I'm not. You need me to identify the target. I'm the only one who knows him."

"No problem. I downloaded a photo of the guy before we left." She held up her iPhone to show a photo of a man who looked familiar, but for the moment I couldn't place him. "Besides, it's probably best you're not there in case he recognizes you. Remember, we don't want this to come back on the Devils."

I tried to close my ears, to not hear what I was hearing, for I knew with a certainty that it was my death warrant. But it also settled in my own mind that I must do my utmost to ensure Jid came out of this alive.

"Professor, can I speak with you?" I said in a low voice while I moved away from the others. I didn't want them knowing what I was about to tell him.

He hesitated for a second before following me into the hall. "Make it quick."

"I know Larry is a valuable part of your life, and you do what you can to protect him."

"What do you want?

"You would protect someone Larry deems just as valuable, wouldn't you?"

"Like who?"

"The boy. Jid is his son."

It took a few seconds for this to sink in, and when it did, his body jerked with the shock. "How do you know? Larry hasn't lived on the reserve for more than sixteen or seventeen years."

"I imagine he came back to visit friends, even girl-friends, before he was locked away thirteen years ago. Jid is almost thirteen. Larry could've got his girlfriend pregnant before he was arrested."

"But he would've shared this with me."

"Maybe his girlfriend never told him."

"The timing is there, but that doesn't mean the boy's his."

"Jid was brought up by his great-grandmother. From the things Larry has said, I think this woman was his grandmother. You just have to look at the two of them together. They have the same slight stature, their faces are the same oval shape with the same eyes, and they share similar mannerisms."

He nodded. "You're right. I've noticed this myself. Okay, so he's Larry's kid. What do you want me to do about it?"

"Keep him alive. I know this isn't going to end well for me, but I want Jid to survive. He has his whole life ahead of him. He's a smart kid. He can become what Larry never had a chance to become. You could be his mentor."

I said this last out of desperation because I thought it would appeal to the man's vanity. There was no way I wanted this supposed professor anywhere near Jid. But I didn't think it was in danger of happening. I figured if he got out of this in one piece, he would end up far from here, either in prison or on the run.

"Okay," came his answer.

FIFTY-TWO

Bébé Jean shoved me out the back door and down the stairs with such force that I almost lost my footing. A last-second grab of a roof support kept me from doing a face plant into the snow. As it was, I landed in a less than ladylike fashion at the bottom of the steps with my legs spread out like a drunken sailor and my arms pumping frantically to stay upright. I wasn't going to give him the satisfaction of falling on my bum.

"You come with me," he ordered. Squeezing my upper arm, he thrust me in front of him.

The second I felt his touch, a jolt of revulsion and fear surged through me. I twisted my arm free. "Don't you dare touch me," I yelled, backing away.

I expected him to grab me again, but he must've sensed my panic, for he said instead, "*Bon*. Get your ass to the snowplough."

"Fine, I'll do it. Just don't come near me."

I remained standing for a few seconds longer in an effort to bring my shaking under control before attempting to move forward. I followed the Ski-Doo track toward the front of the house. Jo was loading the machine with

Freddie's help into the back of the bikers' pickup. Jean trudged behind me a safe distance away.

"Auntie, auntie," Jid suddenly called out. "Where are you going?"

I turned to see him standing at the top of the porch steps. The biker stopped too, a good metre or so away.

"Stay with Larry. I'll be back soon," I lied.

"I want to come with you."

As much as I feared being separated from him, he would be safer remaining behind. "It's better you stay here, okay?"

"No, we got to stay together."

"Jid, listen to me. You'll be much safer with Larry. Trust me, okay?"

"What about you? I'm worried. It doesn't feel right you leaving like this." He started walking down the stairs, but Slobo jerked him back.

"Don't worry about me. I'll be fine. Before you know it, I'll be back with you and Shoni."

Growing impatient, Jean began walking toward me. I slowly backed up while trying to maintain my balance in the uneven footing.

"If you want … but I'm scared." Jid's voice wavered.

"Think about tonight's hockey game and scoring the winning goal, okay?" I tried not to look at the startling splotch of red and its deadly message. I wasn't sure what I would say if Jid asked me about the blanket.

"I guess." He was quiet for a second. "Do you know where Shoni is? I can't find her."

"She's outside. Look for her," I called back. But the back door slammed shut before I finished.

Although I could see the crater where Shoni had landed, the surrounding snow was too churned up to tell where she had gone.

Jean started walking toward me.

I spent another second trying to determine if the dog had gone under the porch for protection, but the drifts piled up against the footings looked impenetrable.

When the biker was almost upon me, I turned back around and resumed walking.

The snow was up to the windowsills of the cottage, while the outbuildings looked more like igloos than wooden sheds. Several fir trees had come down under their heavy load, with one cantilevered over the garden shed. The snowplough had buried my truck under another mound of snow. Eric was either going to have to bring an excavator to dig it out or wait until spring for the snow to melt away.

But what was I thinking? I was the one who was going to have to deal with the snow. I was coming back. Somehow, some way, I was going to survive. I wasn't going to write myself off, no way — not yet.

Freddie was attempting to close the door of the truck bed against the back of the snowmobile. It was a tight fit, especially with the ramp squeezed in beside it. It took him three tries before the door clicked closed.

Professor was leaning against the passenger side of the truck, rubbing his head as if it still pained him. Perhaps it had grown into a headache, which wasn't good. A headache meant a possible brain injury, which could get worse. If the man died, there went any chance of keeping Jid alive, or Larry, for that matter. He was as expendable as the boy.

As we tromped past the pickup, Jo stuck her head out from the driver's side. "Hey bitch! Don't even think of escaping. If you do, the kid's dead."

"But he's under Professor's protection." I waited for the man's confirmation.

Instead, "Don't escape," was his succinct reply. Turning his back on me, he climbed into the pickup truck.

"I told Tiger if we're not back in an hour to kill him," Jo added.

The "we" had better include me. But even if it didn't, I wasn't about to do anything that would prevent Jo from returning within the stipulated hour. However, an hour would be cutting it close.

"Lake Robinson is a twenty-five-minute drive from here, but with these snowy road conditions it will likely take longer. Can you make it two hours?"

"Google Maps says it's a fifteen-minute drive, not twenty-five. We can make the return trip easy in one hour."

So I had exaggerated. "But the road into the lake won't be ploughed. Depending on how far in you need to go, it could take thirty minutes to clear."

She shrugged. "One hour it is. If you have thoughts of getting us lost, forget it. I will be following the route on my iPhone."

"If you have a map, why do you need me?"

Ignoring me, she climbed into the truck.

"Walk," Jean ordered, advancing. I ran more than walked to the plough. I opened the door and struggled to pull myself up onto the step of the cab, which wasn't exactly designed for someone at thigh level. I closed the door and leaned against it as Jean climbed into the driver's side with considerably more finesse. But I almost tumbled out when my door abruptly opened.

"Move over," Freddie said, climbing in.

I hastily slid across the seat but was stopped by the gears to the plough filling the middle of the foot well. Freddie squeezed in beside me. I felt as if I couldn't breathe. Panic consumed me. I started to thrash around, and then I felt the cold metal of a pistol against my head. I froze.

"You are beginning to really annoy me," Freddie said. "If we didn't need you for directions, I'd kill you now."

I tried to get my panic under control.

"I thought you weren't coming," Jean said to Freddie.

"The boss lady told me to come. Thought the bitch would need watching while you drove. Looks like she was right, eh?"

FIFTY-THREE

I would admit taking a detour to the police had crossed my mind. But I'd rejected it out of fear that bringing this amount of gun power to the doorstep of the Migiskan police station would result in a battle that would get many more people killed. I could only hope that somewhere along our journey we would cross paths with a police cruiser. But since it was only a few short kilometres along the main road to the Lake Robinson turnoff, I didn't think it likely.

I agonized over the hour turnaround. There were no shortcuts to the lake. I couldn't see how I was going to get them there and back in time, especially with the lumbering speed of Gerry's truck.

"Can't you speed it up?" I asked, watching Jean manipulate the tricky gearshift.

He wasn't lying when he said he knew his way around a snowplough. He'd expertly set the wing blade at the right angle to push the snow completely off my road.

Gerry had only cleared one side of it, so Jean was forced to plough the other side to allow for easier passage. But this slowed us down even more. By the time we reached the main road, the normally three-minute trip had become eight. Fifty-two minutes to go. Thankfully, Migiskan Road was as drivable as a road could be after a major storm.

"Turn right and drive until I tell you to turn," I said. I figured it should take about eight minutes. "Can you get this truck to go faster?"

Though he ignored me, I sensed the trees beginning to move slightly faster past us. And so we plodded along the main road until we almost ran into a hydro truck blocking our way. The crew was removing a half-dead balsam that had fallen on the line. They had positioned the truck in the middle of the road so the cherry picker could be used to lift it off.

"Don't even think about it." Freddie jammed his gun into my side while at the same time shoving my head below the dash.

My skin rippled in protest. "Don't touch me. I won't budge until you tell me."

"Can't stand men, eh? You a lesbie or something?"

Just a victim of a rape, I thought.

"Not a peep," he hissed and removed his hand.

I slowly let out my breath.

I felt the cold rush of air from a window opening.

"How long you going to be?" Jean called out in French. "I got clients waiting for their roads to be cleared."

I was surprised he would risk talking to them. But he'd probably come to the same conclusion I'd reached. The chances were almost nil that these hydro workers were from the area. So they wouldn't be the least suspicious to see someone other than Gerry driving his truck.

"Give us five," one of the guys shouted back.

Shit, another wasted five minutes. If I had any thoughts of suddenly raising my head and shouting for help, the gun against my head was enough to dissuade me.

"Business gotta be good, eh? With all this damn snow. *Calice*, I never seen it so bad," the man said.

"The more the better," Jean chuckled. "I'm raking in the millions." He paused. "Any more of you guys up ahead?"

"*Oui*, a couple of crews from Vermont fixing a downed pole about five k along."

"Vermont? That's a fair distance. Where you guys from?"

"St. Bruno, just outside Montreal. We weren't so badly hit, so we could spare some crews."

"St. Bruno, eh? Small world. My buddy, Pierre Gagnon, lives there. If you see him, tell him Bébé Jean says hi."

"Sure will do. He's the…" The sudden revving of the plough's engine cut off the sentence. The truck lurched forward and then jerked to a stop, ramming the back of my head against the underside of the dash.

"Christ, what did ya do that for?" Freddie exclaimed. "You coulda castrated me."

"*M'excuse.* I hit the gas pedal by mistake."

"Hey, I forgot to tell you," the hydro guy called out. "A lot of cop cars up the road. Not sure what that's all about."

Just when I thought all hope had gone, it raised its welcoming promise.

"Jesus H. Murphy," Freddie muttered.

I heard what sounded like a truck moving.

"How far along?" Jean shouted back.

"A kilometre or so after the Vermont crews. Okay, you can go now. Good talking to you."

The plough rumbled forward. I started to raise my head, but Freddie pushed it back down again and kept it there for another minute or so. Then he released his hand. I took this to mean that I could finally sit up.

I looked back to see the hydro truck disappearing behind a curve in the road, which, apart from Jo's truck, was now as empty as the road in front. Up ahead, I could make out the hill formation and the giant white pine that marked the turnoff to Lake Robinson.

"Bitch, how much farther before we turn off?" Freddie demanded.

I debated telling him that it was a good ten kilometres to see what they would do about the police, but the feel of his gun in my ribs convinced me to be honest. "It's just up ahead."

"Christ, Jean, I don't like it. How do the pigs know we're here? Someone must've squealed."

"Relax. No one talked, unless you did?"

"What? You accusing me of being an informant?"

"*Sacrebleu*, it was a joke. No way the cops know."

"Someone must've told them. Why else they here?"

"Could be any number of reasons. An accident, a burglary."

"A grow-op," I offered, thinking of the one I stumbled onto a few years ago.

"*Oui*, a grow-up. We sure know about them, eh, Freddie?" Jean laughed and was joined by the other man.

"Not one of ours, is it?" Jean asked.

Freddie shook his head. "Nah, we don't have any in this area, though I looked into a possibility a few years back. What a laugh. The pigs could be getting rid of our competition." He broke into another loud guffaw. "But fuck, they're going to ruin our operation."

"*Pas possible*. We'll be gone long before the cops clue into there being one less judge to worry about."

FIFTY-FOUR

It took less time than it took to take a breath for me to connect the dots. "The judge" could only be one person, The Honourable Richard Meilleur, one of the most senior and well-respected judges in Quebec, known for his impartiality and fair-handedness. He was heading up a commission on organized crime and had vowed to unravel every last tentacle organized crime had interwoven into the judicial and police systems of Quebec.

He was indeed a man a gang like the Black Devils would want to silence.

He was also the judge who sent Larry to prison for life. So this hit would be more than a business arrangement for Professor. It would also be personal.

The judge's cottage was a rambling timber building like mine, though not as old, dating from just after the Second World War, when the first cottages were built on the lake. A couple of summers ago, Eric and I spent a delightful evening over dinner with him and his wife on their expansive deck overlooking the lake. But I'd heard that she'd died from cancer in the spring, and the judge hadn't been near his cottage since.

It seemed highly improbable that he would be there in such wintery weather, particularly in a cottage intended only for summer usage. But these gangsters were here, so they must be very certain of his presence. After all, they'd gone through a lot of effort springing their assassin from jail, though I couldn't begin to guess why they would take such a risk for an outsider. Surely there were more than enough gang members walking free who wouldn't hesitate to put their hand up to do the job.

Any thoughts I harboured that their intelligence was wrong were quashed the second I saw that the road into Lake Robinson had been cleared of all snow but for the latest dump. Designated a summer road, it could only mean someone had asked the municipality to keep the road open because they were staying at their cottage.

I looked up the main road toward where the police were supposed to be. A matter of a few kilometres and yet so impossibly far. If only one of them would decide to drive this way. A useless thought, I realized, since there was little I would be able to do squeezed between these two thugs with a gun poking my ribs.

Bébé Jean lowered the blade into position and aimed the truck straight at the mound of snow blocking the entrance to the road. The plough crunched through with ease and continued down the road, sending plumes of white into the air. The judge's property lay at the end of the road, a couple of kilometres away. Another five or so minutes. Thank God, the snow was light, otherwise it would take more than double that amount of time to plough our way in.

Still, the time was accumulating. Twenty-three minutes since I'd been forced to leave Jid behind. That left only thirty-seven before we had to be back at the house. It was still possible, but I had no idea the length of time it would take the tattooed man to complete the job.

What was I saying? I couldn't let him kill the judge. How could I? There had to be something I could do to stop it.

A bump in the road caused the blade knobs to knock against my leg. Maybe I could do something to render them inoperable? If the plough couldn't continue clearing the road, Professor wouldn't be able to reach the judge. But what was I thinking? They had the snowmobile. And worse, it would mean we wouldn't get back to Jid in time.

It took a few minutes for me to realize we were passing cottages. With their driveways filled in with snow and their roofs hidden under the heavy load, they'd merged into the surrounding forest. If I hadn't noticed the flickering red of a wind chime, I would've missed them.

"Christ, how much farther do we gotta go?" Freddie asked. "I thought this was going to be quick."

"There are at least five cottages. We've passed two," I replied. "We have to go through a long stretch of forest before we reach the judge's driveway. He owns all the land at the end of the lake."

"God, I hate this fucking snow," he continued. "It's screwed up everything."

"Why are we not doing it in Montreal, where the guy lives?" Bébé Jean asked. "That was the original plan."

"Too much security. And Jo caught wind that the judge was coming here for Christmas, far away from anyone."

"There will still be bodyguards."

"Maybe one or two guys, but Professor can handle them easy. And the beauty is no one will know the judge is dead until well into the New Year. By then Professor will be long gone with his bitch to his romantic getaway." He snickered.

"It's Costa Rica, isn't it?" Jean asked.

"Nah, the Seychelles. Can't be extradited back to Canada from there. No way the cops will figure it's the Viper. They never do. He leaves the kill site squeaky clean."

As if remembering my presence, he shifted his eyes in my direction. I tried to disappear into the seat. He shrugged. "Guess it don't matter." Which left me feeling decidedly queasy.

"You sure the cops won't connect the killing to us?" Jean asked.

"Nah, no way. That's why we use Viper instead of a Devil for a job like this. I suppose they might suspect, but they'll never be able to prove it." He turned his eyes fully on Jean. "Unless one of us squeals."

Jean stomped on the brake, sending us crashing into the dash. "You accuse me?"

I heard a loud honk from behind as the pickup slid to a stop.

Freddie drummed his fingers on his knee while he kept his eyes fixed on his fellow biker, then he snickered. "No need to get your balls in a knot, Bébé. Just making a point."

The two men continued to stare each other down until Freddie broke it off.

Jean hissed, "Don't you dare accuse me again."

He jammed the truck into gear, and down the road we rumbled.

We passed the last of the cottages and were heading down the narrow, tree-lined stretch of road that ended at the entrance to the judge's cottage. The minute I saw the banks of ploughed snow continuing to line the road, I knew with a sinking feeling that the judge was there.

Snow-laden boughs brushed against the truck on either side, while overhead, several fir trees had collapsed against each other, creating a winter arbor. One had fallen across the road. The plough moved it aside as if it were a matchstick.

Both men were quiet, lost in their own thoughts. I sensed a tense wariness in both.

We rounded a bend and were immediately stopped by another tree blocking the road, a massive spruce with its snow-enmeshed boughs rising a good three or more metres off the road. Jean pushed the plough against it but only dislodged snow. He reversed and tried again. More white powder came loose, but not the tree, while the truck's wheels spun with the exertion. He tried one more time.

"Fuck!" Freddie cursed. "How far away is the cottage?"

"I don't know." I tried to look for markers that would give me a sense of distance, but with everything transformed by the snow, it was impossible to tell. "Maybe another kilometre." I guessed on the far side, hoping that it would persuade them to change their minds about killing the judge. But I'd forgotten about Jo's determination.

She rapped on the window. "Why in the hell are you stopped? Move the damn thing."

"Too big. Did you bring a chainsaw?"

"Hell, no."

I knew Gerry likely had one stowed in his truck. But I wasn't about to tell these guys.

"Try again," Jo ordered.

"Move your truck back so I can get a good run."

I heard the whine of the truck reversing behind us.

"Okay!" Jo shouted.

Jean raised the blade and backed up until Jo shouted, "That's enough."

Then he lowered the blade onto the ground, slammed the truck into gear and moved forward, increasing the speed as the distance to the tree narrowed. The blade rammed into the spruce with a thud. The cab rocked. The tree rocked. The gears groaned. Branches broke sending snow, twigs, and needles flying. The tree moved until it stopped with a crunch and the whine of spinning wheels.

I noticed at the same time Freddie said, "Fuck, you slammed it against another tree. No way we're going to move it now."

I glanced at my watch. "Look, guys," I piped up. "We're running out of time. Only thirty minutes remaining. Why don't you forget the judge for the moment and get back to my place? You can pick up a chainsaw there. I have two."

FIFTY-FIVE

"Shut the fuck up!" Freddie jammed his gun back into my side.

"Easy, Freddie," Jean said. "We don't want to damage the goods before we need to."

Though I felt the pressure ease, I could still feel the hardness of the metal through the layers of clothing.

"Is there a chainsaw on this truck?" Freddie asked.

"How should I know?" I answered.

"Don't play smartass with me." Freddie jabbed harder. "I bet trees fall all the time around here. There's gotta be a chainsaw on this fucking rig. Now tell us where it is."

"I don't know. I've never been in the truck before. But like I told you, I have two saws at home."

"We're not going back, so start looking."

There was no space behind the bench seat. The glove box was far too small. That left under the seat. I bent over and felt around but only encountered a greasy rag and an empty fast food carton that had held something sticky.

"He might keep one on the outside of the truck," I suggested, wiping my dirty hands on the seat's cracked vinyl.

"Freddie, go outside and check," Jean ordered.

But the man refused to budge. Instead he rolled down his window and hollered, "Jo, Viper, see if you can find a chainsaw somewhere on the outside."

After several minutes of watching the two of them through the side-view mirrors scanning every inch of the truck, Jo finally called out, "Found it."

She held up an orange and white Stihl chainsaw with a blade that was almost double the length of mine — actually of Eric's. I was too unnerved by the whirring blade to own one myself.

"Anyone know how in the hell to use it?" she asked.

"*Oui*, I do," Jean said, jumping out of the cab.

Not wanting to remain alone inside with Freddie, I lifted my feet onto the bench seat and scooted past the blade knobs after him.

"Hey, get back here," Freddie shouted.

"You better climb out too. Your friend's going to need help clearing the tree away."

With the minutes ticking off in my head, I was desperate to get this tree removed. But I was afraid to do the math, for deep down inside I knew my buddy was running out of time.

I jumped down onto the firmness of a freshly ploughed road and hurried after Jean. He began severing the massive boughs from the trunk, sending wood chips flying. As each came loose, I pulled the branch free from the tangle and handed it off to Freddie, who tossed it over the snow bank. I had no idea where Jo and Professor were. I only knew they weren't helping.

Once Jean had exposed about a metre-and-a-half section of the trunk, he began cutting it into manageable lengths. As they dropped to the ground, he rolled them away with his boot. Once finished, there was more than enough room for a person to walk through, but not the plough. He was starting to cut into the next layer of branches when I felt more than heard a presence behind me. I turned to find Jo astride the Ski-Doo with Professor sitting behind her.

She was shouting. But with the combined noise of the chainsaw and the Ski-Doo, I had no idea what she was saying.

Professor jumped off, pushed me out of the way, and walked up behind Bébé Jean. "Stop," he yelled into his ear.

The saw jerked in the man's hand and almost fell to the ground, narrowly missing his foot. He pushed the brake to stop the blade's action and whirled around, yelling in French at the tattooed man. "Don't you dare do that again," followed by a string of "*tabernac, calice*" and other unique Quebecois swear words.

He turned off the saw.

"What do you want?" he shouted in French.

"Stop sawing. There is enough room to take the Ski-Doo through. Jo and I are going on ahead. You and Freddie wait here for us."

"But I'm supposed to take care of the bodyguards."

"The only person going near the cottage is me. I won't even let Jo near it."

"What happens if they surprise you?"

"They won't. Look, you guys brought me in to do the job without a trace, and that's what I'll do. Though with the mess you've made at the woman's house, I don't know how you'll be able to keep the Devils out of any of this shit. But that's your problem. I have a job to do, so let us through." He pulled out a pair of latex gloves and put them on with a climactic snap.

He returned to the Ski-Doo and climbed on behind Jo. As he slung himself onto the seat, his jacket flapped open to reveal several knives in long slender sheaths attached to his belt. The tools of his trade. They were too slender and deadly looking to be Eric's. Jo had brought them with her.

Jean continued to block the opening. Jo lurched the Ski-Doo forward and screamed at him. The man barely sprang away in time.

"Hell, what did you do that for?" Freddie said, walking up to him.

Jean's response was to wrap his arm around Freddie's neck and jam his gun into his back. "Throw your gun onto the ground," he ordered.

"Hey, buddy, what are you trying to do?" Freddie's voice wavered. "We're on the same side. Remember?"

"No, we're not. I'm a police officer with the Sûreté du Québec. I am holding you for questioning in the murder of two prison guards and the escape of three incarcerated convicts."

"Fuck."

"I repeat. Throw your gun onto the ground."

"Always knew there was something not right about you."

The gun bounced off Jean's boot. He winced and kicked it out of the way.

"Meg, pick it up."

I did as told and almost let it fall back to the ground, so startled was I by the weight. Never having held a loaded pistol before, I wasn't sure what to do with it.

"Point it at him, and fire if he moves, okay? But try not to hit me."

"Sure," I said with considerably more bravado than I felt.

I was terrified that I would accidentally kill the man who had become my saviour. Grasping it with two hands, like they do on TV, I pointed it at as best I could at the captured man.

"Freddie, I'm going to let go of your neck very slowly. But I still have my gun on you."

Bébé Jean released his hold.

"Now, step away very slowly."

Freddie started walking.

"That's far enough," the cop ordered. "Turn around and reach down very slowly, and remove the gun from your ankle. If you so much as make any other movement, I will shoot. Meg, keep pointing the gun at him."

I was so worried that Freddie might overpower Jean that I forgot I was holding the gun and let it point away. I aimed it back at the gangster.

Once again he dropped his pistol beside his feet.

"Walk backward until I tell you to stop," Jean said. Keeping his gun trained on the retreating man, he followed him until he reached the gun.

"Okay, that's far enough." He kicked the gun in my direction. "Meg, get this one too."

I now had two guns in my possession that I didn't have a clue how to use. This second pistol was even heavier. There was no way I could aim both guns properly, so I slipped the new one into my jacket pocket and hoped I didn't accidentally shoot my foot.

"Now, Freddie, I remember you bragging about the knife you hid on your other ankle. You used to say, 'A man never knows when he will need backup.' So reach down and pull it out very slowly and throw it on the ground."

Freddie threw it at his captor in an attempt to stab him, but Jean easily dodged it.

Not wanting to let go of my two-handed hold on the gun, I kicked the knife out of reach into the snowbank. I was still trying to digest the fact that this man who epitomized the stereotype of a biker was an undercover cop.

"Now, what are we going to do with you, Freddie?"

"The boss is gonna kill you when he finds out."

"I don't think he'll get a chance to do that. He'll be in prison by the time he discovers his golden-haired boy set him up."

The cop reached into the inside pocket of his leather biker jacket and pulled out some plastic zip ties. "My backup is to keep a couple of these handy. Never know when you might need them." He grinned. "Now walk nice and slow to the other side of the truck."

Jean kept a good couple of metres behind Freddie as the two of them squeezed between the snowplough and the pickup truck. Not sure what I was supposed to do, I decided to return to the front of the truck and meet them on the other side. That way I would be facing Freddie head on and not aiming the gun at Jean's back.

Perhaps it wasn't the smartest move, for when I inched past the wing plough, I found the two men scuffling on the ground, frantically trying to reach Jean's gun lying half submerged in the snowbank a few feet away.

I had a clear shot of Freddie's back, but when I tried to pull the trigger, I froze, afraid I would accidentally hit the cop. By the time I summoned up my nerve, the opportunity was gone.

The two men continued to flail at each other. At one point Jean's fingers were within inches of grasping the gun, but Freddie kicked his arm away. With the two men blocking the way, it was impossible for me to retrieve it.

Petrified of shooting the wrong man, there was little I could do other than watch and pray for the right outcome. Then it came to me. I could fire into the air and startle them into stopping. Maybe it would give me a clear shot at Freddie.

I gingerly placed my finger on the trigger, pointed the gun over their heads and fired into the forest. A grouse exploded from his roosting spot under a tree. Snow tumbled off branches. But the men kept fighting.

Then Freddie stopped, raised his head, and looked in my direction. Blood streamed from his nose. Before I could pull the trigger, Jean grabbed his jacket collar and smashed his head against a tire. The gangster collapsed into a senseless heap.

"*Merci*," Jean shouted.

He dragged the unconscious man over to the wing blade. Placing him in a sitting position, he pulled the man's hands behind his back and attached him to one of the metal arms with a zip tie. For extra measure he zip-tied his feet together.

"There, that should hold him," Jean said between gasping breaths. "Give me the Glock."

"The what?"

"The big gun."

I passed him the heaviest gun, which he tucked into his waistband. He walked over to where his own had sunk into the snow bank and pulled it out.

"Stay here and keep the Smith & Wesson pointed at him until I get back."

He turned to leave.

"Hey, where are you going?"

"To stop them from killing Meilleur."

"But what about Jid? The hour is almost up."

He gave no indication that he'd heard me as he disappeared through the gap in the sawed tree.

FIFTY-SIX

I didn't wait two minutes, let alone five. Freddie wasn't going anywhere. He was out cold. When he finally came to, he would barely be able to move, let alone break free. Given the extent of his nosebleed, I'd say the poison would also help to keep him immobile.

I had eleven minutes to get back to the house to save Jid. Though I had no idea how I was going to do this on my own, I couldn't sit here and wait for the cop's return, if he did return. The way my luck was going, he would end up getting killed along with the judge, and I'd find myself facing two very angry assassins intent on putting an end to their only witness.

I scrambled into their pickup, a much more luxurious model than mine. I didn't blink when I saw there was no key in the ignition. The time I'd lost my keys, Jid had shown me how to hotwire my truck.

Within minutes I had the ignition punched out with the help of a screwdriver found in the plough's glove compartment and the right wires connected to get the engine going. Unfortunately, with only one side of the road ploughed, it would be impossible to turn the truck around without getting stuck. I would have to back up the entire way to Migiskan Road.

Backing up wasn't my forte in the best of conditions. With this narrow, twisting road, it was going to be even more challenging, particularly with the pervasive whiteness blending everything into a featureless expanse. I slowly depressed the gas pedal and inched the vehicle backward, careful to keep the wheels from veering into the deeper snow. A couple of times they slid in, but I was able to stop before they dug in too deeply.

The seconds seemed to be ticking by faster than the truck was creeping backward. At this rate it would take more than eleven minutes just to cover the kilometre or so distance to the main road. So I picked up the pace.

The truck was handling well. I felt I had reversing under control. I passed the first of the five cottages. And the next one. But I got a little too cocky and a little too impatient. I lost my focus, applied too much pressure to the pedal and ended up grounding the back wheels in the snowbank.

I tried to move forward. Nothing but the sound of spinning tires. I stopped, put the gear into reverse, and slowly inched back then tried to move forward again, but without success. In frustration, I stomped on the gas and succeeded only in digging the truck in deeper.

I counted to ten and told myself to slow down. Getting stuck was far from a new experience, and I'd always managed to get unstuck, except for the one time the back tire had dropped into a ditch. It had needed Eric with his come-along and Grand Cherokee to rescue me. But that wasn't going to happen this time.

I jumped out of the truck. It didn't look as if the tire was caught in a ditch, but it did look as if I was turning the front wheels too much. So I climbed back in, positioned the tires straighter, and began a slow back-and-forth rocking motion by putting the gear into reverse than into first, and so on. After three or four times, the truck sprang free.

I continued the slow backward crawl, this time ensuring my mind remained fixed on the task at hand. Within minutes I'd passed the remaining cottages and was backing onto the main road. I had four minutes to get to Three Deer Point.

I rammed the truck into gear and sped down the road toward my lane. Going after the police was a non-starter. They were in the opposite direction and might no longer be there. Nor did I consider driving to the reserve to get Will Decontie and his constables. That would take at least twenty minutes. By then Jid could be dead.

The hydro truck was gone. They had been my last resort. I was going to ask them to go after the police. Not now. I would have to rescue my buddy on my own.

As I charged up my road, I tried to formulate a plan, but my mind was in too much of a whirl. At least I had the wherewithal not to drive right up to the house, but to stop short of it, behind a clump of spruce trees. I jumped down from the cab and quietly closed the door before remembering I'd left the gun lying on the passenger seat.

I hastily retrieved it and then remained by the truck, listening for sounds that would tell me what was happening in my house. But all I heard was the stirring of the pines and the whisper of snow sliding off a nearby tree. From farther down the lake came the faint whine of a Ski-Doo.

I walked along the drive until I could make out the house through the trees. I pulled branches aside to get a better view. The house seemed almost too dark and too quiet. Was I too late?

I tried to determine the best way to get inside without alerting Slobo. The back door was too risky. He was likely in the kitchen or the den. That left the only two remaining entrances, the front door or the dining room door.

The damage caused by the tree ruled out the front door, while the deep drifts would make accessing the dining room door slow and difficult, unless I used the verandah. But if the Serbian happened to be in the living room, he would see me. To complicate matters, the steps onto the verandah were blocked by the gnarled branches of the pine, so I would have to climb over the railing. Not an easy undertaking in this deep snow.

A face suddenly appeared in Eric's office window. I ducked. The height told me it wasn't Jid. Likely Slobo on the lookout for his girlfriend. The face vanished.

I could just make out the edge of the red blanket covering poor Gerry. His attempt to save us had ended in disaster. Why wouldn't my attempt end the same way? This monster was a hardcore killer. Did I really think I could outsmart him and spirit the boy away out from under his gun? But I had no choice. I had to save Jid.

If only I knew the boy was still alive. Even though Professor had placed him under his protection, I didn't trust the Serb. He hated the other man. I could see him killing the boy out of spite.

I had one more worry. If the undercover cop failed to stop the assassination, Jo and Professor would return to Three Deer Point. Then it would be three of them against me.

Enough dithering. I had to act now.

FIFTY-SEVEN

I crept closer to the house and halted behind the white mound that was my truck. I could just make out where Slobo had started clearing the snow off the front of the vehicle. But if he were wanting to use it, he'd need a lot of muscle power to remove it from its icy prison, something I didn't see him expending any way other than in fighting.

It looked as if the wraparound verandah was relatively snow-free where it abutted the house. Although this would provide an easier passage to the dining room door, I would have to sneak past a wall of windows without being seen. Although I wasn't comfortable with the risk, I felt I had little choice. It was the easiest and quickest way to get into the house.

My first challenge was to cross unseen the open expanse to the path Jid and I had created in our aborted escape. Unfortunately, it would place me in full view of the windows in Eric's office and the den. Another risk I had to take.

I pulled the pistol from my pocket, although I wasn't certain I could actually use it. I waited another minute to ensure Slobo had left the office. It proved to be a smart move when a dark shadow appeared in the den window. My heart skipped. It could be Jid. The person was nowhere near the height of Slobo and seemed too short to be Larry. But maybe this was wishful thinking on my part. Still it was enough to spring me into action. Jid was alive.

Gripping the gun firmly, I sprinted along the snowmobile track to where we had broken through and scurried along our path to the side of the house. I was about to steal around to the front when the back door slammed, its sudden sound cutting through the muffled silence like a rifle shot.

I plastered myself against the stone foundation and waited, not daring to breathe. Because the back part of the house was recessed, they wouldn't be able to see me, unless they ventured onto the snowmobile track.

Boots echoed on the porch's wooden planking and then thudded down the stairs. I pressed further against the wall. When the Serbian came into view, I dropped down behind a hump of snow that was a global pine. I steeled myself for the man to appear along the snowmobile track. The most I could do would be to bury myself in the snow covering the pines and pray he wouldn't see me.

Wait a minute. I had the gun. What if I missed and he shot me instead? That would be the end of Jid. Could I chance it? I'd never fired a gun before. I'd flunked archery at summer camp because I couldn't hit the target. Still, I had to try.

I poked my head above the shrub. The man was standing with his back to me only a few feet from the bottom of the stairs. He was zipping up his jeans. I dropped my head the second he turned in my direction. It was easily fifteen metres away. Could I hit him?

I lifted the heavy pistol up with both hands, willing them to stop shaking. Just as I was about to stand up to fire, I heard the thud of his boots on the stairs. The back door closed with a resounding bang.

It took several long minutes for me to settle down before I could start moving. A conflicting mixture of disappointment and relief overwhelmed me. I had come that close to killing a man. Even though this monster was the most odious man I had ever encountered, I didn't think I had it in me to kill him.

I rounded the corner and started walking along the front of the house. Though Jid and I had left a deep trench, it was still hard going and slowing me down too much. I worried that at any moment I would hear the sound of Gerry's snowplough returning. I had no idea whether it would be the cop driving, or Jo. I only knew I didn't want to be standing in full view when it arrived.

When I reached the office windowsill, there wasn't much I could do other than duck my head, keep walking, and pray no one was inside. I stopped when I reached the snow-covered trunk of the downed tree. Though the verandah roof hadn't completely collapsed, I couldn't see an opening large enough for me to squeeze under it so I could climb onto the verandah. But there looked to be room on the other side of the tree.

As I clambered over the trunk, I noticed how firmly wedged it was against the house. I pushed on it a few times with my full weight. It didn't budge. Thick, sturdy branches ran up the trunk almost as if they were stairs. I decided to use this unexpected gift. I would climb onto the roof and get into the house the way Jid and I had escaped: through the window. The second floor would also be safer. The cold would keep the Serbian downstairs.

I used to be a master at tree-climbing, but that was when I was a tomboy intent on impressing the boy living next door. It came to a sudden end when I fell out of a particularly challenging maple and broke my arm. Fortunately, this pine was at about a forty-five-degree angle, so climbing it wouldn't be as difficult. Since it had fallen when the blizzard was almost at its end, there was only a modest amount of snow to deal with. Within minutes I reached the verandah roof and was testing it to ensure it would hold my weight. While several roof joists had broken and were detached from the wall on the other side of the broken tree, they looked to be still intact in the direction I wanted to go.

I tentatively crawled onto the roof. It held. I stood up and shuffled through the snow toward the side of the house overlooking the frozen expanse of Echo Lake. Thankfully, the snow muffled any sound my boots would make. From the direction of the Forgotten Bay Fishing and Hunting Camp, I could hear the Ski-Doo. Although it sounded louder, I didn't think it was coming my way.

I did, however, hear the faint whine of another motor some distance behind me. It was too close to be a vehicle on the main road. Gerry's snowplough was returning. It had better be the cop coming to my aid.

I hastened around the corner to my bedroom window.

FIFTY-EIGHT

The window stuck before I'd managed to slide it up a third of the way. I might have lost weight, but squeezing through such a narrow gap wasn't going to happen. I jiggled and thumped it as quietly as I could, but it refused to budge. I couldn't even pull it down. I tried the window of the next room, and up it went, miraculously, as if the slider had been greased.

I was expecting to feel warmth, at least a warmer temperature than outside, so was taken aback when I felt air as cold if not colder coming from the room. Though the power had been out since yesterday afternoon, I was still surprised by how far the temperature had plunged.

But it was okay. This arctic chill was on my side. I could be assured that Slobo would be downstairs, along with Larry and Jid, in a room with a fire.

Fortunately, the door to the hall was closed, so I scrambled over the windowsill into the room without fear of discovery. I removed my boots, tiptoed to the door, and opened it a crack. It seemed safe enough, so I opened the door fully and listened. The house was quiet — almost too quiet as if it were empty. Yet I'd seen Jid very much alive less than five minutes ago ... or had it been Larry instead?

I ran down the hall to the stairwell. If Jid were alive, he would be in the den or kitchen. I should be able to hear him from the top of the stairs. But before I was halfway there, footsteps rang out directly below me. I scurried into the first open doorway and brought the door almost to a close.

"Where the fuck Jo?" the biker muttered. "She late."

He started up the stairs. "Fuckin' cold. I hate it. Hate fuckin' country. I go back to Serbia."

By the time he reached the top of the stairs, I'd completely shut the door. I assumed he was coming upstairs to use the bathroom and then remembered his visit outside.

He knew I was in the house!

I searched the room for a place to hide.

He hobbled down the hall toward me.

The house was too old for closets, and the armoire too narrow and low for me to fold my frame into. That left the narrow brass bed I used to sleep in when a child. I jammed myself under it and prayed.

The footsteps continued past my door.

I heard him enter my bedroom and the sound of drawers opening. He was raiding the drawers, probably for warm clothes. I relaxed.

The footsteps came out of the bedroom and down the hall toward me. They stopped.

"Window is open," he muttered.

Shit. I'd forgotten to close it.

"Snow on floor," he mused.

Double shit.

I listened to him walk into the room where I'd come through the window.

I suddenly remembered my boots. I'd left them next to a chair. Maybe in the low light he wouldn't notice.

"Larry, is boy with you?" he shouted from the hall.

Thank God. Jid *was* still alive. So too Larry.

"Yeah, he's with me in the den," Larry answered. "Why?"

I knew where they were.

"I have strange feeling," Slobo answered.

The Serb's footsteps halted outside my door. Panic set in. The door opened. I knew I should move farther out of sight, farther against the wall, but I couldn't. I waited, expecting at any second to feel his vile touch as he dragged me out from under the bed.

Instead, the door clicked shut. I heard him padding, one foot lighter than the other, back down the hall to the stairs and down them.

I slowly let out my breath. Only then did I remember the gun.

FIFTY-NINE

I lay under the bed, quivering from head to toe, while the memory of the man's grasping fingers and scraping hardness consumed me. What a fool I was to think I could save Jid from this … this personification of evil. There was no way I could leave the safety of this room. Fear had taken over.

If only I'd gone after the police or headed to the rez to get Decontie. But I'd been too impatient, too certain that Jid's time had run out. Now his rescue was in jeopardy because I'd convinced myself I could do it all on my own.

But I couldn't, despite the gun. I'd be too afraid to fire it, too worried I would hit Jid, too cowardly to actually kill someone.

I breathed in deeply and tried to focus on counting to calm my racing heart. My jacket had formed an uncomfortable lump under my back. I attempted to smooth it out, but my hands were shaking too much. I could feel the iciness of the floor creeping through my jeans.

But I couldn't just lie here and wait for something to happen. I had to do whatever I could to save Jid. Since I couldn't rescue him myself, the only other option was to retrace my steps to the gangsters' truck and drive out to get Decontie.

I lay a few minutes longer, summoning up my courage. After Slobo descended the stairs, I'd heard nothing more from below. He was waiting for Jo. She could be arriving at any moment.

I pushed myself over the cold planking until I was free of the bed. It took me several tries before I was steady enough to stand up. While I could escape onto the verandah roof through the window in this room, I needed my boots from the other room. My hand was trembling so much, I could barely clasp the door handle. I nudged it open, waited another minute before daring to step into the hall. I heard movement coming from the den, but no voices.

I tiptoed as silently as a mouse along the hardwood toward the open door of the neighbouring bedroom. A floorboard creaked. I stopped, held my breath, and waited. No reaction. I continued.

I turned to go through the doorway when a voice suddenly rang out.

"Leave me alone!" Jid shouted.

At the same time the roar of an engine sounded from the front of the house.

"Jo!" Slobo shouted. "About time you come." I heard him hobble down the hall toward the front door.

Without another thought I was running to the top of the stairs in time to see the man's back disappear into Eric's office. I raced down to the den. It was only as I entered the room that I realized I was holding the gun. Jid and Larry stared at me, open-mouthed.

"Quick. We've got to go." I gestured frantically for the two of them to follow.

Jid responded, but Larry remained seated on the sofa.

"Run upstairs and wait for me in the room with the open window."

The boy scrambled up the stairs. Larry didn't move. He seemed listless, with his body leaning to one side and his hands lying limply on his lap.

"You'd better hurry. He could be back at any second," I urged.

"Forget about me. Take the kid."

"No, you have to come too."

"He won't hurt me, but he's gonna kill the boy."

"You can't stay."

"I'm hurtin' real bad inside. I'll only slow you down. I'll make a diversion while you get outta here with the boy. Now go!"

"Not so fast, bitch." I could feel Slobo's hot breath on my neck at the same time as the metal barrel jammed into my back. I flinched but had the wherewithal to do the only smart act I'd done since this nightmare started. I hid my gun in my pocket.

"Come here, kid, or I kill the bitch."

I heard Jid's patter coming down the stairs.

"Please, don't hurt my auntie." His voice wavered. He came up beside me. I wrapped my arm around his thin shoulders and held him close.

He was alive. That was all that mattered.

"You can do whatever you want with me, just let Jid go," I said. "He's only a boy. He can't harm you."

"Shut fuck up. Get your ass over there."

He pushed me toward Larry. Maintaining a tight grip on Jid, I sandwiched him between his father and me. If Slobo fired his gun, Larry or I would be hit before his son.

The man limped into the room and stood directly in front of us. "What I do with you?"

"You give them to me," came a familiar voice from the hall. Professor and his writhing snakes stepped into the room. Both arms ended in taper-thin stilettos.

The Serbian didn't turn around. He'd been waiting for him.

"Not so fast, Mister Professor," Slobo said, enunciating every letter of his name. "They belong to me. Where Jo?" He kept his gun aimed at us.

"I hope you said your proper goodbyes. You won't be seeing her anymore. She's dead."

SIXTY

While the two enemies jousted, Larry slumped over onto Jid and against me. For a brief moment, I felt his hand in my jacket pocket, and then he struggled to sit upright.

"You bastard," Slobo hissed, his face twisted in fury. "You kill her." He raised his gun and started to turn around to face Professor.

Larry lunged from the sofa, my gun in his hand. He fired at the same time as Slobo's gun went off. With a quiet "Oomph," the Serbian crumpled to the floor, almost on top of Larry. The silver hilt of a knife stuck out of his back, next to a tiny red bullet hole.

Professor sauntered toward the dead man. "Actually, it was Bébé Jean who had the pleasure of getting rid of the bitch." He extracted his knife and wiped it with a blood-stained cloth removed from an inner jacket pocket. "They cost too much to throw away." He smiled and then leaned over his lover.

I didn't ask where Jean was. I figured the only way that Professor could be here was by killing the cop.

He gently nudged his friend. "Larry, you can get up now. We have to leave."

"I think he's dead."

"No, that can't be. The bastard's shot whizzed past my ear. It wasn't anywhere near P'tit Chief." He ran his hands gently over his friend, searching for the wound and found none. He slapped him on the face. "Come on, wake up. Don't scare me like this."

I knelt down beside Larry, searched for a pulse, and found none. "I'm sorry, Professor, he's gone. He's not going to wake up."

"No, it can't be. We were going to spend the rest of our lives together basking in the sun. I was going to teach him the best the world has to offer. Wake up, *mon petit chou.*"

I noticed fresh blood at the site of Larry's injury. "He died saving you. I think when he went after the Serbian, he tore something inside."

Professor moaned and collapsed onto his lover.

For a few seconds I felt sorry for the man. Then, grabbing Jid's hand, I pulled him off the sofa.

"We have to get out of here."

I had no idea what Professor would do with us when he stopped his mourning, but I didn't intend to wait around to find out.

Jid pulled back. "I want to say goodbye to him." His eyes were brimming with tears. "He's my dad."

"I know. He died trying to save you. But we have to go."

"No. I want to help him on the way to the Creator."

"Okay, but be quick."

He pulled his amulet through the neck of his sweatshirt, loosened the drawstring, and shook some dried tobacco onto his palm. He knelt down beside his father, gently closed his eyes, and sprinkled the tobacco onto his eyelids and his forehead, while chanting softly in Algonquin. Professor stopped his moaning and joined the boy with his own chanting, which sounded vaguely Gregorian.

Larry likely wasn't the kind of man Jid had dreamed of for a father, but when he finally met him, it didn't matter. What mattered was that for a few brief hours the two of them had been able to be father and son.

I tensed at the faint sound of footsteps in the kitchen.

"Jid," I whispered. "Someone's here. Come over by me."

Terrified that Freddie had somehow freed himself, I backed against the wall next to the door and placed Jid on the other side of me.

"Do you want this?" He held a gun with the grip, waiting for me to grasp. It was the one his father had taken from me.

I gripped it firmly. This time I knew I would shoot.

I listened to the patter of footsteps slowly coming down the hall in our direction. They stopped and went into the dining room and then came back out and continued toward us.

I placed my finger on the trigger and pointed the gun at the opening.

A floorboard creaked. A male voice muttered.

The footsteps stopped right at the opened doorway. I could hear the man breathing as I pressed farther against the wall.

I steeled myself to make the killing shot.

"*Sacrebleu*," he muttered.

I saw the gun barrel before I saw the man.

"Stop!" I shouted. "Jean, it's me."

As I slowly lowered my gun, he turned his away from me and pointed it at Professor. The cop motioned for Jid and me to move away.

The tattooed man remained seated on the ground with the head of his dead lover on his lap. Without a single glance or sign indicating that he knew his freedom was about to end, he continued caressing the still face while chanting softly.

"Guy Charbonneau, or should I call you Professor, raise your hands slowly in the air," Jean ordered.

Unlike guns, knives are much easier to tuck into unlikely spots. While I'd seen him remove the stiletto that had killed Slobo, I didn't see where he had hidden it.

Professor continued to ignore the cop.

"Do it now!" Jean yelled. With his feet braced and his finger on the trigger, he pointed his pistol straight at the man's snake-covered head.

Professor brushed the hair from Larry's unseeing eyes and kissed him full on the lips. Then he slowly lifted his head and stared at Jean. For what seemed like interminable minutes, he kept his unwavering amber gaze on the cop. Without shifting his eyes, he eased his hand down toward his waist. A gun roared. The snakes quivered and lay still as the tattooed man gradually slumped to the ground. His blood pumped out onto his lover.

Jean waited for the body to stop twitching and then stepped over Slobo to reach Professor. He felt the pulse. "Dead."

He pulled out one of the man's arms, expecting, as I did, to find a knife. The hand was empty. So too was his other hand, except for a slender brown feather that looked to be a match with Larry's earring. We both saw the silver gleam of a hilt sticking out from his shirtsleeve.

"I was so sure he was going to throw a knife," he said.

"I think he wanted it to end this way," I replied.

"Meg, Meg! Are you okay?" came a shout from the kitchen. "What in the hell is going on?"

Eric! Eric was here. I ran.

SIXTY-ONE

Yesterday the sun came out for all of one hour and added a momentary sparkle to an otherwise depressing day. But it wasn't enough to raise me from the dreary depths into which I had sunk. Today's grey skies only made me more miserable.

This morning Eric had had to remind me that today was Christmas Eve. But I merely shrugged and said, "So what." I didn't feel in the least Christmassy. Nor did I want to bother with the big day. We could skip it and head straight into the New Year without a stop at New Year's Eve for all I cared.

Thank God, my sister had let us know they wouldn't be coming. With our phone service still out of commission, she'd contacted Will at the police station via emergency channels. I guessed that, as a judge, she had privileged access. She told him that as a member of the judiciary, she couldn't be seen having anything to do with a crime scene. Only as she was terminating the call did she remember to ask how I had fared. So much for sisterly love.

The power was still out. When it did come back on, Eric and I would have one godawful mess to clean up. I fully expected to be greeted by burst pipes, flooded floors, carpets soaked in blood, police tape, chalk outlines, and boot prints smeared over the hardwood floors. As an added touch, I'd probably find a bullet hole or two in the cherry panelling.

I wanted no part of it. I would rather stay here in Eric's cozy bungalow and never go near Three Deer Point again. The den, where Eric and I relaxed from life's ups and downs, would never be the same again. I would never be able to rid my mind of the images of the three bloody bodies splayed out on the carpet nor forget the never-ending night spent in hell trying to keep Jid and me alive.

When the police kicked us out of Three Deer Point, we were lucky to have Eric's house on the reserve to retreat to. Reluctant to sell, he'd been renting it out since moving in with me. Fortunately for us, the house was between renters. Though it was empty of furniture, thanks to Will we had a mattress, a couple of well-used armchairs, and a small table.

Within an hour of our taking up residence, the police chief arrived with his van jammed with items from his basement, including a kettle and other cooking utensils and some groceries, which brought a smile to Eric. Will also brought his two brawny sons to clear a path through the deep drifts from the road to the front door and carry the furniture inside.

In the interests of keeping warm, we set up house in the living room and placed everything close to the fireplace. Thanks to the firewood left behind by the renters, this room was bursting with heat, so much so that I finally felt warm enough to crawl out from under the duvet.

Shoni was nestled in my lap. She hadn't strayed far from us since Eric found her shivering and whimpering on the back porch. He figured she'd hidden under it until she smelt his familiar scent and knew safety was at hand. She seemed to have survived her ordeal with little outward effect other than a skittish reaction to sudden loud noises. It didn't seem to have dampened her kisses, either. She was forever lathering both of us with wet, sloppy licks. I took this as her way of saying she was very glad her life had returned to normal.

Jid, Eric, and I, along with the puppy, fled as the police overran the house. We were barely given enough time to gather clothes and other personal belongings before we were hustled into the back seat of Will's official SUV. During the drive, I let Eric and Will do all the talking. I wasn't up to speaking, nor was Jid. We simply sat in the back seat on either side of Eric, clinging to him as if we never wanted to let go, while we tried to come to terms with the last twenty hours. We probably would for the next while to come.

Will drove us straight to the Health Centre to ensure we hadn't suffered any serious health problems. Apart from bruises, a cut or two, and chafed wrists, we were both physically okay. Mentally was another matter, but the nurse didn't attempt to explore the possible repercussions to our mental well-being. She merely suggested that if we needed counselling, it was available through the Health Centre.

Eric had held me close and whispered that he would be there when I needed him, and always would be. But that was about all that was said between the two of us. I wasn't yet up to discussing the nightmare, nor did I want to broach the events leading up to his door-slamming departure. So we kept our conversation to day-to-day banalities. It was fine by me, but I wasn't so certain about Eric. Still, I knew him to be a very patient and understanding man. He would wait until I was ready.

After the medical examination, Will, along with an SQ officer, interviewed Jid and me and took our statements. Jid's interview was cut short when his aunt stormed into the room, demanding, as the boy's official guardian, that he be released to her care immediately. She shouted that it was my fault her nephew was almost killed. If I hadn't lured the boy to my house, if I hadn't let those murderers in, her nephew would never have been exposed to such danger. Eric had tried to calm her down, but without success.

It ended with her dragging a distraught Jid out of the Health Centre with a warning that she would never allow him to come to my house again. I was too stunned to try to dissuade her. Knowing how much he disliked his aunt, I was deeply worried about the effect this additional stress would have on him.

Both Eric and Will tried to convince her not to be so rash, but legally there was nothing they could do to stop her. At least Eric was able to convince her that Jid should spend time with Summer Grass Woman. The highly respected elder had helped me at a difficult point in my life. I knew she would provide the kind of healing Jid needed.

I already missed him, his impish grin and his *joie de vivre*. Even Shoni acted as if she missed him too when she ambled restlessly through the house, as if in search of him. When I got my energy back, when I felt like my old self, I would do what I could to bring him back into my life.

After they left, the SQ cop and Will continued to drill me about the ordeal. I told them everything I knew. The only event I kept from them was the rape. The monster was dead. There seemed little need to bring it up.

I hadn't yet found the right moment to tell Eric. I didn't know if I would. It made me feel dirty and ashamed. I blamed myself for winding the man up. It was better to keep it to myself, and maybe with time I could bury it so deep, I would convince myself it never happened.

I heard stomping on the front porch. I tensed, knowing it couldn't be my husband.

It was too soon. He'd left less than an hour ago to make the two-and-a-half-hour drive to Ottawa to pick up his daughter at the airport. We'd debated whether she should come and in the end decided it was a time for family. Unlike my sister, Teht'aa wouldn't mind camping out in her father's empty house. I liked her. We had become good friends. It would be nice to focus on something other than the nightmare. Besides, she would be a good buffer between Eric and me should things become awkward.

A loud knock rang through the house and with it the unwanted memory of the knock that started everything. I froze. Was I always going to react with fear whenever someone knocked at my door?

The SQ officer had asked me several times why I'd opened the door to two such unsavoury strangers. It was as if he didn't think my reason for wanting to help the injured man was good enough. Eric didn't comment one way or the other. He'd merely kissed me on the forehead and said everything was going to be okay. But was it?

The knock sounded again.

SIXTY-TWO

I relaxed when I saw the blond-framed visage of Bébé Jean through the door window. I was still having difficulties reconciling this man who looked the epitome of a Black Devil with the undercover cop he had turned out to be.

"I'm on my way back to Montreal," he said, rubbing his ungloved hands to keep them warm. "I wanted to let you know that we've finished the investigation at your house. It's all yours." His English sounded as if he was born to it. The French accent must've been part of his cover.

"You look cold. Would you like to come in and have a cup of hot tea before you set out?"

"Thanks. Sounds good."

Shoni scurried out of his way, despite his attempts to pat her. It was going to take some time before she would be used to strangers, particularly strange men.

"I'm afraid we've left your house in a mess," he said, enclosing his hands around the hot mug as he sat in the other chair. He angled it closer to the fire.

"I've expected as much. Though given all that has happened, I may just sell it. I'm not sure I can live there again." I sat down and rewrapped the duvet around me. The puppy resumed her place on my lap.

"You have a beautiful house. It looks as if it has been in your family a long time. If you don't mind my saying, don't make any quick decisions. I find with crimes of this nature that time is a great healer. Often victims later regret decisions made in the heat of the moment. So wait until you've had a chance to mull things over."

"You sound like my husband. That's what he said last night when I mentioned selling."

"Eric Odjik, isn't it? I remember when he played hockey. Even though I'm a Canadiens fan, I'll never forget the winning goal he scored against us in the Stanley Cup. That was some goal."

"You don't look old enough."

He laughed. "It's amazing what a bottle of peroxide can do." He ran his fingers through his scraggly blond hair. "Tools of the trade. A nice man, your husband. We had a good chat yesterday when he dropped by the house."

"I didn't know he'd gone."

"He came to pick up the Ski-Doo he left on Tuesday."

Something else I didn't know. I'd assumed he'd arrived in his Grand Cherokee.

"Apparently the SQ were blocking the entrance to your road and wouldn't let him through because of the ongoing operation. So he came in by Ski-Doo via the lake."

"Probably one of the fishing-camp machines."

I thought back to the Ski-Doo I'd heard. I'd been so happy and relieved to see him that I never thought to ask how he'd managed to arrive at just the right moment.

"I haven't had a chance to thank you for saving Jid

and me. If you hadn't come when you did, I don't think I would be talking to you today."

"Thanks. I will admit it was touch and go whether I'd reach you two in time. But from the way you were holding that Smith & Wesson when you almost shot me, I think you would have handled yourself very ably." He chuckled in a way that so reminded me of Eric.

He'd only been gone an hour, and already I was missing him.

"I've been so focused on myself, I never thought to ask about Judge Meilleur. I assume you reached him in time."

"Remember the cops the Hydro guy mentioned? They were setting up a perimeter around his cottage."

"But we saw no evidence of them on the road into his place."

"They came in via Ski-Doo from across the lake. The intent was to keep their presence unknown in order to capture Professor. Before I left Montreal, I let my contact know that the location of the hit had changed to the cottage."

"How did Professor manage to escape?"

"I think he sensed something wasn't right. Before they reached the cottage, he made Jo turn around and go back. Jo tried to run me down, but I jumped out of the way. As she turned the machine to come after me again, I shot her. Professor tossed her body aside and took off before I could shoot him. I ran like hell back to the snowplough. I tell you, I don't think that old snowplough ever went so fast. I was very worried I would be too late."

"Lucky for us, you weren't."

I went over and kissed him on both cheeks in Quebecois fashion. "Many, many thanks from both Jid and me."

"How's the kid doing?"

"I'm not sure. He's with his aunt. He's a good kid with a lot of inner strength. I think he'll be fine. To go through what he did and to lose a father on top of it will be doubly hard for him."

"Yeah, I heard Larry was his father. Tough." He took a sip of his tea. "How are you doing?"

"It's been difficult, but I'll survive." The puppy slipped off my lap onto the floor.

"How are you feeling?" Though I hadn't seen any outward signs of discomfort, I thought I should ask. "I should let you know that I put mouse poison in the scrambled eggs."

He laughed. "So that was it. I thought you'd done something with the food. Apart from a few stomach cramps, I've had no adverse effects, but I didn't eat anywhere near the amount of eggs the other two did. It helps to explain the extent of Slobodan's blood loss. I'm afraid he left a lot behind on your carpet. Freddie's nose took a long time to stop bleeding, too. He's using it to accuse me of police harassment. What a guy. I guess I'll have to make sure they give him the antidote, and I'd better take it too, although it's unlikely the poison will do either of us much damage. I think humans have to ingest a few boxes before it can cause serious harm."

"I didn't think it would, but I felt it was worth a try. I assume that you had nothing to do with the prison break."

"God, no. If I had, it never would've happened and three men would be alive today."

"Do you know anything about Professor? I found him a very intriguing man, full of contradictions."

"He's been on our radar for a very long time. One of your classic hitmen, but he was so damn good, we could never catch him. The only offense they could nail him on was tax evasion on the money he'd locked away in the Caymans. I gather several million was involved. The assassin business must be good. When I discovered he would be doing this job for the Devils, I knew it was now or never. The main reason for inserting myself in the operation."

The puppy padded toward the man, her nose in the air, sniffing. But she chickened out before she got within touching range.

"Do you know why Professor became a hitman? After all, he had a very respectable job as a university professor."

"I believe he got his taste for blood while he was living in France. He was a champion fencer. Though he didn't win a medal at the Olympics, he ended up in the top five. When he left the country he left a couple of bodies behind, one killed by a sword, the other a stiletto. The French police suspected him, but they couldn't prove it. They brought him to our attention a couple of years ago after a French national was killed in Quebec City with a similar MO to the stiletto death in Nice. He was very good at his job. He never left so much as a trace behind, DNA or otherwise."

Shoni approached again and was within sniffing distance of his legs before she scampered away. Jean dangled his hand as an invitation for a pat.

"It still doesn't answer the question of why?"

"I think it is a simple answer of liking it and being good at it. The money didn't hurt either."

Finally Shoni grew brave enough to sniff his hand. He held it very still while she gave it a thorough once-over. She approached closer and received a delicious ear rub for her courage. Next she was on his lap, licking his face.

The puppy was going to be okay. I hoped I would be able to say the same about me.

"I know he liked the finer things in life. Maybe a professor's salary wasn't enough to support the kind of lifestyle he wanted. Do you know the reason for the snake tattoos?"

"Sorry, I can't help you there. But maybe it was to get the message across that he was as fast and deadly as a snake. It sounds as if you might have liked the guy."

"I wouldn't go as far as to say liking. Though he scared me, he treated Jid and me well, apart from one or two instances, not like that dreadful Slobodan."

"Yeah, if a guy ever deserved to be dead, he did. He was a mean son of a bitch. Exactly the kind of enforcer the Devils like to use. He's left a lot of bodies behind too. Not as many as Professor, but enough, and they weren't always tidy, instant kills like Professor's. He was also a suspect in a couple of rape cases, but they could never pin them on him." As he mentioned the rapes, he kept his gaze steady on me.

I squirmed and concentrated on the flames licking the glass window of the fireplace.

"Not sure if anyone asked you about the ripped clothes we found in your bathroom during our investigation."

I continued staring at the fire. Should I tell him? "Sorry, no one mentioned anything to me. I'm not sure what clothes you are talking about?"

I felt his eyes fixed on me, but I ignored them.

To fill the silence, I asked, "What do you know about Jo?"

"Not much. She was a biker chick. Got her jollies by hanging around the clubhouse. If she were a male, she would have become a full patch member. But being a female, she couldn't. So she used Slobodan to satisfy her thirst for danger and for blood. I don't think she loved him, but he was sure turned on by her."

"Since she wasn't a real Black Devil, how did she manage to be in charge of such a big operation?"

He chuckled. "Easy. After Slobodan went to jail, she took up with the boss. He had her running a number of activities usually handled by a Devil. Needless to say, there were a few bruised egos within the gang." He placed the puppy on the floor and stood up. "I should be on my way. A long drive ahead of me."

I followed him to the door. "What happens to you now? I don't imagine you can go back to being Bébé Jean."

"You've got that right. With every Devil in the province out gunning for me, I'm going to have to lay low. But I can only take a desk job for so long." He shrugged a typical Gallic shrug before opening the door.

"By the way, what is your real name?"

"Better for both of us if you don't know." He reached into his pocket and pulled out a scrap of paper. "Do you have a pen?"

I ran back into the living room to retrieve one from my purse.

Placing the paper against the wall, he wrote a phone number on it. "It's not easy going through what you've just been through. Sometimes you need to talk to someone who can relate. This is the number of my counsellor. She is very good and has helped me through a couple of difficult situations. She can help you too."

He started to leave and then turned back. "Please, don't keep it to yourself. I know from experience that it will only eat at you until like a cancer it becomes too big to handle. If you don't think you can talk to her about it, talk to someone you are close to, like your husband. He's a good man. He'll understand."

Before I could respond, he was striding down the walkway to his car. With a final wave he was gone.

As I walked back into the living room, I noticed a strange noise coming from the kitchen. It took me a couple of seconds to realize it was the fridge.

Hallelujah, the power was back on.

SIXTY-THREE

"Merry Christmas, my *Miskowàbigonens*." Eric rolled over, wrapped his arms around me, and planted a big kiss on my lips.

I tried not to flinch and willed myself to respond the way he wanted me to, but the images of the monster wouldn't release their hold on me.

"A very Merry Christmas to you too." I caressed his dimples, kissed the tip of his nose, and jumped up off the mattress before he decided to add more zest to his holiday greeting.

"I'll start coffee. Why don't you make us the perfect Christmas breakfast? Teht'aa should be here soon."

The two of them had arrived later in the afternoon than expected. I'd begun to worry that they had been involved in an accident. But when I saw the bags of groceries coming into the house, I forgave him.

We spent an enjoyable Christmas Eve dinner catching up on the latest happenings in his daughter's life in Yellowknife, including a new man, before she had to rush off to visit with friends.

I swore every time I saw her she was more beautiful, with her flowing raven locks, sculpted facial features, and flashing almond eyes, the same soft grey as her father's. She was tall and slim; her dimples were the only other feature she had inherited from him.

Since our makeshift sleeping accommodations didn't promote privacy, she was staying with a friend. She'd promised to join us for breakfast.

"Come on sleepyhead, get up. I'm hungry." I threw my pillow at him.

I donned my heavy Aran cardigan over my flannel nightie. Not exactly sexy, but it was warm. Though the baseboard heaters had been churning out heat all night, the house still hadn't reached a comfortable temperature. I tossed some birchbark and a log onto last night's coals and hoped a fire would start on its own.

With his mane of grey-streaked hair spread over the pillow, Eric yawned and stretched and then kicked off the duvet. Normally he didn't wear anything to bed, but last night he'd kept on his boxers and T-shirt.

"Why don't you put on your wool slacks and cashmere sweater?" he said.

"Why? We're just having breakfast."

"Ah, but it's a day to dress up and celebrate in style."

With a single leap he bounded off the mattress and proceeded to do squats.

"You make me tired just watching you. How can you be so energetic at this hour of the morning?"

He chuckled. "Keeps me young. I'm going to have a shower, and by the time I finish, I hope you'll be ready to go."

"Go? Where?"

"Oh, did I forget to mention that we wouldn't be having breakfast here this morning?" His dimples erupted.

Before I could ask again, he wrapped his arms around me and held me so tightly, I could hardly breathe. "I tell you, when I heard those gunshots, I thought my world had ended. I was certain you were dead."

I gave him a lingering kiss and enjoyed it. "I love you more than you can ever imagine."

"I don't need to imagine at all. I love you even more." He responded with another temperature-raising kiss. "Maybe we should delay breakfast." He started to pull me toward the mattress, but I extricated myself. "I thought we were in a hurry. You'd better have that shower."

Since his return, neither of us had mentioned our less than loving parting. Worried it could open a Pandora's box, I was keeping my mouth shut. I still didn't know the identity of the woman nor did I want to.

"Okay, okay, but get ready for an extra special Christmas celebration later." He licked his lips lasciviously.

Even though I knew he was joking, I couldn't stop myself from stepping back. He'd parodied the monster too perfectly.

To hide my discomfort, I rummaged through the suitcase in search of my sweater.

Twenty minutes later, fully attired in our Christmas best, we were buckling ourselves into the front seat of the Jeep with the groceries in the back seat and Shoni on my lap. "So where are we going?"

"You'll see."

"What about Teht'aa?"

"She's meeting us there."

I assumed we were going to Will's. It made sense to share Christmas breakfast with Eric's best friend and his family. But we turned in the opposite direction and headed out of town. SUV-high banks of snow flew past as we sped along Migiskan Road. The remains of a broken pole that had snapped during the storm lay stretched along the side of the road.

"Surely we're not driving all the way into Somerset."

"You'll see."

I tensed as we neared the turn-off to Three Deer Point and wondered when I would gather the nerve to see my house again.

He slowed and turned in.

"Oh Eric, I don't think I can do this."

"It's going to be fine. Trust me." He reached for my hand and held it tightly.

I didn't think I could ever be able to look at the snow-banks lining my road without thinking of Gerry. I'd not yet spoken to Claire, but Eric had visited her and passed on my condolences. His memorial was planned for the day after Boxing Day. I would go.

"Surely we're not having breakfast here. It's going to be a mess." I gripped his hand tighter. Shoni, as if sensing where we were going, whined.

"Trust me."

I squeezed my eyes closed as we rounded the final bend. I could still hear the gunshots, the cruel laughter, the threats.

"It's okay, Meg," Eric said softly. "You can open your eyes."

I took a deep breath and opened them. "The tree, it's gone!"

"Yup, Will's boys cleared it away yesterday."

While the branches had been taken away, the trunk, sawed off into lengths, lay stacked along side the driveway. The broken roof was propped up, but it looked so precarious I wasn't certain anyone should walk under it. A piece of plywood had been hammered to the outside of the broken window. Some of the planks on the steps had been replaced. But apart from these minor blemishes, Great-Grandpa Joe's cottage looked the way it had looked for over a century: magnificent, especially under its mantel of snow.

Maybe everything *was* going to be okay.

We gathered up all the groceries and walked up the steps with Shoni trotting behind us.

"Are you sure the roof is safe?" I asked.

Eric gave one of the supports a hefty tug. It didn't move. "We'll have to wait until spring to do a proper repair, but in the meantime this should survive another dump of snow."

Before Eric could open the door, it sprang open.

"Merry Christmas, guys!" Teht'aa opened her arms in greeting. But she wasn't alone. Beside her stood Jid, beaming just as broadly. He flung his arms around me. "Oh Auntie, I'm so glad to see you."

Not caring whether I broke something, I dropped the bags and hugged him as if I never wanted to let go. I could feel the tears trickling down my cheeks. I kissed the top of his head and whispered, "I love you, *nigwisis.*"

There, I'd done it. I finally voiced what I'd been thinking for a long time. I called him my son.

I felt Eric's arms go around both of us and knew he'd likely had a hand in springing Jid's release.

"All right, already," Teht'aa said. "Plenty of time for a love-in later. It's cold out here."

The house was filled with the smell of bacon and freshly baked bread and the scent of spruce. The hall floor gleamed with a fresh polish. A fire crackled in the living room, but I kept my eyes averted as we passed the den. The kitchen shone as if it had never seen a dirty dish ... or a murderer.

"Someone has been hard at work," I said.

"Teht'aa organized it," Eric replied. "Some of her friends and their mothers spent most of yesterday afternoon and evening cleaning up."

"But what about the pipes? There must have been water everywhere."

She laughed. "Yeah, but not as bad as it could've been. The cops turned off the water. Stephen came by last night and replaced the broken ones in the bathroom, so we have water."

"Teht'aa, how can I ever repay you?" We hugged as only sisters could hug, though technically we were mother and daughter.

"Okay guys," she said. "Breakfast is almost ready. Grab a seat and enjoy."

The surprises didn't end with breakfast. Afterward, Eric led us into the den, where the Christmas tree stood ablaze with multicoloured lights, glittering tinsel, and gleaming ornamental balls.

"I decorated it yesterday." Jid beamed.

"It's beautiful. The best tree ever."

In pride of place, at the top of the tree, next to my plastic Santa Claus, hung the birchbark beaver that had belonged to his father when he was a child.

My thoughts were so taken up by the tree that I forgot about the bloody carpet. It was gone. I hoped never to be seen again. In its place was an oriental carpet from the living room.

Underneath the tree were Christmas presents.

Eric pulled out a beautifully wrapped box, a striking departure from his usual minimalist approach. "Merry Christmas, my *Miskowàbigonens*."

Inside was something I'd longed for: a velvety-soft doeskin jacket, the beading delicate and intricate, the fringe long and wavy.

"Try it on."

It fit perfectly. I twirled.

"I had it made for you in Regina."

The minute the words were said, I knew the identity of the woman whose ears were probably still ringing after being so rudely disconnected.

"I'm so, so sorry. I've done you a terrible wrong."

"Sssh…." He kissed my lips closed and held me as if he never wanted to let go. "It doesn't matter. All that matters is that we are together and always will be."

I felt the tears trickle down my cheeks as I hugged him just as tightly.

ACKNOWLEDGEMENTS

As with all my books, I couldn't have written *A Cold White Fear* without the tremendous support of others. I'd like to thank Stephen McGregor, Guy Petit-Clair, and Chris Manning for the time they spent answering my many questions. I mustn't forget the Internet. Where would we authors be without the myriad websites that help expand our knowledge?

The critical eyes of Vicki Delany and Barbara Fradkin once again proved invaluable. Thanks, ladies.

I'd also like to thank my editors Allister Thompson and Carrie Gleason and my publisher Dundurn for making this book happen.

Finally a special thanks to my husband, Jim, for his enduring and patient support. He has helped to make this writing adventure so much easier.

IN THE SAME SERIES

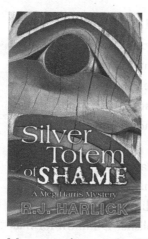

Silver Totem of Shame

The murder of a young Haida carver reawakens sibling rivalries best forgotten and sends Meg Harris and her husband to Haida Gwaii in search of the boy's family and his killer. As the search progresses, a totem pole carver sets out to depict the ancient tale of a long-ago chief's treasure and how it incited deception and shame. Meg unravels a tangle of betrayal and clan rivalries that not only reach back to when the Haida were mighty warriors, but continue to the present day.